Owning a place, putting down roots. Finding someone to spend the rest of your life with.

That life had never been for him in the past. Could it ever be? Probably not, but Thomas could enjoy the here and now and take the memories away with him when he had to leave.

"When I was in town, I noticed posters for the Founders Day Celebration. I think you and I should go. Take Johnny. What do you say?"

"I haven't been to that in years."

"Then you ought to go. You need a break, something fun."

Esther was already shaking her head, but he reached over and put his hand over hers on the horn. "Please. I want to take the baby. I want here him looked over _____ to go with me. While _____ ke in the sights."

"So what you're _____ baby?"

Grateful that she _____ led away from his touch, he grinned. "Yeah, it's for the baby."

"Then I guess I can't say no." She gifted him with a smile and placed her other hand on Johnny's small back. For a moment, the three of them were linked by touch, and he had to remind himself that it couldn't last.

Erica Vetsch is a transplanted Kansan now residing in Minnesota. She loves history and romance and is blessed to be able to combine the two by writing historical romances. Whenever she's not immersed in fictional worlds, she's the company bookkeeper for the family lumber business, mother of two, wife to a man who is her total opposite and soul mate, and an avid museum patron.

Books by Erica Vetsch

Love Inspired Historical

His Prairie Sweetheart
The Bounty Hunter's Baby

ERICA VETSCH

The Bounty Hunter's Baby

HARLEQUIN® LOVE INSPIRED® HISTORICAL

Recycling programs
for this product may
not exist in your area.

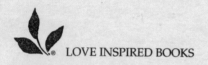 LOVE INSPIRED BOOKS

ISBN-13: 978-0-373-42512-9

The Bounty Hunter's Baby

www.Harlequin.com

Printed in U.S.A.

And they that know thy name
will put their trust in thee: for thou, Lord,
hast not forsaken them that seek thee.
—*Psalms* 9:10 (KJV)

Thank you to Carmen Hyde and Roxane Walker
after their help with all things dairy goat.
This book is dedicated to my mom, Esther,
for whom the heroine of this story is named.
And to Peter, as always.

Chapter One

Folks said Thomas Beaufort could track a house-fly through a hurricane, and though he admitted that might be a *slight* exaggeration, he felt it wasn't too far off. His reputation as a bounty hunter was unmatched, and he intended to keep it that way. The only blot on his otherwise excellent record was about to be erased.

"Well, Rip," he whispered to his half Catahoula cur, half mystery mutt, "looks like somebody's home. We've got him this time."

He and the dog—named after famous Texas Ranger Rip Ford—lay side by side on a sandy ridge in the heart of Texas brush country, looking down on a weathered shanty forty yards away. A thin wisp of smoke leaked from the stovepipe, and a pair of horses stood in the weak shade of a mesquite inside a pole and brush corral, the only signs of occupancy.

Thomas swiped with his shoulder at the sweat

trickling down his temple. Jase Swindell had led him on a wild chase since escaping from the prison up in Huntsville almost a year ago. Thomas had been tracking him off and on for months, taking quicker jobs when they were offered, but never forgetting about his main objective. Every time he got close to making an arrest, Jase slipped away. But not this time. Thomas had him now.

Nothing moved, not a breath of wind to stir branches or cool his skin as the sun pounded the Texas landscape. Thomas surveyed the area once more before easing back from the ridge, keeping low and drawing Rip along with him. He made sure his horse, a sorrel with white socks named Smitty, was tied securely well back from the ridge.

"We'll circle around on foot to that thicket and get close, and then we can rush the door, all right?" Thomas had grown accustomed to thinking out loud, talking to the dog as if he were human. Might as well talk to Rip. Not like there was anyone else to converse with. The bounty hunter life suited Thomas most days, but he had to admit, it could be a mite lonely at times.

He tucked his rifle into the crook of his elbow and checked his sidearm. Chambers full. Thomas took a deep breath, going over his planned moves, trying to anticipate Swindell's reactions and how to counter them so they both lived through the next few minutes.

Firming his resolve, he holstered the pistol, settled his hat securely on his head, and made a crouching run for the tangle of brush and thorns just ahead. Rip followed on his heels, snaking into the undergrowth.

Cautious and smooth, Thomas approached the

cabin, bending limbs out of his way, stepping carefully so as not to snap a twig or rattle a branch. He steadied his breathing, listening to the heavy thud of his heart in his chest. How many times had he done this—crept up on a fugitive, got the drop on him and clapped him in irons? He stood just back from the edge of the brush, studying the cabin, looking for signs of movement behind the tattered curtains hanging in the broken windows.

Nothing. If not for Rip, he'd think the place deserted. Easing forward, he crossed the dry, open yard and stepped lightly onto the porch. A fly buzzed past his nose, but he ignored it, concentrating, letting his experience and instinct guide him. Gathering himself, he plunged his boot into the door, shattering it at the frame, and leaped into the cabin.

"Hands up, Jase!" The door banged against the wall and shot back toward Thomas. He shouldered it aside, raking the room, swinging his rifle from side to side. Rip bounded inside, fangs bared, and skittered to a halt.

Swindell rocketed to his feet from where he'd been kneeling by the bed, his eyes wide, face filthy with sweat and dirt. A woman lay on the bunk.

A woman?

The outlaw crouched in front of her, and Thomas couldn't risk a shot, not with his rifle. The bullet might go clean through the fugitive's miserable hide and hit the woman.

A low moan came from the bed, followed by a lung-racking cough. Rip, who had been snarling and barking at Thomas's side, went silent.

A strange sensation skittered up Thomas's spine, that feeling he got when something unexpected and unwelcome was about to happen.

In that moment, Swindell leaped toward the open back door of the shack. Thomas snapped off a shot as Rip bounded after him. The room filled with the smell of burnt powder, and the woman screamed. Thomas bolted after his quarry, but as he passed the bed, the woman grabbed him by the sleeve.

"Don't shoot him!" she begged.

Knowing he had to get outside, he shook off her grasp. If Rip didn't get to Swindell in time, the outlaw would surely shoot the dog in order to escape.

Thomas jumped out into the sunshine as Rip hurled himself at Swindell, who was trying to climb into the saddle. The dog's powerful jaws clamped down on the man's left forearm, half dragging him from the horse's back. The outlaw used the butt of his drawn pistol to club the dog, sending Rip to the dust in a yelping, tumbling heap. Thomas raised his rifle and snapped off a shot, too quickly, and knew it went wide. Swindell legged his horse into a gallop, racing toward the cover of the thickets fifty yards away, snapping pistol shots over his shoulder as he shouted to his mount.

Thomas steadied his breathing, knelt in the dirt and took careful aim at the fleeing killer. A bullet from Swindell's gun whined past his ear, thudding into the shack behind him. The sun glared into his eyes and he blinked, focusing hard on the rapidly diminishing horse and rider. As Thomas held his breath and began to squeeze the trigger, something slammed him in the back, knocking his aim off, sending the bullet whining harmlessly into the air and loosening his hold in his rifle. The Winchester bucked into his shoulder and clattered to the dirt.

He whirled as the woman toppled into a heap at his feet.

Snatching his rifle, he raised it again, but Swindell was gone, disappeared into the brush. Anger clawed up his windpipe. How had a simple arrest gone wrong so quickly? He took his hat off and whacked his thigh, sending up a cloud of dust. "Lady, I'm going to arrest you for obstruction of justice, aiding and abetting a known fugitive and interfering with a peace officer."

The woman didn't stir, and he frowned, kneeling and putting his hand on her shoulder to roll her over. He leaped back, noting her round belly. "Bullets and buckshot, lady!" What on earth was Swindell doing with a woman way out here, and a woman near to bursting with a child at that?

She clutched her stomach and moaned, eyes squeezed shut.

"Tell me you're not having a baby now." Thomas jammed his Stetson on his head. They were miles from anywhere, and what he knew about birthing babies could be poured into a thimble and still leave room for a decent-size cup of coffee.

Rip approached, stiff-legged and slow, sniffing and growling. Thomas ran his hand over the mutt's head, looking for signs of injury where Swindell had clubbed him, but other than a jerk of his head when Thomas touched the spot, Rip seemed all right.

"Let's get her inside, boy." He bent and scooped

the woman into his arms. Even being so close to her time, she weighed next to nothing, her bones sharp under her skin. He edged the door aside, shoving with his boot when it ground against the uneven floor.

The smells of burnt grease, unwashed bedclothes and neglect hung in the air. A sun-rotted curtain hung at the broken window, unmoving in the still afternoon air. Thomas set her gently on the rumpled bedding. "Stay put while I tend to things outside."

She stared up at him with frightened eyes, her hair straggling over her face and shoulders. "Did he get away?"

"Yeah, for now, thanks to you." He headed outside to retrieve his horse. Keeping his rifle handy, he scanned the area. Swindell had been hightailing it south, but the nearest settlement that way was well over a hundred miles. From what Thomas had seen, the outlaw had no supplies with him, so he'd need to head to a town soon. Which meant he was probably headed to Silar Falls or Bitter Creek, swinging wide around the cabin and riding to the northeast by now.

Thomas hoped the trail led to Bitter Creek. He hadn't been to Silar Falls in five years, and he doubted his welcome would be cordial.

He would have to get the woman on her horse and take her in, but she would slow him considerably. She looked ready to pop, and he wanted her under a doctor's care, pronto. Untying his sorrel gelding, he led the horse to the corral and caught the remaining horse, leading them both to the cabin. The sooner they got started, the sooner he could get back on Swindell's trail.

"All right, let's go." Thomas pushed open the door.

"We need to make tracks if we're going to reach town before nightfall."

The thin, white-faced woman stared back at him, frightened, her tangled hair hanging half over her face. Her tatty dress rode above her knees, and she closed her eyes, her hands gripping her pregnant belly. Through tight lips, she groaned, "Help me. Please."

Silar Falls, Texas

Esther Jensen bent over her scrub board, back aching, hands stinging, scrubbing yet another pair of pants.

"Only ten more pairs to go," she muttered. Dropping the denims back into the water to soak a bit more, she turned from the scrub tub, picked up her wooden paddle and went to the heavy, iron kettle chained to a tripod over the fire. She swirled the shirts and drawers and socks as they rolled and tumbled in the boiling water. How many hundreds of times had she filled that pot, lit the fires, hung out clothes, collected her coins, only to get up and do it all again the next day?

Her life stretched out before her, an endless procession of buckets of water and miles of clotheslines, an abyss with nothing to break her fall. Wiping her reddened hands—forever chapped by harsh lye soap—on her apron, she blew her hair out of her eyes.

"You're not very good company today, Esther Marie. As melancholy as a morose mule," she chided herself, looking up from the laundry. She tried to stay positive, to remember her blessings, but some days were easier than others.

She surveyed her little kingdom, the legacy of her

departed father. A sturdy stone house, a weathered barn, a shambling bunkhouse, a windmill with more baling wire than nails holding it together. Five years was a long time. Five years since her father had passed away, since the ranch hands had left, since she'd found herself alone on the edge of town and needing to make her own living, a living that didn't stretch to building repairs or hired help.

The road into Silar Falls went by her place, but few folks stopped in…mostly the cowboys who dropped off their clothes to be washed and mended. None of them ever really saw her; some didn't even say hello, just plopped down their bundles, touched their hat brims and rode on.

If she stood on her porch, she could watch them all the way into town, less than half a mile on a straight road. Half a mile, but it might as well be a hundred for as often as she traveled it. She went to town only to pick up and drop off laundry. That and a monthly trip to get supplies composed her entire social life. If it wasn't for her friendship with Sarah Granville and Trudy Clements, both older women who had stepped in to help when her father died, she might not talk to another person for weeks.

She hefted a basket of newly washed laundry and headed to the clothesline to peg it out. "It's not like some handsome prince is going to ride down that road, sweep you off your feet and take you away from all this."

Esther had half the shirts hung up when the sound of hooves on the hard-packed road made her turn around.

Another cowboy. He must not need much washing

done, since the bundle in his arm was so small. She didn't recognize him as a regular. Shading her eyes, she watched him, even as she stooped to pick up another heavy, wet shirt.

Before she could dig a clothespin out of her apron pocket, a huge dog bounded up out of the road ditch alongside the rider. He loped ahead, turning through the gate and headed her way. His brindled coat and powerful build sent a memory ricocheting through her heart.

The shirt fell from her numb hands into the dirt, and her knees took on the firmness of damp washcloths. It was Rip. And if Rip was here…

Thomas Beaufort.

The pain she had often pushed to the back of her mind over the years came rushing forward like a stampede. A curious, empty feeling opened in her chest, crowding out her breath. She couldn't move as he rode closer. He would go past her gate and on into town. He wouldn't stop.

And she didn't want him to. Not after she'd stood in almost this same spot five years ago and watched him ride away, taking her heart with him.

No, more like leaving her heart in the dirt at her feet as he chose a bounty hunter's life over her. He had informed her of his intentions without showing even a hint of emotion. Had she imagined that he had come to care for her? She had fallen in love with him so easily, and she had thought he felt the same, though nothing had been spoken between them.

She jerked, her limbs suddenly awakening from their numbness, and stalked to the porch.

Rip trotted up the lane toward her, tail wagging, tongue lolling, as casual as if he hadn't been away for years. She remembered when Thomas first brought the dog to the ranch, a little fuzz-ball baby, all yips and puppy fat and mismatched eyes. Thomas had been one of her father's employees in those days, thoughtful, kind, winning her heart with no effort at all.

The dog bounded onto the porch and nudged her leg, letting out an exuberant bark. She prayed Thomas would ride on by without a look, even though she knew she was lying to herself. She wanted him to ride up. Perhaps if she saw him again, she could finally put to rest her feelings for him. Perhaps he wasn't as handsome and kind and capable as she remembered. Her breath stuck in her throat when he turned off the road and into her yard.

He pulled to a stop. "Miss Jensen. Esther. It's good to see you again." He smiled, the dimple in his left cheek showing in spite of a few days' growth of whiskers.

A wave of nostalgia, for all those times when he'd smiled at her and sunbeams had burst in her heart, washed over her. She steeled herself, remembering the hurt he had caused her, and she crossed her arms, hugging herself.

"Hello, Thomas." Esther was proud of her flat, disinterested tone. She'd rather show up in church in nothing but her shift than let on that she had ever fancied herself in love with him.

"Hello, Esther." He cast a glance over the warped boards on the porch, the cupping shingles, the weedy yard, so different from the prosperous young ranch he'd ridden away from. "What happened here? Where are the ranch hands?"

Shame licked through her at her run-down place, but she raised her chin. "Gone. If you're looking for bandits or rustlers here, this place is a dry hole."

He frowned, cocking his head. "Is your father around?"

Esther was helpless to stop the wave of grief that cascaded through her.

"My father is dead. He died a week after you left."

Thomas at least had the grace to appear shocked. "I didn't know. Esther, I'm so sorry."

She backed up a step as he moved to dismount. "I can't wash your clothes. I don't have time for any more customers at the moment, so you had best ride on." She motioned toward the bundle in his arms.

"Wash my clothes?" Puzzlement froze him, leg swung over the saddle, halfway to the ground.

"That's what you came for, isn't it? That's all anyone comes here for these days." She motioned toward the washtubs and clotheslines. Pushing her straggling hair off her face with her shoulder, she wished she didn't look quite so much like she'd been washed over a scrub board herself...then chastised herself for caring at all what Thomas Beaufort thought of her looks. *Where's your pride, girl?*

"I'm a laundress now." She infused the statement with all the dignity of a duchess.

Rip looked from one of them to the other, head tilted to the side. He gave a little whine, no doubt picking up on the tension in the air, and plopped his rear on the porch.

Thomas didn't even slow his steps. "Esther Jensen, would you just hear me out? I came to you because you're the only person I could trust."

"Trust?" Her voice went high. The last thing she would ever do was trust Thomas Beaufort, or any man, ever again.

Without another word, he peeled back the fabric in his arm to reveal the sleeping face of a baby, and from the looks of it, fresh as a bean sprout.

Her veins felt as if sand trickled through them, draining out and leaving her empty. Thomas had a baby? Where was his wife? All those dreams and ideas that Thomas had shattered when he left her five years ago exploded into finer bits of dust.

She opened her mouth to ask, when the baby stirred and gave a pitiful little mewl.

Thomas shot her a terrified look. "Can we at least go inside? I want to get him out of the sun."

The baby began to cry in earnest, and the sound pierced her lonely heart.

Esther stepped aside, and Thomas tromped up the steps and into the house. Rip wriggled close, hopeful, but she shook her head. "Stay." She pointed to the floor, and the big dog dropped down and put his chin on his paws, looking up at her with his mismatched eyes, one tawny yellow, one pale blue, both sorrowful and pleading.

Thomas jostled the baby, who continued to cry. Esther laced her fingers and pressed her thumbs to her lips.

"What do I do?" His brow wrinkled. "Hush, little fella."

So the baby was a boy. "Where is your wife?"

"Wife? I don't have a wife." He shot her a be-wildered look and adjusted the crying baby in his arms to no avail.

She didn't know whether to be relieved or disgusted. "Then where did you get a newborn?"

"I plucked him out of a cactus flower, where do you think? I was hot on the trail of…a fugitive…when I came on a woman in trouble. I helped her deliver her baby last night." He quit bouncing and started swaying, speaking over the baby's wails.

"Where is she then?"

He shook his head. "She died early this morning. She was a consumptive, and with the strain of the birthing…"

Esther couldn't stand the crying any longer, and she reached for the newborn. "Give him to me." Though she had little experience with babies, something in her needed to hold him. She cradled him against her shoulder, fitting his little head into the hollow of her neck. His dark hair was plastered to his head, and his eyes were screwed shut. "Didn't you even wash him off?"

Thomas held up his hands. "There was no water at the cabin where I found them, and when I did reach a creek, I didn't think it was proper to just dunk him in. I figured getting him to shelter was more important. I wet my bandanna and wiped his face, but no, I didn't take time to give him a full-blown bath."

"Dip some of the water from the stove into the basin." Esther soothed the baby. "Have you fed him yet?"

"With what? All I have is some jerky and beans." Thomas grabbed the porcelain basin off the washstand and strode to the stove. "Do you have a cow?"

Esther sat in her rocker under the window, laying the baby on her lap and peeling back the man's shirt wrapped around the infant. "No."

She had sold the cow to help pay the taxes on the property the first year after her father died. "I have a can of milk. In the cupboard."

Thomas brought her the basin and the cloth that hung on the peg by the washstand. The baby continued to snuffle and whimper, so helpless and new Esther's eyes burned, and she blinked fast. She dipped the corner of the cloth into the water and wiped the baby's face and neck. "He needs a proper bath, with soap."

Rip whined from the open doorway, and Thomas chuckled. "He's taken a shine to the little fella."

"That's fine, but he still has to stay outside." Esther unwrapped the baby further, finding a bandanna fastened around him as a diaper. It needed to be changed. "I'm pretty sure you have to warm up milk before you feed it to a baby this small. Open that can and get it heating on the stove. You'll need to thin it with a bit of water."

Thomas found the can, a saucepan and her matches. With a minimum of effort, he had a fire started in the stove and the milk warming, as efficient as ever. She had always admired his resourcefulness and capability, but to have him using those skills in her kitchen, as if no time had passed, had her battling resentment. He dusted his hands together. "What else can I do?"

"Here, hold him while I fetch some things." Esther transferred the baby into Thomas's arms, ignoring the jolt to her heart as their hands touched. The items she wanted were in the trunk in her bedroom, and she refused to let Thomas in there. She went to the end of her iron bedstead and knelt in front of the trunk—the one her mother had brought with her from Virginia as a new bride, first to Tennessee, then to Missouri. After she'd died, Esther had used it when she and her father had come to Texas for a fresh start.

Inside the trunk was a pair of clean towels, a safety pin and the last slivers of castile soap she'd been hoarding. She paused, placing her hands flat on the domed trunk lid. Thomas was back, with a newborn. Her head whirled, and her mouth felt dry. She needed a moment to collect herself, to think. But the baby cried again, a weak, hopeless little sob, and she pushed herself up, gathered her things and returned to the main room.

Thomas, worry lines bunching his forehead, patted the baby, his big hand dwarfing the child. Esther relieved him of his tiny burden, and Thomas stepped back, wiping his palms on his jeans. "I'll go tend to the horses."

Esther spread a towel on the table and laid the baby down. She soaped a washcloth in the warm water from the stove's reservoir, testing it to make sure it wasn't too hot. The baby snuffled and squirmed, turning his head every time her hand brushed his cheek. He had hazy blue eyes that didn't seem to focus too well, and a sweet little chin that quivered. She swirled the soapy cloth into all the creases and crevices and quickly rinsed him off. Before he could grow chilled, though it was a mighty warm day, she bundled him into a soft, clean towel, raising him to her shoulder and inhaling his fresh, brand-newness.

Thomas ducked back inside, this time remembering to remove his hat. He carried his saddlebags slung over his shoulder and his rifle in his hand. His holstered pistol rode his right hip, and bullets studded his gun belt.

Esther bristled at the sight of the firearms. She hated guns. Hated what they represented and what they did to people. Thomas carried his arsenal to hunt men. Guns never used to bother her, but now she could barely stand the sight of a pistol.

"Can't you leave those outside?"

"Leave what outside?" He glanced toward the doorway, where Rip sat, looking in.

"The rifle. And your sidearm." Particularly his sidearm. She cradled the baby against her shoulder. "I don't like guns."

"I never leave my guns unattended." He leaned his rifle in the corner. "Guns never bothered you before."

"A lot of things have changed since you left."

She settled into the rocker, the pan of milk beside her on the table. Using her smallest spoon, she dripped milk into the baby's mouth. His eyes opened, and he swallowed, pushing half the milk out again. Esther wiped the dribbles from his chin and gave him a few more drops. He smelled so good, felt so sweet in her arms. Her heart, cold and lonely for so long, warmed a bit, which made her pause. *Do not let yourself get attached to this little scrap of humanity, Esther. He isn't yours, he never will be, and they're both leaving soon. Leaving is what Thomas does. It's what every man does.*

Thomas leaned over her shoulder to watch. "Say, he's really putting it away. At this rate, he'll grow six foot tall by morning."

Discomfited to have him so close, Esther breathed in the scent of leather and sunshine and that unique something that was just Thomas. Against her will, she was thrust into the past when all she wanted was this man, the safety of his embrace, the warmth of his smile. Once upon a time, she had prayed her future would center around Thomas Beaufort, and all her dreams had been tied up in him.

But not now.

"At this rate we'll be out of milk before sundown." Her voice snapped like a clotheslined sheet in a high wind.

"Guess I'd better get some more then, huh?" Thomas still hovered at her shoulder, reaching down to put his finger into the baby's tiny hand. When the minute clasp closed around his finger, it was as if something squeezed Esther's chest.

Thomas chuckled. "Got himself quite a grip, doesn't he? But he can't go through life wearing nothing but a dish towel. Can you make a list of things a baby needs?"

"I don't know what a baby needs. I've never had a child before." *And likely never will.*

"You'll know a mite better than me." The reasonableness in his tone chafed. Her hard-won serenity had been upset by his arrival, and here he was acting as if nothing had happened in their past, as if no time had gone by. "If you have a wagon or buckboard, I'll go hitch it up and we can head to town to get the little fella outfitted."

Her first instinct was to refuse. Trips to town were painful reminders of her change in status, and going into Silar Falls with Thomas would be too much to bear. The infant in her arms stretched, arching his little back and sinking into a relaxed bundle. He snuffled, and his lashes skimmed his cheeks as he blinked slowly, completely helpless and trusting as he lay in her arms.

He needed help. He needed her.

Thomas was right. She could see this child properly clad and provisioned, but she'd have to go into town with Thomas to see it done.

She looked up from spooning the milk. "What are you going to do with him?" It was the question she'd been wondering since she first saw the baby in his arms.

Thomas knelt beside her chair, putting his big hand over hers on the towel-wrapped infant. "Esther, I know it's a lot to ask, and you have no obligation, but I need someone to help me. His mama left him in my care, but I don't know what to do. It was all I could do to get him here alive and squalling. I need someone to look after him until I can find his relatives."

His "oh my" brown eyes looked deeply into hers, and she shivered at the power he still had to move her. She suppressed the tremor that rippled through her, wanting to thrust the baby into his arms and put some distance between Thomas and her feelings. His hand on hers, so warm and familiar, was the first touch she'd felt in a long time. When she realized just how good it felt, she shrugged him off.

"Will you help me, Esther?"

"For how long?" She closed her eyes, inhaling a deep breath to steady herself, calling herself all kinds of foolish to even think of letting him back in her life. How long could he stay before she betrayed herself, betrayed that she had once loved him?

"I don't know, exactly. I should get back out on the trail, but I'll put out feelers and try to find someone in the little gupper's family willing to take the boy." He cupped the baby's head, and the tenderness in his eyes threatened to tear down a layer of protective bricks around her heart. "Please? I don't have any-where else I can turn. We need you."

It felt so good to be needed. Even though she knew she should refuse, that she should send him and his problems packing, she found herself giving in. "I'll help you, for the sake of the baby, for a week or so, until you can make permanent plans for him."

She could do this. She could help Thomas get this baby fed and outfitted without jeopardizing her heart once more, without regretting letting her guard down.

Couldn't she?

Chapter Two

"The buckboard is in the barn, but you'll have to catch the horses. They're in the trap." And a merry chase they would lead him, too. Esther usually had to bribe the horses with a carrot or two to get them to come to her in the pasture, or "trap" as the cowboys used to call it. The trap was the only fenced pastureland on the Double J Ranch. At one time, there had been more than thirty horses there, mounts for the many ranch hands her father had employed, but now, only the harness team remained. With good grazing and Silar Creek running across one corner, the horses mostly fended for themselves there.

Thomas nodded. "I'll be back as soon as I can."

Figuring she had plenty of time, Esther rocked slowly, the baby snuggled against her shoulder. Regret warred with anticipation, and she took herself to task. "You had best keep your wits about you, girl. He won't stay. He can't. You heard him five years ago. He never wants to be tied down."

And here she was, listening for Thomas to return,

the same way she'd waited and watched five years ago when he rode away, praying he'd come back to her.

The baby stirred and nestled against her again. He was warm and smelled of soap and milk and newborn. She'd fashioned a diaper out of a dishcloth and wrapped him in one of her oldest, softest bath towels. Now that his hair was clean, she marveled at its fineness…like dark thistledown, and if she wasn't mistaken, a bit curly. Cuddling him, she couldn't believe how quickly things could change. Was it only this afternoon that she saw her life stretching out day after day with nothing to vary the monotony?

"You sure have a sense of humor, Lord."

Rip inched toward her on his belly, creeping inside. Thomas had left the dog behind when he'd gone for the horses, or more accurately, Rip had refused to leave the baby. He was draped half inside, half outside the door, lying on the threshold, watching Esther and the boy with hopeful eyes, sneaking into the room a bit at a time when he thought she wasn't looking.

The dog's ears perked up, and he swiveled his head to look out the doorway. The sound of hooves on the road made Esther's stomach flip. Thomas hadn't been gone long, surely not long enough to accomplish his errand. Had he forgotten something? Or was it one of her customers?

She hurried to the bedroom and laid the sleeping baby in the center of the bed. Rip snuck in and sniffed the baby, tail wagging, eyes soulful. Esther ignored him and went to the door.

It wasn't Thomas.

Four cowboys, all spit shined and slicked for a

night on the town, turned into her gate, each one with a duffel tied behind his saddle.

Danny Newton rode in the lead. She bit her cheek. He was Esther's least favorite customer. Brash and bold, he leered and smirked every time he came by, leaving her with a creepy-crawly feeling and a desire to bathe when he left. His father owned the Circle Bar 5, the ranch adjoining hers to the south, and he had designs on her property as a gift for his son.

"Evening, Miss Esther." Danny pushed his hat back, revealing dark blond hair and sun-browned skin. His pale blue eyes pierced her, perusing her from hem to hairline, pausing a couple of times on their journey. Heat rushed to Esther's cheeks. "Nice night."

She rubbed her hands against the sides of her skirts, gripping the faded fabric. He was insolent, full of bravado in front of his friends. He swung out of the saddle and removed his hat.

"You're looking fine tonight, Miss Esther. You ready to take my father's offer?"

"I've already declined his offer too many times to count."

He rubbed his thin mustache in that gesture she knew so well, the one that preceded some remark she would hate.

"Only a matter of time. The tax man is coming around." He stuck his thumbs into his back pockets, insolent as he eyed the buildings. "Your ranch is going downhill on a fast horse. You could always save my pa the purchase price and just marry me." He winked and gave her a smirk. "You *should* marry me. After all, it's what your daddy wanted, and mine, too."

She gritted her teeth. "Leave your laundry if you're going to. And you still owe me for last week's. I don't work on credit, so don't forget to pay up before you go. As to your continued insistence that we marry, I wouldn't have you if you came with a money-back guarantee."

One of the men laughed, and a flush charged up Danny's cheeks. His eyes snapped, and he leaped onto the porch, grabbing her wrist and hauling her up against him.

"Let me loose." She spoke through tight lips, unwilling to let him know how much he was hurting her...and scaring her.

"It's high time someone taught you a lesson, little lady." His breath scoured her cheek. He smelled of pomade and aftershave and sweat and horse.

From behind her, a low growl crawled over her skin, freezing her blood. Rip bounded out of the house, ears flat against his head, teeth bared. His body crouched to spring, every muscle bulging under his brindled coat.

Danny dropped her wrist like a hot rock. He backed up a step, hands held low, eyes wide. "Whoa. When did you get him?" He stared at the dog, easing back another step.

Esther pressed herself against the front wall of the house. Rip advanced on Danny, head low.

"That's enough." One of the riders cocked his pistol. "Call him off, ma'am."

The sight of his drawn gun sent a sick shiver

through her. Why hadn't she bitten her tongue? She knew what Danny could be like. Things escalating had been her fault.

Would the dog obey her? "Rip."

The canine stopped advancing but didn't cease his growling.

"Rip. Come." She patted her leg.

Slowly rising from his crouch, relaxing his lips to cover his teeth once more, Rip sidled to her, never taking his eyes off Danny. Esther risked touching the dog's head. "Good boy."

Danny's face was a hard mask. "Next time you sic that dog on me, I'll put a bullet between his eyes."

"I'd think twice about that if I was you." Thomas's voice came from the side of the house, and he rounded the corner, pistol trained on Danny. His dark eyes glittered, and his hand was steady.

Esther's heart lurched. Thomas with his gun in his hand. Her view narrowed, and her heart thrummed so loudly in her ears it was almost as if she was under water. The gun filled her vision.

"Beaufort? I hadn't heard you were back." Danny's eyes narrowed as he looked from Thomas to Esther and back again. Thomas and Danny hadn't gotten along too well back when Thomas was a hand here. Of course, not too many people got along with Danny, not unless his father paid them to.

"I didn't feel the need to check in with you first, Newton." Thomas's gun and gaze didn't waver. Esther gripped the doorframe to steady herself.

"You just passing through, or are you staying on?"

"If you can explain how it's any of your business,

I'll tell you my plans," Thomas said, his eyes dark and intent.

Danny stood still a moment, as if gauging his situation, and then edged off the porch. "Boys, we're wastin' time. Throw your bags down and let's mosey. We're going to have us a night on the town."

Esther pressed her hand to her middle, thankful that in a few moments they would be gone. One by one they pitched their duffel bags onto the porch. Both Thomas and the dog regarded them all as if memorizing their faces, and a shiver skittered down Esther's spine and settled in her knees.

"I believe the lady mentioned a payment that's due?" Thomas's soft voice sliced the air like a saber.

Danny froze, scowling and sizing Thomas up. Finally, he dug into his vest pocket, removed a coin and flipped it Esther's way. Thomas's hand shot out and caught it before she could react, holding it up. A silver dollar.

"That the right amount?"

She nodded. "That will cover what he owes and this week's laundry."

"What about the rest of them?"

"They're current."

"Fair enough. Time for you boys to go." Thomas motioned with his pistol toward their horses. The gun was like an extension of his hand. "And when you come back, you'll mind your manners, I'm sure."

The men were just preparing to mount up when a weak cry came from the house. The baby! She'd clean forgotten about him.

Danny jerked around at the sound. "What's that?"

Thomas stepped in front of Esther, nudging her backward toward the open doorway. She put her hand on his shoulder and stood on tiptoe to keep her eye on Danny.

Rip trotted into the house and then emerged again with a whine. The infant's cry grew louder and unmistakable.

"A baby? Where'd you get a baby, Esther Jensen?" Danny shouted, making Rip growl and lower his head once more.

Thomas stood his ground. "I believe it's past time for you boys to be moving along."

Danny's eyes darted from Thomas to Esther and back again, calculating. "If you're figuring to horn in here, Beaufort, you'd best be the one moving along." He poked his boot into his stirrup and swung into the saddle. "I aim to have this ranch one way or another, and soon. I don't know where that brat came from, or how long you're staying, but you both better be gone pronto." He sunk his spurs into his horse's sides, and the animal surged into a gallop, the rest of the men following, sending clouds of dust into the air.

Esther let out her breath, tension trickling away. When she turned to go to the crying infant, Thomas followed.

"What's going on here, Esther? Why is Danny Newton after your ranch? And why does he think he can get it?" Thomas holstered his weapon and crossed his arms.

Esther wrapped the baby in the towel again and lifted him to her shoulder, crooning to him, trying to ignore the panicked flipping of her heart. "It's nothing. Nothing I can't handle." Hopefully he hadn't overheard about the taxes coming due. Esther had practiced the most severe economy this year, and she had almost enough to meet the tax bill, barring any unforeseen events, but that was her problem, not Thomas's.

After all, he'd be gone soon.

Thomas had his hands full with the frisky team. Clearly it had been a while since they'd been harnessed and hitched. He remembered them from his time as a ranch hand. The bay was shaggy and the black scruffy, and both could use a good currying and trip to the blacksmith, but he used a firm voice and steady hand, and they gradually gentled.

He brought the horses and buckboard around the house, still tense from the encounter with Danny Newton and his crew. Thomas and Danny had never been friends, but they hadn't been enemies, either. How often did Esther have to deal with customers treating her poorly? And why was Danny hoping to get his hands on her property?

The news that Elihu Jensen was dead had rocked him. When Thomas had ridden away five years ago, the rancher had been in good health, with a profitable ranch and big plans for his daughter's future. Plans that hadn't included Thomas.

The condition of the Double J shocked Thomas. The disrepair and despair everywhere was a punch in the gut. The weather in south-central Texas could be hard on buildings and equipment, but this seemed extreme for only five years. If he was going to stay, he could fix up a few things. Too bad he couldn't spare the time. Jase Swindell's trail grew colder by the minute. He might be halfway to the Rio Grande by now.

Esther emerged from the house, the baby in her arms. Her eyes looked pensive, and a little furrow had developed between her eyebrows. Thomas helped her into the rig; the touch of her hand in his sent a familiar jolt up his arm. Climbing aboard himself, he glanced at her hands as he picked up the reins. They were so different than when he'd first known her. Then they had been pale and slender, moving constantly when she spoke. Often she wore fingerless lace gloves, wielding a fan or some fancy needlework as she rocked on the porch in the evening. Now they were reddened and work worn, the hands of a woman older than the twenty-four years he knew her to be.

He chirruped to the horses, slapping the lines.

Rip rode in the back, sticking his snout between Thomas and Esther from time to time, sniffing the wind. Sunshine slanted toward the horizon as dusk approached, and Thomas drove into town from the south, turning right onto the main street. He studied Silar Falls, comparing it to his memory.

Not much appeared to have changed, perhaps a couple of new businesses, but on the surface, things seemed the same.

The brightest lights shone from Big Aggie's Saloon, halfway down the block. He recognized Danny Newton's horse tied at the hitching post out front. The saddle and harness shop had closed for the day, and the telegraph office was shut up tight. One team and wagon waited down by the livery. At the west end of the street, the church steeple pierced the pink and orange sky.

Thomas hopped down and tethered the team before circling the buckboard to help Esther alight. She didn't meet his eyes, keeping her head down and walking up the steps to the store. He followed and reached the door in time to open it for her.

As they stepped inside, Rip followed, tail wagging, determined to stick close to Esther and the baby. The proprietor, Frank Clements, looked up from his ledger. "Evening, Miss Esther. Don't often see you at this time of day. I was about to close up and head upstairs." He tucked his pencil behind his ear, and Thomas smiled at the gesture he remembered so well. The shopkeeper's eyes widened when he noticed the bundle Esther carried, and his eyebrows shot up when he saw the dog.

Thomas held out his hand. "Hello, Frank. Been a while. How's your wife?"

The shopkeeper blinked, tearing his gaze away from Esther and Rip. "Well, as I live and breathe. Thomas Beaufort!" A smile stretched his cheeks. "How long has it been, son?"

"Too long." Thomas shook his hand, happy to be remembered, though he'd only spent one summer in Silar Falls. "Glad we made it in before you closed. We need to pick up a few things." Glancing around, he hooked his thumbs in his gun belt. Nothing seemed to have changed inside the mercantile, either. The candy jars still sat beside the glass display case of fans and scarves and combs. Canned goods stood in pyramids on the shelves behind. The sharp tang of vinegar from the pickle barrel mixed with the scent of beeswax polish and new boots.

Thomas snapped his fingers and motioned to Rip to lie down. The big dog dropped to his belly, watching and waiting for the next command. "Wait there and don't make a nuisance of yourself, boy."

Esther eyed the stock on the shelves, her lips pressed together. The baby slept sweetly in her arms, and she gently rocked from side to side. Thomas wondered if she was even aware she was swaying.

"What can I do for you?" Frank pressed his hands on the countertop, leaning forward, the lamplight gleaming off his bald dome. He was clearly curious about the baby, but he didn't ask. From what Thomas remembered about Frank, the store owner didn't have to ask. If he waited, the information he wanted usually flowed his way. That or his wife ferreted it out.

"Esther?" Thomas turned to find her fingering a bolt of fabric, a wistful expression on her face.

She started and then collected herself. "Frank, we need some supplies for this baby."

"Be glad to help. Flannel, canned milk? Bonnets and booties?" Frank asked.

"Do you have any diapers made up? And some sleeping gowns?" Esther asked.

Frank shook his head. "I have flannel lengths for sewing them up yourself, but nothing ready-made."

Esther sent Thomas a what-do-you-want-to-do look.

"Can you sew?" He tried to remember if he'd ever seen her making garments. Seemed to him she'd been a fair hand at fancy needlepoint stitching, but her dresses and such had come from a dressmaker. He'd been told by her father to drive her into town several times for fittings and the like.

"Yes, I can sew."

"Get whatever she needs, Frank." Thomas stifled a yawn as weariness crept over him. He hadn't slept in more than forty-eight hours, and his eyes felt like he'd rubbed them full of sand. "I'll have a look around while you pull things together for Esther."

He perused the groceries, remembering how bare Esther's cupboard had been when he'd fetched the lone can of milk off her shelf. She was doing him a mighty big favor. The least he could do was add to her larder. If she would let him. She could be a proud little minx.

Edging past a table full of ready-made menswear, he paused beside a shelf holding lengths of fabric, letting his rough hand trail across the blues and purples and yellows. The bolt Esther had been touching caught his attention. Pale blue with little pink flowers scattered over it. A smile tugged at his lips. Wouldn't Esther look something in a dress made of this?

From across the store, Thomas studied her, taking in her clothing. She wore a greenish dress so faded from washing it was almost gray. It was too big for her, drooping on her slender frame. The scuffed tips of a pair of sturdy boots peeked out from beneath her hem. And she wore no hat or bonnet. When he'd known her before, she'd worn pretty gowns with lots of ruffles and lace, and she had shoes and parasols to match. Gloves and bonnets and fans. Her father had given her everything she could want. He remembered back to the blue dress she'd worn to the church social the night before he left Silar Falls. Her hair had been all piled up, and her eyes shone. Every young man in the place, Thomas included, couldn't take his eyes off her.

Maybe he should've stood up to her father all those years ago. When Elihu Jensen had learned that one of his hired hands was falling for his lovely daughter, he'd taken Thomas aside and given him an ultimatum: ride on and leave Esther alone, or be run off.

"You're penniless. There is no way you can support my daughter. You're a nobody, and I have bigger plans for her. Pick up your pay and your bedroll and clear out. She's too young to know her own mind right now, and she deserves better than a saddle tramp."

And because he'd been young and impressionable, Thomas had listened. He hadn't been in a position then to support a wife, certainly not one as well off as Esther had been. He had no skills beyond cowboying. And he loved Esther and wanted the best for her. Though it had about killed him to leave her, he'd gone. He'd become a bounty hunter after learning new skills, but he'd never forgotten her.

He'd known then he wasn't good enough for her, that she deserved better than him. He was a nobody who didn't even know who his parents were. A foundling, a drifter. As a bounty hunter, he was accustomed to being seen as a necessary evil, moving on the outskirts of society, a manhunter who most folks didn't want to associate with.

And still not good enough for Esther Jensen.

"How many yards of this flannel?" Frank asked Esther.

She shifted the baby to her shoulder. "I don't know. How much do you recommend? We need diapers and gowns and blankets."

"Let's call in the expert." Frank headed for the stairs at the back of the store and hollered up. "Trudy? Can you come down for a minute?"

Frank's tiny wife bustled down the steps, wiping her hands on a dish towel. "Yes?" Her dark eyes darted quickly, lighting on Esther. "Why, Esther Jensen, it's so nice to see you. It's been weeks, child. You don't come in nearly often enough. And who is that there with you? A baby? My lands, child. Where did you get yourself a baby?" She embraced Esther and then hugged her again.

"He's an orphan." Esther's arms tightened around the boy. "We're looking after him until Thomas can find his people."

"Thomas Beaufort." Trudy's smile lit the store. He snatched off his hat and nodded as she advanced on him with her arms outstretched. Trudy hugged everybody, he recalled. "I remember you. It's good to see you back in these parts. Frank told me he heard you had a big arrest not too long ago. The Burton Boys? I try to keep up on all the news, especially when it's about someone I know."

"Yes, ma'am." Not only had he captured the four-man gang of outlaws, he'd earned himself a hefty bounty in the process.

"Trudy." Frank held up a length of flannel. "They

need to outfit the little guy, and you'd know what they need better than I would."

"Of course, of course. Let me see." Trudy, though bird-like and small, tended to blow through a room like a tornado. Esther was bustled over to the dry goods counter, and Trudy exclaimed over the baby, putting her arm around Esther's waist and talking nineteen to the dozen.

"Isn't he beautiful? And you need a complete lay-ette? Of course you do, what with this little sweetheart being dropped in your lap, as it were. I remember when my first was born. I didn't have so much as a safety pin to call my own, traveling in that bouncy wagon across the plains. I cut up my best flannel pet-ticoat to make diapers." She continued on, talking and whisking bolts of fabric onto the counter. Her shears *snicked* as quickly as her tongue, cutting lengths and folding them. "Do you need me to include a pattern for the gowns? Thread, needles, bias tape? Of course you do. I have just the thing."

With the women occupied, Thomas motioned for Frank to join him. He had questions he didn't want anyone overhearing.

"Frank, you still know everybody in town?" Thomas reached for a couple of cans of peaches and set them on the counter.

The storekeeper picked up a feather duster and flicked it over a row of McGuffey readers. "Can't think of anybody I don't know." He grinned. "Course, if I could think of them, I'd know 'em, right?"

"Has anybody heard anything about Jase Swindell lately?" Thomas kept his voice low.

Frank stopped dusting. "That who you're after now? Jase Swindell?"

Thomas nodded. "Off and on for almost a year. Since he killed a guard while busting out of Huntsville. Seems he runs to Mexico, but he doesn't stay there. Keeps coming back north." The liaison with the woman was most likely responsible for that. Now that she was dead, would Swindell come back to Texas ever again?

"We heard about the escape." Scratching his chin, Frank thought hard. "If he's been anywhere in the county, I haven't gotten wind of it. When him and his gang got caught the first time, the rest of his kin around here lit a shuck for the hills, cleared out. Only one left is his sister, Regina. And she isn't right in the head, from what I hear. Does her shopping over in Spillville, so I don't hear much about her."

"Nobody else who used to run with the Swindells? Nobody around here who would hide him?"

"No, can't think of anybody. He left a lot of victims and no friends hereabouts. Like Esther, poor thing. You could've pushed me over with a twig when I heard her pa shot himself."

"He did what?" Thomas cringed as the question came out too loudly, and Trudy and Esther turned toward him. Lowering his head and his voice, he asked, "Esther said he was dead, but she didn't say how."

"Well, she wouldn't, would she? When the rustlers wiped out Elihu's herd, he just didn't have the strength to go on."

Thomas braced his hands on the countertop. Elihu had killed himself after his cattle had been rustled.

Elihu's cattle had been rustled by the Swindell Gang, led by Jase Swindell.

Thomas looked down the store to where Esther cradled the baby.

Jase Swindell's baby.

How could he tell her?

Frank flicked the duster over another shelf. "Elihu left a note, telling Esther he was sorry, and begged her to forgive him and to do everything she could to hold on to the ranch. It was the talk of the county for months. The hands all quit. Sheriff Granville suspected at least half of them had to be in on the rustling. Poor Esther's been taking in laundry and scratching out a living out there alone for the last five years." Frank rubbed his palm across his bald head. "How long did you ride for the Double J?"

Thomas shrugged, his mind still reeling as he put all the pieces together. "Just the one summer five years ago. But I didn't punch cows. Jensen hired me on to fence a pasture. I spent three months driving post holes and stringing wire." And watching for glimpses of the boss's daughter.

"Esther sure took her daddy's death hard, especially since it was by his own hand. Some folks in town weren't too nice to her right after it happened. Always thought that was a shame, since it wasn't her fault. But folks feel peculiar about suicide. I wondered if she could make it when she set up as a laundress. From what she spends in here, she's barely keeping body and soul together."

Guilt hooked its claws into Thomas's chest. Esther, poor and struggling, didn't fit what he'd known about her. And he'd left her to struggle on her own.

"Frank," Trudy called out, hands on hips as she scanned the shelves of fabric. "Did you sell the rest of that cotton sheeting? Or am I looking at it and just can't see it?"

Frank went to help, and Esther edged toward Thomas. "She keeps piling things onto the counter. I can't seem to hold her back," Esther whispered. "Surely a baby doesn't need so many things. It's going to cost the earth."

Thomas shrugged. "She's raised three kids. I reckon she should know what one baby needs. Don't worry about the expense."

"Don't worry? I don't think you know how things add up." She bit the side of her thumbnail, the crease between her brows deepening. Frank's assessment of her financial situation hit him again.

Which made him more determined than ever to help her.

"Peaches?" Esther picked up one of the cans he'd put on the counter. "I remember those were your favorite." The wistful hint to her voice tugged at Thomas, harking back to happier days when she had surprised him with a peach cobbler for his birthday.

"Still are, though I don't get them often, being out on the trail all the time."

"Don't you have a home base?" she asked. "Are you always moving from place to place?"

He shrugged. "No home base. I go wherever the trail leads, me and Rip." The dog's head came up at the sound of his name. "We stay in hotels or boardinghouses or sleep out, depending on our quarry. We're never in one place too long. Been like that all my life."

"That's sad. I might have lost a lot, but I still have my home. I don't know what I would do if I lost that, too." Bleakness entered her eyes, and Thomas wanted to put his arms around her and the baby and tell her everything would be all right. But he had no right to do that and no assurance that things *would* be all right.

The baby began to fuss, and Trudy bustled over. "Let's go upstairs and get him changed before you head home. And I imagine you could use a cup of tea. While we're at it, let's look through my storage trunk. I might still have some baby things left over from my own children."

Thomas smiled at how Trudy managed everyone, so kind that you half didn't mind her being a bit pushy. He was grateful to have Esther out of the way for a bit so he could get on with his plans.

By the time she was ready to leave, Thomas had made several trips out to the buckboard. He slid his purchases under the tarp and returned for Esther's bundle of baby things.

"I'm sorry it's so much." Esther frowned.

"And I'm pretty sure I told you not to worry about it. You and Rip head outside, and I'll settle up." When she'd gone, Thomas reached into his vest pocket for his money pouch. He handed Frank a fifty-dollar gold piece. "Put the rest on Esther's account, will you? And, Frank, I'd just as soon the whole town didn't know I was back."

Frank smiled, nodding, and made a note in his ledger. "I'll keep it under wraps. And I'll tell Trudy, too."

"Thanks, and if you remember anything about Jase Swindell, get word to me."

"Where will you be? The hotel? The boarding-house?"

"I'll be staying out at Esther's tonight." He paused. "In the bunkhouse."

Letting that sink in, Frank dropped the money into the till. "Trudy worries about that girl out there all alone. How long are you planning on staying?"

"That depends. I need to see about contacting someone from the baby's family, and I need to get back on Swindell's trail." He picked up the paper-wrapped bundle of baby things. Once Thomas was on the porch, Frank locked the door behind him and pulled the shade, flipping the Open sign to Closed. Esther stood by the horses, patting the black's nose. The last rays of sunset had dwindled, and the outline of her hand against the horse's nose stood out, fragile and light.

"Say, you know of anybody who has a milking cow for sale?" Thomas asked as he helped her into the buckboard.

"A milking cow? I don't know of any for sale. You'd have to go to San Antonio for one, I imagine. Anyway, isn't a cow a big expense? I can get by with canned milk for the baby. It's just for a few days until you get him to his family." She smoothed her skirts as she settled onto the seat.

"Maybe, but wouldn't fresh be better?" Thomas leaped aboard and picked up the reins.

"I suppose. If you're set on fresh milk, there're some Mexicans south of town who have a herd of goats. You can probably get one of those cheap. It still seems a waste of money for such a short time though."

As they rode back toward Esther's place, he considered his options. He had planned to leave the baby with Esther and strike out after Jase Swindell first thing in the morning, hoping this was the time he finally caught him, and quickly before he could do any more harm.

But that left a sizable burden on Esther, especially since she was making her living as a laundress. Could he spare a few days from the hunt to check out Jase's sister over in Spillville or, failing that, to try to find another relative? No matter what, Thomas refused to take the boy to an orphanage. He had spent the first twelve years of his life in an orphanage, and there was no way he would do that to a child if he could help it. If he couldn't find any of the boy's kin, perhaps he could find a family who would adopt him. That wouldn't take too long, surely, not with a healthy little boy. The minute the boy was settled, he would hit the trail again.

But he found himself hoping things wouldn't be sorted out too soon. Thomas felt an obligation to do the best he could for the baby, but he also felt an obligation to Esther for helping him out. She'd suffered and struggled the past five years, and he could make things easier for her over the next few days.

Contentment settled over him once he made up his mind to stay for a few days, something he hadn't felt for a long time.

Chapter Three

Esther shifted the baby in her arms as Thomas pulled the buckboard into the yard. In the dark, the place didn't look so bad. Though the porch boards had warped in the sun and the roof could use some attention, the stone house was sturdy, built to withstand a tornado or Indian attack.

What it hadn't been able to withstand was the weakness of her father. Faced with financial ruin, he hadn't been strong enough to bear it. He had been too ashamed to know that he'd been duped by his ranch hands, been robbed and that he was now land-rich and cash poor.

And when it had all come to light, Esther had been left to endure it alone. Her father's last wish was that she do everything she could to keep the Double J, and she'd given the last five years of her life to that task. Alone. No family, no ranch hands, her father dead, and the man she had fallen in love with gone. Even God seemed far away.

Thomas wrapped the reins around the brake handle

and hopped down. "Let's get you and the little guy out of this night air."

She shouldn't thrill to the touch of his hand on her elbow as she climbed down. She shouldn't take such comfort in having someone to come home with in the dark. And she certainly shouldn't let her guard down and start caring about either of these males, because they would be gone in a few days, and she would be on her own again.

Rip's tail thumped her leg as she passed him on her way inside. The June night, cool now and pleasant, drifted in through the open doorway. Esther tucked the receiving blanket Trudy Clements had given her higher around the baby who snuffled and yawned in her arms. She smiled as she laid him in the basket, yawning too. Washing clothes was hard work. She rose early, and in order to save on kerosene, usually went to bed early, too.

When she lifted the lantern and shook it, only a little kerosene sloshed in the bottom. She needed to make it last as long as possible, so she set the lantern aside and scrabbled in a drawer for a candle, stuffing it into a holder and lighting the wick. The soft glow illuminated the sparseness of her kitchen. The house had already been on the property when they bought it. Her father had made plans for a larger, fancier house, but it had never been built.

Thomas entered the house, his arms full of packages. "The baby still sleeping?"

She studied Thomas in the lamplight, taking in his dark hair—in need of cutting—and his dusty clothes and tired eyes. He'd filled out and grown taller in the years since she'd seen him. He had turned twenty just before he left, a year older than herself. Now he was a man, full-grown, in his prime. And handsomer than ever. She pulled her thoughts away from that direction.

"Yes, though he's making noises like he might wake up soon. I don't have a cradle, so I thought a basket might do for him to sleep in." She motioned to the laundry basket she'd padded and lined and set beside the rocker. Rip stood guard over the sleeping baby.

Thomas deposited the parcels on the kitchen table. "Silar Falls hasn't changed much. Frank looks about the same, don't you think?"

"I suppose. I don't spend much time in town." Esther untied the string around the bundle of baby items, rolling the twine carefully and setting it aside. She did the same with the brown paper. These days, she wasted nothing, and she would find uses for both the paper and string. Unable to resist, she trailed her work-roughened hands across the snowy-white flannel. "This will make some soft gowns and blankets." She opened the fabric to test the length. "Trudy said we'd need a couple dozen diapers."

"That should get the little tadpole started." Thomas squatted beside the basket. "He sure looks better cleaned up." He brushed the back of his finger along the baby's round cheek. The boy snuffled and wriggled and gave a squawk, turning his head toward the touch as if seeking something. "He can't be hungry again, can he?"

Esther found the glass feeder bottle among the fabric, carefully wrapped against breakage, and washed it out. Thomas withdrew a knife from his pocket and flicked it open, puncturing the top of one of the cans of milk and pouring it into the saucepan she gave him.

"I'll see to the horses." Thomas wiped his knife on his pant leg before closing it and returning it to his pocket and heading outside again.

While the milk heated, Esther changed the baby, who fussed and squirmed as she tried to fasten on another dishcloth as a diaper. "I'll get to sewing you up some real diapers soon."

A baby was definitely adding to her chore list. And Thomas was adding to her disquiet. Used to being alone, having a man, a dog and a child in her house, especially after dark, unnerved her. The sooner Thomas got on his way, the better for her peace of mind.

She hurried to the stove to check on the milk. Still not warm, so she poked another piece of kindling into the firebox. Thomas's boots thumped on the porch floor, and when she turned around, her mouth opened on a gasp.

He set a crate on the table and unpacked it quickly. Foodstuffs covered the surface. Canned goods, sacks, boxes. It looked as if he'd brought the entire general store into her kitchen. He ducked outside and came back with a flour sack over his shoulder and another parcel under his arm.

"What is all this?"

"Supplies." Thomas let the sack thump to the floor and set the parcel on a chair since the tabletop was full.

"How much are you planning to eat? Or are these for the trail when you get ready to leave?" Esther picked up a sack of Arbuckle's coffee beans. She hadn't had coffee in ages, and her mouth watered at the thought.

Thomas pushed his hat back and scratched his head. "I won't be hitting the trail right away."

She set the coffee beans on the table as if they were made of glass. Her insides stilled like the coppery air before a summer thunderstorm. "What are you going to do, then?"

"I'm going to stick around Silar Falls for a while." He shrugged. "The little fellow can't exactly travel at the moment, and even if he could, where would I take him? I'll need some time to track down his family."

"And in the meantime? Will you take him to the hotel in town or a boardinghouse?" Neither place was ideal for an infant.

"You said you'd help me with him, remember? Until I could make other arrangements?"

"I thought you meant feeding him and getting him properly clothed. You'll be riding out tomorrow, right?" He couldn't mean to stay. That was too much to bear. "Or were you going to leave him here while you locate his family?" Even as she said the words, she knew she wouldn't escape this encounter unscathed. The longer the baby stayed, the more she would grow attached. Then Thomas would ride in, take the baby and leave her alone again.

Before he could reply, the baby's fussing turned to a full-blown wail. They needed to tend to him before they sorted out this situation. And it would give her some time to marshal her thoughts.

"Sit," she said.

Rip plunked his rump on the floor, looking up at her alertly, tongue lolling, and Esther almost laughed. "Not you, silly." She swept over to the basket and picked up the baby, handing him to Thomas and nudging them toward the rocker. "Hold him while I fix his bottle."

Thomas took the child, sinking into the chair and cradling the infant as if he were made of soap bubbles. The baby's face screwed up and reddened, his cries sounding so heartbroken.

"What should I do?" he asked.

Esther didn't miss the panic in his voice, and it was a bit comforting to find something he wasn't confident about.

"Rock him, pat him, sing to him."

The chair creaked as he set it in motion, and Rip got up, pacing and bumping Thomas with his nose, giving soft whines as if to say "make that puppy stop crying." Esther tested the milk—finally warm enough—and poured it carefully into the bottle. Figuring out the tight, rubber nipple took longer.

"Can't you hurry? He's about to throw a shoe or something." Thomas shushed the baby.

"You haven't tried singing."

"I can't carry a tune in a bucket with a lid on it. He'd probably cry harder." Thomas raised his voice above the wailing.

She finally snapped the nipple into place over the neck of the bottle and handed it to him.

"Aren't you going to feed him?" Worry clouded Thomas's eyes.

"I have full confidence in you." She smiled, taking a bit of pleasure in his being flustered.

Rip whined again, and Thomas grimaced. "That makes one of us. Hush that caterwaulin', buster." He shifted the baby to lie more securely in his arm and offered the bottle.

After a bit of fumbling and fussing, the baby caught on and began sucking with long, steady pulls. "There you go. You're making hay now."

The tenderness in his voice affected Esther, as if she'd just taken a sip of hot chocolate on a chilly day, warming her when she didn't even realize she was cold. She turned back to the laden table.

"This is an awful lot of food." More than she would purchase in a whole month on her own. She hefted a can of peaches. How long had it been since she tasted something so luxurious? Not that she'd considered canned peaches a luxury once upon a time.

Until it had all come crashing down. Her throat went tight and her insides cold again.

Thomas looked up from the baby. "I figured if I was going to impose on you, I should at least provide some grub. Your cupboard looked a mite bare."

She stiffened. "I don't need charity."

"Now, don't get into a lather. It isn't charity. I'm the one who brought more mouths to feed. Five if you count Rip and the horses. I pay my own way, same as you." He gave her a be-reasonable look that had her pressing her molars together. "It's really for the baby, when you come to think about it. Taking care of him is bound to be hard work, and you need to keep your strength up. And I have to eat, too. Anyway, what's a little food between friends?"

Friends. Was that what she and Thomas were? He had such a logical way of looking at things, downplaying things. And he was usually right. But this was too much. There was enough food to last for weeks, well beyond the time he would be here. She opened her mouth to refuse, but he cut in.

"Oh, just take it. It's not like I can take the stuff back to the store. It will go to waste if you don't use it." He held up the bottle. "Look at that. Half gone already. He sure likes his grub, doesn't he?"

Stifling the feeling of being pushed around, Esther said, "I think you're supposed to help him get his wind up." She cast back to what she'd seen mothers do. "Little babies can't get their air out by themselves. You have to sort of pound on their backs a bit."

Thomas gave her a skeptical glance and set the bottle on the edge of the table. He lifted the fussing baby to his shoulder and gave him the lightest of taps with his fingertips.

"I think you have to do it harder." Esther crossed her arms at her waist.

"I'm afraid to break him. He's lighter than an oat stem." He patted again. The infant squawked and bobbed his head like a baby bird, bumping his nose on Thomas's shoulder. "You sure about this?"

"I'm sure. He'll have awful gas pains if you don't help him burp. Try rubbing in circles."

The infant cried harder. "Mad about being taken away from his feed trough, isn't he? Wish he'd just belch and get it over wi—" Before Thomas could finish the word, the baby obliged, sending a currant of milk sloshing onto his shoulder and down the front of his shirt.

Esther couldn't help but laugh at the expression on Thomas's face. The baby quit crying, almost as if his feat surprised him. She was still laughing when she took the boy. "Good job, little one. You sound like a range-hardened cowhand." She wiped his mouth and chin, snuggling him close while Thomas peeled his sodden shirt away from his skin and looked around for a towel.

"I already sacrificed my other shirt to wrap him up after he was born, and now he's christened this one."

Hospitality demanded that Esther come to his aid, but she had a hard time forcing the words out. "There are clean shirts in the bureau in my father's room. You can borrow one of those, and I'll wash yours tomorrow. You can put that one to soak in the washtub." Esther pointed to the second bedroom door at the back of the house, and took Thomas's place in the rocker and offered the bottle to the baby again.

"I'm making a lot more work for you. I'm sorry." He disappeared into her father's room and returned, buttoning up a faded blue shirt that was tight across the shoulders and chest. He left the cuffs unbuttoned and rolled up the sleeves. Seeing him coming out of her father's room made Esther's heart ache. Her father wasn't coming back, and she wasn't being disloyal by loaning out one shirt. She tamped down her feelings, striving for the calm demeanor she'd been practicing ever since that moment the ranch foreman had come to the door to tell her that her father was dead.

"Sorry about the extra work," Thomas apologized again.

"A couple more shirts won't tax me." This time, Esther took the precaution of putting a cloth against her shoulder before burping the baby.

"Thank you for letting me stay on while I figure out what to do with him. That's the good thing about the way I live. All I need is six feet of space to spread my bedroll."

"You plan to stay here?" She brushed a kiss on the baby's hair, unable to stop herself. He was just so sweet. The notion of Thomas staying on the ranch sent her senses reeling, and she concentrated on the infant in an effort to get herself under control.

"Sure. Where else would I go? I want to be close to keep an eye out on the little guy."

Esther nestled the baby into the curve of her arm, grateful that he had dropped off to sleep again, when a thought occurred to her. "You aren't staying in the house."

Thomas's eyes went wide. "Of course not. I'll be out in the bunkhouse, like I used to be. Probably in the same bunk that used to be mine." He scrubbed his hand against the back of his neck. "I figure a few days, a week at the most, and I'll have sorted out what to do with the baby. Then I can get back on the trail."

If he planned to sleep in the bunkhouse tonight, he'd have his work cut out for him. Nothing on this ranch was the same as it had been when he'd worked here, not the buildings, not the livestock and certainly not her.

"That's fine." She lay the baby in the basket and

put her hands on her hips. "Since you provided the fixin's, I might as well make some supper. Then I'm headed to bed. It's been a long day, and I am looking forward to a good night's sleep."

Thomas shouldered his saddlebags, snapped his fingers at Rip and headed out into the moonlight. He rubbed his stomach. That was the best meal he'd had in a long time. Biscuits, fried ham, red-eye gravy and green beans. Someone had taught Esther to cook during the last five years, since he recalled her saying once that she was glad they had domestic help because she barely knew a whisk from a wagon wheel and was hopeless in the kitchen.

Tumbleweeds and brush clogged the yard and piled up in the corners of buildings and fences, but the moonlight hid most of the faults of the buildings and grounds. He checked on the horses in the corral beside the barn, making sure they had water. The ground inside the rails was overgrown, so they'd have plenty of fodder for the time being.

A shame about this place, really. It had so much potential. Good grass, good water, close to town. When he'd worked here, it had been a prosperous ranch. Plenty of cattle, good horses, a full crew.

So much had changed since he was a stripling kid, digging post holes, stringing wire, taking the jokes and ribbing of the older cowhands, barely dreaming of something more than working for fifteen dollars a month.

Falling in love with the boss's daughter.

Yep, a lot had changed. He was older, more trail

worn. The Double J had gone to seed. And he had shouldered a responsibility that had him leg-roped to one place for the first time in years.

And yet, one thing hadn't changed a bit. Esther Jensen still had the power to stir him. From the moment he'd first laid eyes on her years ago, his heart had started thumping and his wits had scattered to the wind. Her, with her brown hair and light brown eyes, the sassy toss of her head and the swish of her skirts, everything about her fascinated him.

But more than her heart-stirring looks…she had been kind. Kind to everyone from her father to the Mexican girls who cooked and cleaned for them. And lively. She loved to ride, and she was good with animals. Orphaned calves, dogs, young horses, she had a knack with all of them. Her love of animals was more than half the reason he'd gotten Rip and brought him home when he was just a puppy.

She just seemed to make the world a brighter place for being in it. She had made his life brighter, too.

And now he was back, however briefly. This time he vowed to leave her better than he found her, to try to make some amends for the hurt she'd suffered.

Thomas shouldered his way into the bunkhouse, grimacing as the door sagged on its hinges and ground along the wooden floor. He let his bags drop and dug in his shirt for a match, striking it with his thumbnail and holding it up to survey his temporary sleeping quarters.

"This is not encouraging." He found a battered lantern with a little kerosene in it on the table and lit it, shaking out the match flame. Turning up the wick, he spied the bunk he'd been assigned when first hired on. The one right by the door, where the wind and dust and cold seeped in and where every cowhand passed by on his way to his bed. Lowest in the pecking order got the bunk by the door.

Rip nosed about, investigating corners. He sneezed and flapped his ears.

"Little dusty?" Thomas asked. He kicked the bunk, then picked up the mattress and shook it, wondering how many rodents might be nesting inside. Maybe he'd be better off in the barn or in his bedroll under the stars. This place needed a thorough cleaning before he could sleep here.

"Let's check out our other options." He snapped his fingers at Rip, picked up the lantern and his bedroll, and headed outside.

The barn wasn't any better. No hay or straw, and if he didn't miss his guess, bats had taken over the loft. He blew out the lantern and hung it on a peg inside the barn door. "Guess it's outside for us, pard."

They skirted the meager woodpile and the washtubs and kettles, ducking under the clothesline, as they headed toward the house. "The porch will be better than the dirt, don't you think?"

A soft light glowed from Esther's bedroom window and then went out. The bedsprings creaked, and then the only sound was the wind in the grasses and a far-off coyote yip.

Quietly, Thomas spread his bedroll on the porch floor and stretched out on it. Sleep dragged at his eyelids as Rip circled and flopped down beside him.

Thomas buried his hand in Rip's fur, glad for the warmth the big dog gave off.

Even with all he needed to think about, Thomas couldn't keep his eyes open. Long days on the hunt, a sleepless night delivering a baby, a desperate ride to get the little fellow to help and an encounter with the only woman he had ever loved had taken their toll. Time enough tomorrow to think about what he should do about the baby's future, about getting back on Swindell's trail and about helping out Esther as much as she would let him.

Chapter Four

It seemed Thomas had barely closed his eyes when he was jolted awake. Rip bounded to his feet, letting out a low woof that had Thomas drawing his gun from the holster he'd placed at his side before falling asleep.

He scanned the starlit area in front of the house, wondering what had roused him. Years of hunting bad men had taught him to be on guard, but lack of sleep had dulled his wits. His head felt as if it had been stuffed with sawdust.

Then the sound came again. The baby was crying. Rip whined and went to the door.

Thomas forced himself to relax, laying the gun on the floor. If he got to the little fellow in time, perhaps Esther wouldn't even wake up. He levered himself up and placed his hand flat on the front door, easing it open.

He was just bending over the cradle when her bedroom door opened and candlelight shone over him.

"What are you doing in here?" She gathered the lapels of her housecoat around her. Her eyes glistened in the candle flame, dark and wide, and her hair tumbled about her shoulders in a river of chocolate-toned curls.

His breath snagged in his chest. He'd never seen her with her hair unbound before. Her bare toes curled against the floorboards, and the flush of sleep rode her cheeks.

"I heard him crying." He lifted the baby out of the basket.

"From clear out in the bunkhouse?" She had more starch in her voice than a brand-new, store-bought shirt collar.

"The bunkhouse isn't fit to live in right now. I rolled out my blankets on the front porch." Thomas cradled the baby's head in one palm, his little rump in the other. "Hush there, little fella, there's no need to get all worked up."

The baby disagreed. He drew his legs up, eyes screwed shut, mouth wide as a fresh-hatched bird. "Is he hungry again? What time is it?" Thomas squinted at the clock on the wall. "Seems like he just ate."

"He did, not more than an hour ago." She gathered her hair into a bunch on her shoulder. "Does he need a new diaper?"

"Not so I can tell." Thomas shifted the baby to his shoulder, grappling with the child, the blanket and his own awkwardness.

"Maybe he needs to bring up more wind?" Esther used her candle to light two others on the table.

Thomas patted the infant, but it didn't seem to make any difference. "Is he in pain?" The thought of something so little and helpless hurting made Thomas's gut clench.

"Let me try." Esther took the child, cradling him, crooning and shushing. She rubbed small circles on his little back. "Don't cry, baby." She looked up. "We really should give him a name. We can't keep calling 'baby.'"

Thomas paced, scratching his cheek, his whiskers rasping. "His mama didn't live long enough to tell me what she planned to name her son. Any suggestions?"

"Did she tell you anything at all? The baby's father's name?"

He stopped. "She said his name was Jason."

"Jason." She swayed, rocking the baby. "Maybe we could pick a name with the same first letter. What about John? That's a good, sturdy name. He can be Johnny when he's little and John when he grows up." She had to raise her voice over the pitiful cries.

"Johnny." Thomas tested the name. "I like it."

John Swindell, if she only knew.

"What can we do for him?" Thomas hooked his thumbs into his back pockets. "He's killing me with that crying."

Esther took the baby to the table and laid him down, peeling back the blankets. "Maybe he has a pin sticking him." She checked him over, but the safety pins were closed. Being unwrapped seemed to make things worse. Johnny's face reddened, and he jerked his legs up toward his little tummy.

"Maybe wrap him up tight like a papoose."

Rip paced and whined, tall enough to get his muzzle up near the edge of the table, sniffing. He let out a low woof.

"We're trying, fella." Thomas scrubbed the big dog's head.

As Esther cocooned Johnny and lifted him up, he brought up a stream of sour milk that hit the floor. The crying stopped, reduced to a bout of hiccups and snuffles. "I guess his tummy *was* upset."

"Think he'll sleep now?" Thomas grabbed a towel from the shelf near the stove. "I'll clean up. You sit with him." He steered her toward the rocker and then knelt to mop up the mess.

Esther settled Johnny in against her chest, his head tucked under her chin. In the candlelight they looked like they could be mother and son. Something squeezed in Thomas's chest. If he hadn't ridden away five years ago, would she have ever considered marrying him against her father's wishes? And if they had, would they have kids? Would she be sitting there with his son in her arms?

Knock it off. Those are pipe dreams. The fact is, you left, and it was for the best. She deserves better than you.

"I'll fetch some water." Thomas picked up the bucket beside the door and headed out toward the windmill and pump. The moon had already started its descent, and stars coated the sky. Far away a coyote yipped, and its mate answered.

The path to the windmill was hard-packed, and Thomas imagined Esther had walked it hundreds of times, filling up washtubs and kettles day after day. What she needed was a pipe and spigot, so the water from the tank would flow down to where she washed the clothes without her having to carry it.

He hooked the windmill to the pump handle, letting water gush out into the tank for a moment before sticking the bucket under the spout. Already he was tallying materials and the tools needed to plumb a line. Shouldn't take more than a day.

When he returned to the house, Esther was asleep, the baby snuggled in her arms. Thomas set the bucket down gently and tossed the soiled towel into it to soak. He eased into a chair, content to watch Esther and Johnny sleep. A yawn cracked his jaw, and he rested his elbow on the table and his head on his fist for a moment. Surely now, everyone could settle down and get some rest.

Esther squinted at the clock, wondering if it was even worth it to go back to bed. For what seemed the hundredth time that night, Johnny cried out. She'd tried feeding, rocking, changing, singing and every-thing else she could think of. Thomas had tried, too.

"It's got to be his tummy. Maybe it's the canned milk that isn't agreeing with him," Esther said, want-ing to cry herself. "It's the only thing left I can think of."

Thomas ran his fingers through his hair, making it stand on end. Red rimmed his eyes, and his whiskers darkened his cheeks. "That's it. I'm heading out at first light to get a nanny goat." He rubbed his hands down his face, yawning. "I feel terrible feeding him something that upset his innards so much."

Esther nodded. The only place Johnny seemed to get any rest at all was in the center of her chest with her housecoat wrapped around them both. The poor little mite had thrown up repeatedly, his abdomen hard, his legs drawing up tight. They'd washed him from head to toes twice to get the sour milk smell off, using up the last of her special soap in the process.

Thomas had stayed with her all night, even when she knew he would probably love to bolt from the house and find somewhere to get some rest. He'd even shared in the walking and rocking and patting, though Johnny seemed to want Esther most. Rip had worried and walked right along with them, and now the big dog lay sprawled next to the rocking chair.

At long last, dawn began to pink the sky, fingers of light reaching through the front windows and chasing the shadows to the corners of the room. Thomas leaned over and blew out the almost guttering candles.

Johnny slept on, his tiny fist resting on Esther's collarbone, his cheek pillowed in the hollow of her neck.

"I'd grind beans for coffee, but I'm afraid of waking him up again." Thomas eased down onto one of the wooden chairs, putting his head on his crossed arms on the table. "Who knew one little baby could rout two grown adults, horse, foot and artillery? If I had known I wouldn't get back to my bedroll, I mightn't have been so quick to leap out of it when he first started to cry."

She didn't know whether to be glad or exasperated that Thomas had elected to sleep out on the porch. When she'd come out of her bedroom and seen him bending over the baby, he'd nearly frightened her out of her wits.

But now…

Tousled hair, bristled chin, rumpled clothing, sleep-deprived and in need of coffee, he'd never looked so appealing to Esther.

"I know it's Sunday, but after last night, I don't think I'll be going to church. Unless you want me to hitch up the buggy for you." He said the last on a yawn.

"Don't bother. The church has been without a preacher for months. Folks in town have a prayer meeting that moves from house to house, but I don't know who is hosting it this week."

She felt herself drifting toward sleep and forced herself to open her eyes. "I'm going to try putting him in the basket again. Hopefully he'll sleep long enough for me to dress and start breakfast."

Thomas let out a snore.

Esther smiled. In the words of her Kentucky grandma, he was worn slap out.

Carefully, holding her breath, she eased Johnny into the blanket-lined basket. He stirred and relaxed, staying asleep, and she exhaled.

She gently closed her bedroom door, glancing in the mirror on her bureau. With a gasp, she reached for her hairbrush. She looked like she'd been dragged through a knothole backward. Her mop of curly hair had bushed out like a sagebrush, and dark smudges circled her eyes. Working to tidy her hair, she gazed out her bedroom window. Standing on tiptoe and angling her head, she could just see the porch floor where Thomas's blankets lay, half tossed aside from where he'd jumped out of them.

His rifle lay on the boards, and his pistol at one

end of the bedroll, the cartridge belt wrapped around the holster.

A chill chased up her back at the sight of the pistol. She hated guns, but pistols especially.

Her hands went slack on her half-fashioned braid as she remembered back to that horrible day. Thomas had been gone from the ranch for almost a week, and at that time Esther still hadn't given up hope that he would return. She'd been fixing her hair then, too, hoping to look pretty just in case Thomas came back.

Carlita had called to her from the front room, and her heart had skipped a beat as she finished pinning up her braid.

Bark Getty had stood in the doorway, his hat in his hand, shifting his weight from boot to boot. The ranch foreman hadn't come to the house often.

"Good morning, Mr. Getty. My father isn't here. He was up at first light and out of the house. I'm not sure if he went to town or if he is out on the range." She rolled down her sleeve and buttoned her cuff.

"That's why I'm here, Miss Esther." He looked at the floor, out the window and over her shoulder, but not in her eyes.

"Would you like a cup of coffee?" She tried to ignore the skitter of unease that brushed her skin.

"No, thank you." He twisted his hat brim. "Miss Esther, I don't want to have to tell you this, but your pa…"

"What?" Her hand went to her throat and unease turned to panic.

"He's dead, ma'am." Mr. Getty finally met her eyes, his troubled under their heavy brows. He brushed his hand down his long, dark whiskers.

"Did he fall from his horse?"

"No, ma'am. It wasn't an accident. He…" He took a deep breath. "Your pa shot himself."

She would never forget the shock, the pain, the bewilderment. Nor the sense of betrayal. How could he leave her that way? On purpose and so finally?

Esther didn't remember much of the following days, except for the overwhelming grief. Others had prepared her father's body for the funeral. Others had prepared the meal, the service, the gravesite. She hadn't wanted him buried at the cemetery in town, and no one had objected to having him buried on the Double J. In fact, she surmised that some folks were glad not to have a suicide victim buried on church grounds.

His suicide was just one in a cascade of shocking events for her. The foreman had come to her to tell her that the bulk of her father's cattle had been rustled, and the banker had informed her that there were considerable outstanding debts in her father's name. She had no choice but to order the last of the cattle rounded up and all the horses, too. With the exception of the buckboard team, every animal on the place had been sold, along with most everything else of value. Within a month, the ranch hands had departed, and Carlita and Maria sought work elsewhere.

A week after the funeral, she'd mustered the courage to go into her father's room. That's where she'd found his note. The one that apologized for leaving her, for his lack of courage, for not seeing what was happening right under his nose. And he'd begged her to do everything she could to hold on to the ranch.

For the first time in her life, Esther had to fend for herself. Her few friends had urged her to sell her home and move into town, but she had stubbornly hung on, vowing to fulfill her father's wishes. And each year, it had gotten harder. This year she might have to admit defeat. The taxes were due in about six weeks, and at the rate she was earning, she would be short the total amount.

She finished braiding and pinning up her hair. Thankfully, the baby slept on, and so did Thomas. They might've had a rough night, but somehow, as it always did, the sun came up, lifting Esther's spirits. She could always cope better when the sun was up. It was at night that her cares and problems pressed in and swelled. The Bible verse about God's mercies being new every morning came back to her.

"I could use some mercy right now, Lord. Thank You for the sunshine."

And with sunup came chores. She wouldn't worry about breakfast now, not with Thomas and Johnny finally asleep. Easing from the house, she paused for a moment to breathe in the fresh morning air. As quietly as she could, she rolled Thomas's blankets and tied them, leaving them propped up against the side of the house. She couldn't make herself touch the pistol.

Eight trips to the pump saw the washtubs and kettle filled, and she unpacked the bundles of laundry Danny Newton and his men had brought yesterday. If she could get a couple tubs of wash done first thing, she could use her afternoon to sew for Johnny. She smiled at how quickly the name had stuck.

Having kindled the fire under the kettle, she dumped

Danny's shirts into the water. Her woodpile was shrinking at a depressing rate. Soon she would have to head out into the mesquite thickets with her hatchet and lay in another supply, doing even more backbreaking work than bending over a scrub board. It was something she put off for as long as possible. She shaved a few slivers of homemade lye soap into her washtub, dipped some hot water from the iron kettle and got to work.

"Why didn't you wake me?"

She jumped and whirled, her hand to her chest. Thomas stood there, looking still half-asleep.

"You scared me, sneaking up like that." Her heart raced. "Is the baby still asleep?"

"Yeah, though he's getting restless like he's going to wake up any minute." Thomas yawned and stretched. "I wanted to be up at first light." He frowned, and she smothered a smile. Lack of sleep obviously made him as cranky as a little boy.

"You needed some rest. It's only been an hour or so since you dropped off."

"You need sleep, too, but here you are scrubbing clothes and looking way too fresh and prettier than you've a right to, considering the night you just went through." He rasped his whiskers, making a sandpapery sound so masculine Esther's breath skidded in her throat. She knew she shouldn't let him affect her, shouldn't take his compliment to heart, but he'd never told her she was pretty before. Tucking that thought away to ponder later, she reached back into the washtub.

"My customers won't care that I had a broken night. They'll expect their clothes to be clean when they come pick them up. I'm behind already, so Sunday or not, I'm going to work." She wrung out a soapy shirt and dropped it into the rinse water.

"You need one of those mangle wringer things." He stretched his arms over his head, yawning again. Her father's worn, chambray shirt pulled tighter across his chest and shoulders.

She averted her gaze. "Those 'mangle wringer things' cost money."

"Uh-oh," Thomas tilted his head. "Sounds like little Johnny's tuning up again. That's why I didn't want to fall asleep. I'm headed out to find a cow or a goat or a sheep or a mountain lion if it comes to that…some beast to provide fresh milk that will hopefully be better on his innards than that canned stuff."

Esther walked back with him to the house, trying to ignore the fact that he stopped on the porch to strap on his sidearm and pick up his rifle.

"I'll be back as soon as I can. If you get a chance, and Johnny lets you, take a nap."

"I don't need a nap. I'll be fine."

"Then take one for me. I could use one." He winked and strode out, snapping his fingers for the dog to follow. Rip hesitated, looking from the baby to the open doorway, before trotting outside.

Esther picked up Johnny, going to the window to see Thomas headed for the corral, Rip at his side.

"He'll be back," she whispered against the baby's hair. "But how long will he stay?"

Chapter Five

"That right there is the most cantankerous beast God ever created." Thomas scowled at the goat that stared back and gave a loud bleat. What a nightmare. Goats always looked a little unstable to him, with their horizontal pupils and bony heads, and this one was the most unstable of the lot. At least Thomas had managed to finally get her into the corral.

"She's lovely," Esther said, studying the rust-brown animal.

Thomas studied Esther. She'd fashioned a sort of sling like he'd seen Mexican women wear, and Johnny nestled inside against her chest, leaving her hands free. Stray tendrils of hair had escaped her braid and teased her temples, and bending over her washtubs had put color in her cheeks.

The goat let out another bleat, staring, wild-eyed, as if she was sizing up a target to charge. She'd already butted Thomas a dozen times with her hard little poll. He should be grateful she didn't have horns. She was a complete mishmash of colors with splashes of white on her rust-brown sides, a white face, and black ears and legs. And a very full udder.

"What's her name?"

"Menace? Pestilence? Calamity? Take your pick." Thomas yanked off his hat and smacked his thigh with it. "The Molina family was only too eager to sell me a milking goat. Now I know why. They wanted to be rid of her." He pointed, still scowling. "She kicks and hollers and won't be led on a rope. Bucks like a demented bronco, and every time I get near her, she screams like I'm about to throw her on a barbecue."

"The poor thing. She's probably just scared." Esther knelt along the fence, held out her hand to the goat, and with the other she steadied the baby. "I doubt she's ever had a rope around her neck before. You'd put up a fuss, too."

The goat came right over and gently bumped her head against Esther's hand. Thomas snorted. "Don't turn your back on her."

Crooning, Esther stroked the goat's neck. "I'm going to call her Daisylu." She rubbed the goat's head. "She probably needs milking, and Johnny's definitely going to be hungry when he wakes up. I gave him some sugar water to tide him over, but he needs milk."

Great. Now he had to milk a goat. Thomas was thankful none of the outlaws and bandits he tracked down could see him now, nursemaiding a loco nanny goat. "I'll get a bucket."

Glad he'd tied her to the fence, Thomas went into the corral. The minute he got within ten feet of Esther's precious Daisylu, the animal swapped ends and started bawling. She charged a couple of times, hitting the end of the rope, stomping her foot, bleating and hollering.

"You need to talk nicely to her. Get her to see she doesn't need to be afraid."

"*She* doesn't need to be afraid?" Thomas muttered. He'd never had an animal take such a set against him.

Esther plucked a few weed stems and offered them through the fence to Daisylu, who nibbled them up and looked around for more. "Maybe if you fed her something she'd calm down."

Thomas tried several more times to get close, but Daisylu blocked him each time. Finally, he threw his hands up in the air. "Short of hog-tying her, I don't see this working out."

Esther slipped out of the sling and handed Johnny to him. "Let me try."

"Have you ever milked a goat?" He positioned the baby in the crook of his arm.

"No, but I can't be any worse at it than you are." She grinned, her first genuine smile since he'd arrived on her doorstep. A burst of pleasure shot through his chest, and he grinned back.

"I'll give you that."

With more patience than Thomas could muster with the stubborn beast, Esther crooned and petted and fussed over the animal. The nanny goat leaned against Esther's leg, lapping up the attention. She even closed her eyes at one point, the picture of bliss.

Stupid goat. "I paid good money for her. The least she could do is be grateful."

Daisylu opened her eyes and glared as if to tell him to be quiet. Esther giggled.

In twenty minutes, Esther had a foamy half pail of milk, and Daisylu was released to graze in the overgrown corral. Thomas's horse kept well away from her, something with which Thomas could sympathize. Though he'd turned the team and the extra horse into the trap, he kept his mount in the corral where he'd be handy.

"Just in time." Thomas jostled Johnny, who blinked and squirmed. "The little fella is warming up his dinner bell."

Esther took the baby, and Thomas brought the pail into the house. While she changed Johnny's britches, Thomas followed her instructions and strained the milk through a bit of cheesecloth.

"Since it's so fresh, we won't need to warm it up." Esther wrapped and pinned the dishcloth as if she'd been doing it all her life instead of just over a day. "After he's fed, I need to get to making those diapers. I'm clean out of dish towels now."

"Let me feed him." Thomas used a funnel to fill the nursing bottle. "That's one thing I can do."

He sat in the rocker and took the baby. "Here's hoping this stuff agrees with you better. We don't need a repeat of last night's performance. And I doubt the Molinas would take the goat back, even if I paid them."

The boy looked up at him, taking long pulls on the bottle. Something kicked in Thomas's chest at the complete trust in Johnny's eyes. Though Thomas looked for a resemblance to either Jase or the woman, he couldn't make any out. Here he was holding the child of Jase Swindell, one of the most notorious outlaws in Texas, and he didn't have a clue what to do with him.

Logic said he should head into town and leave him with the sheriff, who could track down Jase's sister over in Spillville and see if she was fit to take the baby, or he should take him over to San Antonio and hand him into the keeping of a pastor there, trusting the church to find a good home for the boy. Then Thomas would be free of his obligation and could get back to the business of capturing Jase Swindell.

There was a sizable reward for his recapture, and if Thomas lagged, some other bounty hunter or lawman would make the arrest, and his hopes of recouping his expenses and making a profit would be out the window and down the road.

And yet, as he held the baby, looking down into his eyes, smelling the scent of Esther's store-bought soap, feeling the grasp of his tiny hand, he found himself throwing logic to the wind. Though the child wasn't his, though he didn't even have a home to call his own, Thomas wondered what it would be like if he kept the boy.

He worried about the child the way he had never worried about another person before. Of course, he'd never had anyone so young and helpless depending on him to make the right decisions.

Thomas didn't want to see Johnny raised in a family of outlaws and no-goods only to grow up to be like them. He refused to leave him in an orphanage where babies this small had a hard time surviving, let alone thriving. What if Johnny never got adopted? Being the child of a wanted felon and murderer surely wouldn't make him the most desirable child in the place. Or, worse, what if the wrong family adopted him and didn't treat him well?

God, protect this little life. He's been given a tough row to hoe. I'm a good tracker, but I'm not following a clear trail here. Help me to make a wise decision about what to do with him.

Esther bustled about, clearing the table and getting out her sewing basket. She unfolded yards of snowy flannel, draping her tape measure around her neck, setting out a pin cushion and shears.

He loved the little arrow of concentration that formed between her brows as she studied the cloth and decided how best to attack it. That was Esther, diving headfirst into a project, determined to conquer it, staying on course and not wavering. She'd always been focused when it came to reaching her goals; that much he remembered well.

"Trudy said sixteen-inch squares, doubled and hemmed, for the diapers," Esther muttered. "I can get two dozen out of this length, which will leave the other for gowns…"

It didn't stop there. She kept up a steady conversation with herself as she worked. Thomas interrupted Johnny's feeding to burp him, which made the little guy cranky. After he finished the bottle, Thomas laid him in the basket, his little rump in the air, to sleep.

"If you need anything, holler. I'm going to see to a couple things outside."

She barely acknowledged him, she was concentrating so hard.

Rip greeted him on the porch, tail wagging, tongue

lolling. The day had heated up nicely, and the sunshine was fierce in the June Texas sky. Thomas headed to the bunkhouse. If he wanted a place to sleep tonight, he'd best get on that first.

Broad daylight didn't improve the bunkhouse's looks at all, particularly since that daylight was streaming through a hole in the roof. Rust furred the potbellied stove in the middle of the square room, and debris and leaf litter covered the floor and piled up in the corners.

"Well, nobody ever drowned in their own sweat. Let's see what we can do." Thomas rolled up the sleeves on his borrowed shirt and got to work.

Two hours later, the place was tidy, if not pristine. He'd raided the tool shed, coming upon a bundle of shingle shakes in the process. The hole in the roof looked to have been caused by a tree falling on it. The cottonwood trunk lay on the ground behind the building, bleaching in the hot sun. All the smaller branches had been cut off and were gone. Perhaps used as firewood? But the bulk of the tree must've been too big for Esther to deal with. He hated to think of her out here struggling with an ax or saw to gather the wood for her wash kettle fire.

He sent the last nail home on the last shingle and pitched the hammer to the dirt below. Before climbing down the ladder, he paused to survey the ranch yard. Tumbleweeds, broken fences, leaning sheds. The windmill needed repairs, the barn, too. A man could work a month of Sundays getting it all fixed up, but he'd sure have a fine ranch when he was done. The only structure still looking stout and steady was the fence surrounding the trap.

Thomas smiled, bringing his knees up and wrapping his arms around them, anchoring his feet to keep from sliding off the newly repaired roof. That pasture fence had been the burr on his shirttail back when he worked here. The boss had put him on fence building, when all Thomas wanted to do was punch cows. Instead, day after day of backbreaking work digging holes, splitting posts out of tough, stringy cottonwood and mesquite and live oak, getting blisters on his blisters, grappling with wire and stretchers and staples. That pasture had seemed a hundred square miles rather than ten square acres.

Thomas had often wondered if Elihu had stuck him with that job in order to see what he was made of. Or had he just seen a skinny drifter who needed money and wouldn't complain at doing a job the cowboys on the ranch despised?

Not that the job had been without its benefits. The work kept him fairly close to the ranch house, and every day he got to see Esther ride out on her blood bay, prim and proper on a sidesaddle. After a week, she came by and chatted for a minute, and those chats gradually turned into her bringing him a cool drink or some fresh cookies. Sometimes twice a day.

By which time Elihu got wind of what was going on and put a stop to it mighty quick.

Thomas took one more look around Elihu's dilapidated ranch and climbed down the ladder and headed for his next repair job.

Esther bundled Johnny into the sling she'd fashioned from a tablecloth, slipping one arm and her head through the tied cloth and positioning him comfortably. His broken sleep of last night, combined with the goat's milk that seemed to agree with his tummy better than the canned, had put him out for almost three hours now, allowing her to sew diapers and cut out some little gowns. It had been a long time since she had spent an entire afternoon in the house.

Thomas had been outside for hours. The sound of his hammer had been a comfort and an irritation, too. A comfort, because it was nice not to be alone on her property, but an irritation that there were so many things in need of repair that it all just reminded her of how alone she would be when he finally decided to leave. What good did it do to repair the bunkhouse when she wouldn't use it? Or the barn when she had no hay crop or livestock to fill it?

Of course, if she couldn't come up with the tax money, due in mid-July, none of this would matter. She would lose her home entirely. Then what would she do? Where would she go?

She couldn't abide the thought of marrying Danny Newton. Could she force herself to accept his proposal just to hang on to the property? The notion abhorred her, and yet, her options were few.

There was always Silar Falls. Sarah Granville, her friend and mentor, often urged her to sell the ranch, buy a little place in town, and move her laundry business there. She'd even offered to let Esther live with her and her husband, Charlie, but Esther didn't want to impose, and she didn't want to live in town. Her father had pleaded with her in his letter to stay in their home, to make the Double J into the prosperous ranch it should be, and to keep it in the Jensen family.

She lifted the lid on the coffeepot, inhaling the rich scent of freshly brewed Arbuckles. She poured two cups, being sure to tuck the peppermint stick from the bag of coffee beans into her apron pocket. It would only be polite to take some to Thomas, wouldn't it? It wasn't as if she was deliberately seeking out his company or checking up on what he was doing. And she'd been cooped up inside, sewing until her fingers hurt. Fresh air would do her and Johnny good.

She headed to the bunkhouse where she'd last seen Thomas, but at the sound of hammering to her left, she changed direction.

He was halfway up the windmill, hammer in hand, nails between his teeth, pounding a cross brace. She set the cups on the edge of the water trough and shaded her eyes, looking up. He stopped hammering.

"I thought you might like some coffee."

He stuck the hammer into his belt and climbed down. She envied him his easy way. When she had been forced to climb the windmill to fix a broken spar, she'd clung to the rungs, praying, squeezing her eyes shut as she got farther from the ground, trying not to look down, trying to keep her head from spinning. And here he was, climbing up and down like a squirrel.

"Much obliged. I was getting parched." He removed his gloves and stuffed them into the space between his hip and his gun butt.

She looked away from his sidearm and drew the

peppermint stick out of her pocket. "I remember how you liked these."

He smiled, the dimple creasing his left cheek. "Arbuckle was a genius, putting these things in the coffee beans. I was always the first one to volunteer to grind beans, because it meant I got the candy." He broke the red-and-white stick in two and held out one piece to her. "We'll go halves."

She took the piece of candy, popping it into her mouth, savoring the burst of pepperminty sweetness. Candy was something way down her list of necessities, and as a result, she hadn't had any for a long time.

"The bunkhouse is right and tight now, and tomorrow, I'll see about cutting up that felled cottonwood." He sipped the dark brew. "I'll need to go to town to get some lumber and more nails before I start on the barn."

Why was he wasting his time?

"You don't have to fix the barn. What's the point? I never use it." She cuddled her arms around the sleeping baby. "It's hardly worth repairing."

"I want to fix it. It's a shame to see a fine barn like this one in such disrepair. Anyway, you might want to use it sometime, or if you decide to sell, having a good barn will bring in more money. How'd it get so run down so quickly?" He took another sip of coffee, watching her over the rim of his cup.

"A storm caused a lot of the damage several years back. That tree fell on the bunkhouse, and the wind tore boards and shingles off the barn. It rained so hard, the ridge behind the barn had a rock slide, which took out one of the corrals." She remembered hunkering down in the corner of her bedroom that night, praying as the storm raged outside, hail breaking the glass out of the western windows of the house, pounding on the roof, flattening grass and chipping bark off the trees. Lightning arced, and thunder boomed, shaking the ground. The blinding flash and deafening crash of the strike that took out the big tree shuddered through her memory.

"Then the drought came. Weeks on end with no rain. Adobe dried out and crumbled, boards shrank and weathered, sandstorms scoured off paint. It was miserable. Dirt sifted in everywhere. With no money to hire workers and buy supplies, I couldn't make repairs. If the house hadn't been made of stone, I'm sure it would've fallen to bits, too."

"Wasn't anyone working here for you by that time?" The brim of his hat shaded his eyes, but she could still see concern in their brown depths.

"No. The crew left not long after my father died. There were few cattle and no money for wages. They had to look for work elsewhere."

"I'm sorry, Esther. I had no idea you were having such a tough time." He set the cup on the edge of the trough and stepped close.

She raised her chin and moved back. "I'm making out. Earning enough to get by on. Speaking of which, I should get back to work."

She couldn't allow herself to become dependent upon him, because he, just like every man, would leave her eventually. She would need to be strong on her own, like always.

Chapter Six

Late that night, Rip barked, hurling himself against the bunkhouse door, trying to get out. Thomas leaped from his bunk, gun already in his hand. Was something wrong with the baby? With Esther?

Orange light flickered through the window, eerie against the black night. Thomas yanked on his pants, stuffed his feet into his boots and flung open the door.

Smoke bit his eyes and throat.

The barn!

Rip bounded across the yard toward the house, barking, while Thomas raced in the opposite direction toward the barn. His sorrel gelding trotted along the perimeter of the corral, head high, white ringing his eyes. The fence was too tall for him to jump, but the flames from the barn were leaping higher and higher, and Thomas feared the horse would attempt the leap to escape the fire.

Thomas opened the gate, grabbed Smitty by the halter and tugged him toward the opening. The sorrel balked, not wanting to go so close to the flames, but Thomas shouted encouragement, pulling on the halter. In a burst, Smitty bolted through the open gate, and Thomas let go. He would round up the gelding later.

That just left Daisylu, who stood spraddle-legged, rigid with panic, bleating repeatedly. Thomas wasn't about to get into an argument with the stubborn beast, so he scooped her up under the belly and ran out of the corral. Daisylu, indignant, bawled and kicked. He struggled with her down the slight slope toward the house.

As he set the goat on the ground, Esther ran from the house, clutching Johnny in her arms. "Thomas! Are you hurt?"

Thomas slipped the end of a clothesline through Daisylu's collar, tethering her. "I'm fine." He sucked in air that wasn't as thickly laced with smoke as that closer to the blaze. "The barn's on fire. Stay here." He gripped her shoulders for a moment, forcing her to look at him. "I don't want you anywhere near that fire, understand?"

She nodded, her face pale in the darkness. Thomas left her, running for the windmill and the water tank. Filling a bucket, he doused a smoldering bush near the corral fence. Working quickly, he made his way around the barn, putting out flames in the grass and weeds. He had to keep the fire from spreading to the tumbleweeds and brush, or the whole county could go up.

It seemed he labored for hours, filling bucket after bucket. Smoke stung his eyes, and his lungs felt scorched. When he returned to the water tank once more, he found Esther there, dunking feed sacks into the water. "What are you doing here? I told you to keep back."

"You can't do it alone." She had taken the time to dress, and before he could stop her, she picked up a bucket of water and doused herself. Grabbing a soaking feed sack, she turned her attention to beating out flames that licked toward the windmill.

Thomas, too tired to argue with her, plunged his head into the water tank, then grabbed a sack and went back to work protecting the bunkhouse.

An hour later, the barn lay in ashy ruins, wisps of smoke leaking from the few timbers still standing. Thomas and Esther stood side by side as dawn pinked the eastern sky. Soot streaked her face, and embers had burned holes in her dress. The whites of her eyes stood out starkly.

"What did you do with the baby?" Thomas asked. He'd been so busy, he hadn't thought of Johnny for ages.

"I put him in the basket. Rip is with him. In fact, I couldn't get Rip out of the house. He kept barking and growling, but he stayed inside. I could see out the window that you needed help, so I left them in there together. I should check on Johnny. He's probably awake by now…"

Esther dropped the battered sack she held and put her hands over her face, shoulders heaving. Thomas gathered her into his arms, tucking her head beneath his chin, just holding her, trying to absorb her pain. *God, I don't understand. How could You let these*

*things keep happening to someone like Esther, who
never hurt anyone?*

She allowed his embrace for a moment and then
pushed herself wearily away without looking at him,
trudging toward the house with her head down. How
much more could this woman take? She'd been buf-
feted from every side, and even now, when he wanted
to help her, she walked away from him, determined
to make it on her own.

And he had no choice but to let her go.

Thomas poked through the ashes, his mind seething.
When he had awakened, the entire building had been
ablaze. Fires lit by accident didn't burn that way. They
started in one place and spread.

He closed his eyes, trying to recall just how the
barn had looked as he came out of the bunkhouse.
Flames in every window, but not yet in the haymow.
As if someone had started a fire in every stall. Thomas
went over every detail of the scene again, and something flickered on the edge of his vision.

A man. Hunched over and running away.

Weary as he was, Thomas hurried over to the
spot where he thought he'd seen the man. If he could
find his tracks, perhaps he could follow him. But the
ground had been scorched and soaked and beaten
with sacks. Any trail there might have been was oblit-
erated by their efforts to stop the fire from spreading.

Who would deliberately set fire to Esther's barn?
Did she have enemies? Who would want to do harm
to a laundress who went out of her way not to bother
anyone with her troubles?

Or was the fire aimed at him? He'd crossed trails

with plenty of bad men, though most of them were dead or in prison now. Only Jase Swindell was on the loose, and why would he burn a barn? If he was smart, he would be across the Rio Grande in Mexico by now. With such a staggering price on his head and his woman dead, he would have no reason to come back to Texas. The outlaw was probably raiding ranchos and haciendas in Coahuila right now. If he gave a thought to Johnny at all, it was probably to be glad he didn't have to be saddled with a baby.

Of course the fire might've been set by a vagrant. Thomas had heard of men who got a thrill from burning things down. Was this a random act of arson aimed at a convenient structure?

Maybe, but something had the hair on the back of his neck standing up. This felt calculated somehow.

But who was the target? Him, or Esther, or just destruction for destruction's sake?

Thomas would have to be extra vigilant until he could discern the truth.

And that would involve an errand to the sheriff's office, something he should've done yesterday.

Catching the team took longer than he thought. The horses were definitely spooked and jittery. Thomas was glad he'd stored the harnesses in the bunkhouse so he could repair and oil them in the evenings or they would've been part of the ashes of the barn.

He washed up as best he could before he left, but short of a full bath, there wasn't much he could do about the smoke smell in his hair. Skirting around Daisylu, who munched grass around the base of the clothesline pole, he stepped onto the porch.

Pausing just outside the door, he listened to Esther talk to the baby.

"You're such a handsome boy, aren't you? I'm sorry I had to leave you for so long last night, but you understand. Sometimes men can be so stubborn. Thomas needed my help, and that's all there is to it. And you had Rip looking out for you."

He peeked inside. Esther rocked in the chair, holding the bottle. She must've milked the goat already. Rip raised his head, keen of ear. Thomas could never sneak up on him, and leaving him here with Esther and Johnny was a comfort.

Laid out on the table in clean piles was the laundry she'd done yesterday morning: shirts and pants and socks and small clothes, all ready for her customers to pick up. How she got so much done in a day, he'd never know.

His own two shirts lay in a stack all their own. She'd washed them, just as she'd promised.

He tapped on the door frame. "Hey, I wanted to let you know I'm heading out."

Her chair stopped, and her head swiveled. The color drained from her cheeks, and her eyes glistened like agates under river water. "Heading out?" She tightened her hold on Johnny, her lips trembling as she drew in a shuddering breath. "You're leaving?"

Thomas tugged off his hat and scratched his head. The fire had clearly put Esther on edge. "I wanted to pick up some things at the hardware store in town, and I thought I'd drop in and see the sheriff. I usually like to check in with the local law when I'm in a town. I find it keeps things civil, and I can get a good read on how the sheriff or marshal feels about bounty hunters in their territory. Not everybody has a good reaction to what I do."

She eased back into the rocker, biting her lower lip. Johnny squirmed and squawked, and she offered him the bottle once more. "I never thought of you needing to check in. Charlie Granville is still the sheriff, though I hear he plans on retiring at the end of the year when his term is up." She put the baby up to her shoulder, patting his back. "Also, I need to apologize about your shirts."

"What for?" He went to the table and lifted one up. "Did the stains not come out?"

"Oh, no, they washed up beautifully." She shrugged, not meeting his eyes. "But, you see, I pegged out the shirts to dry on the line last night, and well, you tied Daisylu to the clothesline pole this morning, and she seems to have nibbled the tails on both your shirts."

He shook out the chambray shirt and surveyed the shredded edge. And the red placket front looked the same. He set his jaw, shaking his head. That conniving cud chewer. "How many shirts did she ruin in all? Will you have to reimburse your customers? If so, I'll take care of it. It was my fault for tethering her where she could reach the laundry."

"That's just it. The only shirts she ate were yours. I can't figure out how she knew which were which. They weren't hanging side by side, and she had to skip over two of Danny Newton's shirts to get to yours."

Was that laughter smothered in her voice?

"I am sorry. I'll make sure she is kept away from the laundry. It's just so odd that she would only chew on those two, when there were so many to pick from…" This time she couldn't quell a giggle.

Thomas clutched the shirts in his fists. He should've known better than to get involved with goats. They were nothing but trouble from sunup to sundown and all night long, too.

But when Esther finally caught his eye, he found his mouth crumpling, and soon he joined her, leaning against the table, laughing like they had in the old days. The tension about the fire eased and trickled out of his muscles.

He changed his shirt, tucking in the ravaged tails, thankful that nobody would be able to tell that a goat had dined on them. Maybe he'd add a trip to the mercantile to his list and get some nonchewed garments.

As he climbed onto the buckboard and headed out the gate, leaving Rip behind to watch over the place, he shook his head. Had Esther really thought he was riding out for good?

Thomas had taken the news about his shirts better than she'd thought he would. Daisylu didn't even have the decency to look ashamed of her actions, blandly munching weeds and letting down her milk for Esther first thing, no longer seeming traumatized by the fire.

Esther put Johnny down to nap and began bundling up the clean clothes and sorting them into the correct laundry bags. She still had the hands' laundry from the Circle C to wash, but they weren't going to pick up theirs until Wednesday. The wizened old cook, a Mexican with skin like dried leather, would drop off more dirty clothes and pick up the clean ones on his way into town to get supplies for the ranch. It was always bittersweet for Esther when Yadier came by, since at one time he had been the bunkhouse cook here on the Double J.

Thankfully, Johnny slept the morning away, allowing Esther to accomplish many items on her to-do list, starting with a head-to-toe bath for herself. She hated the smell of smoke in her hair, and having Thomas in town and the baby asleep gave her the perfect time to scrub it away.

While combing the snarls out of her hair, she pondered her predicament. The barn was gone completely, which, while not affecting her day-to-day existence as a laundress, certainly was a loss to a ranch property. How had the fire started? There had been no lightning, not even a cloud in the sky last night. And no one had taken a lantern in there and left it burning. The building had been empty and silent for several years now, barring whatever critters might've taken up residence there.

Buildings didn't just spontaneously burst into flames.

She shivered in spite of the warming day. Though some people in Silar Falls had been disdainful when her father ended his life, no one had been angry, not even the banker to whom her father owed so much money. And she couldn't imagine anyone she might've offended to such a degree.

Checking on Johnny, who slept sweetly in his basket with Rip on the floor nearby, she tied her hair at her nape. Once it was fully dry she would braid it and pin it up, but for now, she had laundry to wash.

Once she got the fire started and the water toted, and

she was bent over her scrub board, she had no choice but to face the thoughts she'd been pushing aside.

When Thomas had said he was leaving, panic and despair had charged through her. It had been all she could do not to burst into tears.

You know better, Esther. He will leave you soon, and you had better be prepared for it. Don't trust him with your heart again and don't come to rely on him. And do not become attached to Johnny. You're just taking care of him for a few days. It's already Monday, and Thomas said he'd stay a week or so. That gives you four more days. Just get through four more days with your heart intact.

But the way Thomas had held her as she cried after the fire was put out came back to her, the safe feeling of his arms around her, the hard wall of his chest protecting her from harm, the comfort of his hands holding her close, absorbing her hurt and offering solace. She had been alone for so long, without anyone to care about her, even a little, that her heart had wanted to leap out of her chest and right into his safekeeping.

"Morning, Esther."

She whirled, scattering an arc of soapy water that splashed across Danny Newton's chest, making him leap back. "Hey! Watch out." He swiped at a blob of bubbles on his shirtfront. "You sure were woolgathering. I walked right up on you. You should be more careful. I could've been anybody sneaking around."

"What do you want?" The last thing she wanted was to have to deal with Danny today.

"Well, now, I want a lot of things." He scratched the sandy-blond hair above his ear, pushing his hat up to a cocky angle. "For today, I guess I'd like to know what happened to my barn."

"Your barn?" Indignation flared. "You don't own this place, Danny Newton."

"I would if you'd just quit being stubborn and marry me." He tugged at the bright blue bandanna around his neck. "I'm not going to wait forever, you know."

"Don't wait, then. Stop asking. Find someone else to marry and get on with your life."

He set his jaw. "What happened to *your* barn?"

"It burned, obviously." She wrung out the shirt she'd been washing and tossed it into the rinse water.

"Did Beaufort start it?" His eyes narrowed, and he pressed his lips together.

"What? Of course not. Why would you say that?" She picked up a heavy pail of water to pour into the rinse tub. Danny didn't offer to help her the way Thomas did. Instead, he stuck his thumbs into his waistband and scowled.

"He just shows up out of nowhere after all this time and two days later your barn burns? Do you think that's a coincidence? You think he's after your ranch and is hoping to drive you off it?"

"That's ridiculous. Thomas won't settle down in once place. He's not staying long." He never did. "He's just waiting for the baby to get a little stronger. He's in town right now probably sending telegrams out in a search for Johnny's relatives."

"Who is that kid, anyway? And why are you taking care of him? I don't like Beaufort staying out here with you. He might get ideas."

Esther shook her head. Danny was wide of the mark if he thought Thomas had ideas about her. He needed her help with the baby, and after that, he was gone from her life.

Rip stepped out onto the porch. Spying Danny, he went rigid, his mismatched eyes glowing. A growl rumbled in his chest, and his lip raised a fraction to reveal his sharp teeth.

"And I don't like that dog." Danny rested his hand on his sidearm. "He's vicious. Suppose he bites you or that little baby you got in there?"

Esther put herself between Rip and her unwanted guest. "Wait here, Danny. I'll get your laundry. Then I think you should leave."

She returned with his parcel. "Do you want your friends' laundry too, or will they pick it up?"

"I ain't a messenger boy for my hired hands. They want their laundry, they'll pick it up themselves."

"Fine. We're all square on the payment for your order." She turned away to get back to scrubbing, but Danny touched her arm. Rip growled, the hair standing on his neck. She jerked away.

"Why do you always act like I have leprosy or something?" Danny tucked the bundle of clean clothes under his arm. "I'm headed into town to buy a piece to repair a hay rake. How about you come with me? I could take you to the restaurant. When was the last time you had a meal cooked by someone else?"

He wasn't even leering today, and if she didn't already know him, his concern for her might be taken as a kind gesture. Danny was often less belligerent when he didn't have any of his father's hired hands around to posture for.

"No, thank you."

"I'm going to wear you down one of these days. Time's on my side. I've had my eye on this place and on you for a long time, and I can be patient for a bit longer." He resettled his hat and tied his bundle to the back of his saddle. "Not too many more days until the taxes are due, huh? You'd be better off marrying me. That way you can keep your place instead of losing it to the tax man. You know that's all my pa's waiting for, right? For the state to take the land for the taxes and to swoop down and pick it up cheap? Just marry me, and you can stay on your land."

She pressed her hands to her temples. "For the last time, I don't want to marry you."

He swung into the saddle. "What you *want* to do and what you might *have* to do are two different things. How much does this place mean to you? And how stubborn are you going to be? There's an easy way out of your troubles, Esther."

Tipping his hat, he moseyed his horse toward the gate. She watched him go, feeling the net tightening around her. The taxes she couldn't pay, the living she was barely eeking out, the man staying in her bunkhouse and the baby sleeping in her laundry basket.

She snatched up a bucket to fetch more water, storming around the corner of the house. Why couldn't she just live in peace? Why did she feel as if she would forever be paying for her father's sins?

As she passed by the back door, she stopped. Boot

prints stood out in the dust below the bottom step. She shook her head. Had Thomas thought to come in the back door? That was silly. The back door didn't even open anymore. She'd put the Hoosier cabinet in front of the door in order to have more room in her kitchen. Even if he had managed to get the door unlocked, it wouldn't swing open.

She shrugged. *You're too tired to think straight. Best get back to your chores.*

Chapter Seven

Thomas opened the door to the sheriff's office. Sheriff Granville looked over the top of his newspaper.

"Help you?"

"I'm hoping we can help each other." Thomas left the door open, letting sunlight and fresh air stream in. He'd just come from the bathhouse and barber, grateful to have rid himself of smoke, dirt and scruffy whiskers.

"How's that?" Sheriff Granville lowered the paper to his desk.

"You probably don't remember me. My name is Thomas Beaufort. I used to work on the Double J."

The hand the sheriff had been extending dropped, and he gave Thomas a hard look, eyeing his sidearm. "But not for more than five years."

"That's right. I spent a summer there digging post holes and splitting rails." Thomas tucked his thumbs into his pockets, trying to appear as harmless as possible. "I haven't been back to Silar Falls since."

"Name's Charlie Granville." He studied Thomas

hard, and Thomas studied him back. "So what brings you here now?"

"A couple of things, actually. First, I wanted to check in with you. I'm a bounty hunter now, and I like to stop by the local sheriff's office, sort of a professional courtesy." Thomas waited to see how this would be received. He would have either an ally or a roadblock.

Sheriff Granville stroked his silver mustache, pursing his lips. "The question is, are you any good?"

"Yes." He wasn't boasting, but he didn't believe in false modesty, either. The truth was, he was very good at his job. "Better than most."

"You tracking anyone in particular, or are you just passing through?" The sheriff rose, hitched up his pants and went to the stove. "Coffee?"

"Thanks. I'm staying around Silar Falls for a while, but I'm tracking one man in particular as soon as I clear up a little business."

Again the stroking of the mustache. "And who might that be?" He offered Thomas a cup.

"Jase Swindell."

Granville's head came up. "You have any solid leads?"

Thomas sipped the coffee, trying not to wince as the bitter brew hit the back of his tongue. How long had this been sitting in the pot? It tasted like the sheriff had thrown a handful of horseshoe nails to settle the grounds.

"Would you believe me if I said Jase Swindell fell in love?" Thomas shook his head. "He took up with a woman, some gal who had been writing to him in prison. I couldn't believe it when I first heard it, but it turns out it's true. The woman hid him, and they met up at a cabin out in the brush where I found them, planning on making a run to the Big River when I caught up with them about thirty miles south of here."

"What happened?"

Thomas tasted bitterness that wasn't from the bad coffee. "Things went sideways. Swindell got away. He rode off and left the woman."

"So where's she?" Granville looked as if he was storing up every detail, and Thomas got the impression that the man was a better than average lawman who paid attention to the important things.

"She's dead. Died in childbirth a few hours after Jase ran off." Thomas gave a summary of the events at the shack in the brush, delivering the baby and bringing him to Silar Falls, the closest settlement. "So the baby is Jase Swindell's. I hear he has a sister somewhere in these parts, but that she might not be all there in the head. Do you know anything about her?"

The sheriff nodded. "I questioned her, or tried to, when Swindell busted out of jail last year, hoping she had an idea or two where he might run." He shook his head. "What you've heard is right. There's something wrong with her. It's like she never really grew up. She talks like a little girl, plays with dolls and such, and doesn't seem to know real from fantasy. Harmless, but loco, you know?"

"So she wouldn't be fit to take the baby?"

"She isn't fit to take care of a parakeet. You'll have to look somewhere else. What about the mother's kin?

Do you have any notion of who she is? If she has any family?"

"I don't know anything beyond her first name, Anna. I suppose, if I can finally catch up to Jase, he'll know if she has kin."

"Where are you staying now, and where is the baby?"

Rubbing the back of his neck, Thomas shrugged. "I'm out at the Double J. Esther's looking after the baby, and I'm staying in the bunkhouse, keeping an eye on things."

Granville's silver eyebrows climbed. "I wasn't totally honest with you when you first came in here. I know who you are." He gave Thomas a stern, paternal glare. "That gal is mighty precious to my wife and me, and we won't have her upset, so if you have any notion of trifling with Esther's affections or the like, you had better just ride out right now."

Thomas swallowed. "Sir, I have no intention of trifling with Esther Jensen. I just needed someone to help me with the baby. I'll be gone in a few days, and until then, I'm trying to help out Esther around the place. That's all."

The sheriff didn't look like he believed Thomas, but he didn't pursue it.

Setting down the almost-full coffee cup, Thomas went to the notice board to study the wanted posters. "There's something I need to report. Do you know of any enemies Esther might have?"

The sheriff eased down into his chair, making it creak, and propped his boots on the corner of his desk. "Gals like Esther don't make enemies. Folks were a bit scandalized when her pa killed himself, but that's mostly blown over now."

"The reason I asked about enemies is that someone set fire to Esther's barn last night. It's a total loss."

"A fire? Are you sure it wasn't an accident?" Granville's boots came down and hit the floor, and he leaned forward, eyes keen.

"No accident. I'm sure I saw someone running away, and the fire spread much too quickly to be an accident."

"I can't think of anyone who would want to burn Esther out. There's no point in it. If someone wanted to drive her off the land, and there are several folks I know of who are interested in the property, then all they would have to do is wait. Taxes are due in a few weeks, and I can't see how she can pay them. Last year she sold about everything on the ranch that wasn't tied down in order to scrape together enough to meet the tax bill. Unless she's struck gold somewhere on the property, she's as broke as a smashed clock. When she can't pay the taxes, she'll either have to sell the ranch or the state will take it and auction it for pennies."

Thomas nodded. That matched what Frank had told him over at the mercantile. "I met Danny Newton out at her place. He seems keen to get the Double J. Have you heard of him giving her trouble?"

"I've heard him spouting off at the saloon about marrying Esther, but my wife tells me Esther won't go through with that. Her pa wanted her to marry Danny once upon a time, but once Elihu was gone, Esther let it be known she didn't intend to marry Danny or anyone else. And she won't take help, either. I've offered to loan her some money to help pay her taxes, and I know Frank Clements offered her credit in the store, but she's a stubborn thing."

"Don't I know it."

"It's too bad she can't find a steady man to help her out. It's a nice ranch with lots of potential. Plenty of water and grazing. But beyond that, Esther's a good woman who would make a man a fine wife. She deserves a bit of happiness, after all the heartbreak she's had."

Thomas nodded, but his gut churned at the idea of Esther marrying someone. Or was it the thought of her marrying someone *else* that bothered him?

"No sign of who might've burned the barn?" the sheriff asked. "And you didn't chase after whoever it was you saw running away?"

"I was busy putting out the fire and keeping it from spreading. Wound up obliterating any tracks."

The mustache took another mauling. "I'd watch out if I was you. Might be best all around if you brought Esther and that baby to town."

"I don't know that she'd leave the place."

"From what I've seen, every woman digs in her heels every once in a while. They get a notion into their head, and you couldn't dislodge it with a pry bar." Granville shook his head. "Married twenty-eight years, and my wife's still a mystery to me. Anyway, I appreciate you stopping by. I'll keep an ear out for word on Swindell, and I'll ride over to Spillville and see his sister again."

"Don't mention the baby to her." Alarm skittered

up Thomas's spine. "I don't want her coming over to claim the boy just yet. Until I can check her out, I don't want her setting up a ruckus about her nephew."

Granville studied him. "If she's the boy's closest kin, she's got a right to know about him even if she isn't fit to take custody."

"I plan to wait until I have Swindell in irons. *He's* technically the boy's closest kin, and he should have the say in what happens to his son. Until then, the baby's being well cared for." Thomas tried to ignore the wrench he felt at the thought of someone taking the baby away. He should really quell that notion. Johnny wasn't his, and he would eventually have to go somewhere.

Esther moved Daisylu's tether to a fresh patch of weedy grass and drove the picket pin deep into the ground. She gave the goat a pat on the side, smiling as Daisylu butted against her leg for more attention. Toting the bucket of fresh milk to the house, she stopped and shaded her eyes, looking toward town.

A plume of dust rose behind a team of horses, and her heart kicked in her chest. Thomas was coming back. He'd been gone for hours, and even though she had his assurance he would return, the doubts had crowded in.

Johnny lay nestled in his sling, sleeping on her chest, and she feathered her fingers through his dark hair. The goat's milk must agree with him, because his cheeks were already fuller, and he woke only a couple times a night to be fed before falling sweetly back to sleep.

The smell of soot and ash still hung in the air, but the remains of the barn had stopped smoldering and leaking smoke. She turned her back on the wreckage and went around the house to the front door. Setting the milk pail on the counter, she got out cheesecloth to strain the milk before pouring it into wide-mouthed glass jars to take down to the cellar.

Chiding herself, she ducked into her room to check her hair, combing stray wisps back into her braid. Her wide, brown eyes looked back at her, and pink heated her cheeks. *You're being foolish, Esther Jensen. You're not a girl to be primping for a prospective beau. You're a sensible spinster, and Thomas isn't a suitor. Pull yourself together and get back to work.*

The buckboard rattled into the yard, the horses' hooves thudding on the dry dirt. Rip bounded off the porch, and Esther stood in the doorway.

Thomas turned the horses and pulled to a stop, hopping down in an agile movement. The buckboard was piled high with lumber and metal pipes and a crate of oddments.

"What's all that?"

"Some things to fix the windmill better and get water down the slope to where you do your washing. And some more supplies for the house."

Esther's neck muscles tightened. "Take it back."

He stopped, the crate half-raised. "What? Why?"

"I can't afford those things." There had to have been more than thirty dollars' worth of building supplies.

Thomas rested the crate on top of the lumber and pushed his hat back. Puzzlement colored his eyes.

"You don't have to afford these things. They're already paid for."

Her hands went to her hips. "I let you buy the food, since you're helping to eat it up, but how is fixing the windmill and piping water down here your responsibility?"

He scratched his ear. "Well, I'm really doing it for the baby."

She lowered her chin and looked at him out of the tops of her eyes. "For the baby? He doesn't care about the windmill."

"Sure he does." Thomas put his hands in his pockets in a gesture so familiar to her, she almost smiled…and she would have if she wasn't feeling so put out with him. What was the idea, toting things from town? It was one thing to buy the goat, or to repair the bunkhouse roof, since he was staying there, but another thing altogether to throw money at the windmill.

"How do you figure?"

"He likes clean britches, doesn't he? And they've got to be washed, which means plenty of water. I'm the one who added to your wash load, bringing him here. Toting all that water takes time, and it's hard work. You'll have more time to care for Johnny, and more strength, too, if you're not hauling water down that hill all the time. And the windmill…" He shook his head. "No offense, but it's being held together with bailing wire and fond hopes. You get another storm, and it will come crashing down. It might even land on the house. I can't take that risk." He tilted his head and gave her a smile, revealing the dimple that had caught her eye the first time she'd seen him. It made her heart do silly things.

He spread his hands, palms up, appealing to her... in more ways than one. "Please let me do this, Esther. I feel like I'm imposing already, making more work for you. This is something simple, and it really is about keeping you and Johnny safe."

Was her backbone made of pudding? She found herself nodding, giving in to his logic and his charm.

He set the crate of parts on the porch, metal clanking inside. "Fittings and a spigot and some tools to do the job." Esther stepped from the doorway, and Thomas reached out and touched Johnny's head. "The boy been good?"

"As gold. I think the goat's milk agrees with him."

"Any trouble here?"

She bit the corner of her lip. Should she tell him about Danny? If she did, what could he do about it? Danny and the ranch were her problems. If there was one thing the last five years had taught her, it was that she needed to solve her own problems.

"Things were fine here." The question she dreaded hovered on her lips. "Did you find anything out about Johnny's family?"

Thomas placed a second crate on the porch. "Trudy said to tell you hello from her, and she sent along a gift for Johnny. Take a look at these." He dug in the box and drew out a pair of crocheted booties, white, with little blue ribbons. "If those aren't about the most senseless bits of footwear I've ever seen, I don't know what is, but they're about the cutest, too."

He put one on his thumb. "I didn't know baby things could be so small."

Esther took one of the little booties in her hand, resting it on her palm. It didn't escape her attention that Thomas had not answered her question about Johnny's relatives, but since she didn't think she wanted to know the answer, she let it slide. "They're adorable. Do you think she made them just last night?"

"That's what she said." He handed her the second bootie. "Oh, there's one more thing in here. Trudy helped me pick it out." Paper rustled as he handed her a bundle. "I don't want any argument, either."

She tugged the string, loosening the paper, glancing up at him, uncertain. The paper fell away to reveal a dress. Rich blue fabric, with lace trim, a row of covered buttons down the front.

"If you don't like it, Trudy said I could take it back and exchange it. I remember you having a dress this color. You wore it to a church social." He smiled. "You were the prettiest girl in the place. All the hands agreed on that. I could've gotten you some fabric, but I didn't want you to have to sew it up. You've got enough sewing to do with buster here's things." He touched his knuckle to Johnny's cheek.

He remembered a dress she wore five years ago? "I can't accept this."

"Sure you can. My way of saying thank you for helping me. I'd be in a real fix if you weren't caring for the boy."

She wanted the dress. How long had it been since she'd gotten anything new? Years. And yet, she didn't need charity.

"A thank-you gift isn't charity." Thomas stepped off the porch, sending her a frank glance over his shoulder as he went to the horses to lead them up the hill toward the windmill.

How did he do that? Know just what she was thinking?

She raised the sateen to her cheek, closing her eyes at the softness. Not homespun, not hand-me-down and not washed threadbare. Shaking out the folds, she held it up. And not outlandish, either. A dress to wear to church or to town or to visit someone, but sensible for every day, too, since she didn't go visiting anyway.

It was perfect.

"What am I going to do, Johnny? It would be awfully easy to fall in love with him again, if I ever fell out of love with him in the first place, and then where would I be?" Folding the dress, she laid it on top of the box of store goods and took the whole thing into the house. Sorting the contents on the table, she grinned. Two more cans of peaches.

She took the subtle hint and gathered the ingredients for a peach cobbler.

Thomas used his bandanna to wipe the sweatband of his hat. It was hot enough to melt a stove lid today. The windmill repair had taken longer than he thought it would, but it was right and tight now. His current project moved along much better. The hardware store in town had carried everything he needed, pipes, fittings, elbows, spigots and caulking material.

He replaced his hat and looked over the yard. He'd say one thing about having a goat. The grass and weeds were chewed right down until you could play croquet on the lawn around the house.

The next thing on Thomas's agenda was to pull down the burned carcass of the barn and level the ground. If this was his place, he'd be drawing up new plans for a bigger barn, one with room for plenty of horses and at least one milk cow, tack, feed and tool rooms. And a center aisle big enough to drive a hay wagon and team right through.

But this wasn't his place. And if what the sheriff said was true, it wouldn't be Esther's much longer, not unless she married someone who had enough money to pay the taxes. Would she do that? Marry in order to keep her land? Even if she didn't love the man?

Squatting beside the water tank, he smeared the last bit of pitch around the pipe he'd installed. The tarry substance sure was sticky, but it should stop any leaks. He wiped his hands on the grass and hooked the windmill to the pump again to refill the tank. When it was brimming, he detached the windmill and headed down the slope, checking each joint of the pipe as he went.

Esther stood over her scrub board, sleeves rolled up, hair coming loose from her braid. She straightened when she saw him coming. The heat made her skin glow.

"Where's the little gupper?"

"In his basket in the shade." She motioned toward the porch where Rip lay beside the basket, his big paws hanging over the edge of the porch and his tongue lolling. "Where I'll be as soon as I finish this last batch of shirts." Wiping her brow with the hem of her apron, she looked at the pipe running down the hill. "How is it coming?"

"All set and ready to test." He stuffed his bandanna into his back pocket and picked up an empty pail. "Here you go."

"Me?" She hooked a loose hank of hair with her little finger, drawing it off her face in a gesture he found fascinating. So feminine. "But you've done all the work. I thought you'd want to be the one to give it a go first."

He shook his head, offering her the pail. "It's for you...and the baby." He grinned. "Go ahead."

She took the metal bucket and placed it on the wooden platform he'd built below the spout to stop a mud hole from forming. Tucking her bottom lip between her teeth, she turned the spigot. Water gushed into the bucket, thirty yards downslope from the tank.

"It works."

Thomas barely had time to brace himself as Esther turned and threw herself into his arms with a happy squeal, hugging him tight. His hat tumbled to the ground.

"Thank you, thank you, thank you!"

His arms went around her, taking the impact as she hit his chest, and his senses exploded. She fit perfectly into his embrace, warm and soft and sweet. Her hair smelled of sunshine and soap and woman. Better than anything he could remember.

"You're welcome." He breathed it against her temple, his voice gruff and deep.

She eased out of his hold, as if realizing what she'd done, and smoothed her hair and straightened her apron, looking anywhere but at his face. Her embarrassment was adorable.

"You might want to turn off the water before you flood the yard." He bent to pick up his hat, striving to be casual, but his heart still jerked around in his chest, and his arms felt empty. Holding her made him feel strong and protective, made him feel good, as if he was doing and being what he was made to do and be. Being a bounty hunter, protecting the citizens of Texas by rounding up outlaws and putting them in jail made him feel good, but this was something altogether different.

She laughed, turning off the spigot. The bucket had overflowed, and she lifted it by the handle, holding it away as water splashed over the sides. With great ceremony, she poured the contents into one of the tubs just steps away.

"I feel like a whole new woman."

The smile she sent him made him feel ten feet tall. No more hauling water down the hill, no more heavy buckets and backbreaking burden. Thomas grinned at her and turned away to gather his tools.

Rip jumped off the porch and started up the hill with Thomas. "You've had a nice few days of being lazy, haven't you, boy?" Thomas reached out to rub Rip's head, but the dog's ears perked up, he stared off to the south and let out a bark. With a leap, he was in a run tearing across the ground past the windmill and the ruined barn and into the brush.

"Rip, get back here!" Thomas shouted. The dog was well schooled, and Thomas had broken him early of the habit of chasing rabbits, so his running off meant either he had broken training completely or someone was out there. The fire-starter, maybe?

No time to fetch Smitty from the corral. He'd have to go on foot. Thomas ran to the bunkhouse and grabbed his rifle and set out after Rip. After the one bark, the Catahoula mutt had gone silent, another ominous indication that something was amiss. He'd been trained to trail his quarry silently.

Entering the thicket, Thomas put his arm up to ward off branches. Mesquite and blackbrush and guajillo intertwined, nearly impassable in places. He startled jackrabbits and birds, but there was no sign of Rip.

He'd have to risk some noise if he wanted to find his dog. Putting his fingers to his lips, he let out a piercing whistle that he knew would carry. Not five feet away, but unseen, a cow bawled, lunging through the thicket, breaking branches as she stumbled away.

A man could get lost in this tangle. He wished he was on horseback. At least that way he might be able to see over the tops of some of this vegetation from time to time. He'd only gone about fifty feet in and already he was checking the sun to keep his bearings.

Branches rattled to his left, and he turned that way, skirting some blue sage, releasing its heady scent as he brushed against it. The light became stronger and the brush thinned. Rip wriggled under the branches of a spiny hackberry toward Thomas. With his gray-and-black-mottled coat, he was hard to spot in the undergrowth, a trait that had worked well for them in the past.

Thomas snapped his fingers, quietly, and Rip came

to his side, but the dog kept turning its head back the way he'd come. Holding his rifle in front of himself, Thomas crept forward. Sunlight dappled the ground, and the air was still and hot.

He smelled a familiar earthy scent. Fresh horse droppings. The branches were nibbled off a sagebrush, and he found where the horse had been tied to a mesquite. Thomas knelt to study the hoofprints. There were dozens. The horse had been here awhile. Shod, fairly large, not fractious, so trained to stand patiently when tied.

Rip snuffled the ground, working his way farther to the edge of the brush, and Thomas followed. In spite of the heat, a chill chased up his back and across his scalp. Someone had lain here on the crest of the hill, watching the ranch below.

Thomas squatted to survey the ground, and made out a few boot prints here and there in the dirt, but they didn't tell him much, other than that the man was a good size. He'd clearly lain there for a while. The grass was pressed down, and he could make out where something had lain at the man's elbow…a canteen, perhaps? Thomas stood and looked down at the Double J. From this spot, he was about one hundred fifty yards away and a good thirty feet above the house. The windmill, the bunkhouse, the house, Esther's washtubs, all of it was easily reachable with a rifle bullet. Esther worked at the clothesline, pegging out men's shirts. Her apron stood out, white against her work dress.

Thomas didn't recognize the prints, not of the man or the horse. Who would have cause to watch the ranch, and was it the same person who had torched the barn?

Whoever it was wasn't here now, and from the look of the tracks, he'd lit out recently. Probably when Rip scared up his scent. With the sun disappearing toward the horizon, Thomas wouldn't be able to follow until the morning.

Gripping his rifle in one hand, he started down the slope, skidding and starting little rock slides on the steepest bits. By the time he arrived back at the house, Esther rocked on the porch, holding Johnny on her lap. The baby kicked and squirmed, free of his blankets for a time.

Esther eyed his gun, her mouth going tight, and he leaned it against a porch post. "What happened?"

"I took a little walk." He eased down onto the steps. "The brush is growing closer and closer to the ranch house with no hands to keep it cut back. You're going to need to burn some if you don't want to lose all your grazing." He decided not to worry her about someone watching from the ridge. She had enough troubles, and there wasn't anything she could do about it anyway.

"We almost burned it back when the barn caught on fire." She cupped one of Johnny's tiny feet in her palm. "I'm glad you were here."

He was, too. The thought of her here alone trying to put out the fire by herself jangled his nerves. "Have you ever thought of moving into town? Running your laundry from there? Even without a barn, you could still get a good price for this place, and you wouldn't have to worry about the upkeep."

She shook her head, eyes solemn. "I can't. This is my home. It's where my father is buried, and it's the place I've lived the longest in my whole life. You can't understand, since you don't seem to want to put down roots anywhere, but the Double J is the only place where I feel like myself. I can't just walk away from it. It was my father's last wish that I stay here."

Thomas rested his forearms on his knees. For most of his life, he'd moved around, always wondering what was over the next hill. A foundling, he'd left the orphanage at twelve, living hand-to-mouth and taking care of himself. He'd never stayed in one place for more than a few weeks, unless you counted three whole months here on the Double J five years ago. It was also the first place he'd ever considered staying longer.

Truth be told, he was tired of wandering like a tumbleweed in a high wind. He'd like a place to call his own, to put down roots. He was tired of chasing bad men, tired of campfires and bedrolls and eating out of cans. The past few days here on the Double J had been nice. Restful, though he'd worked hard. He liked the sense of accomplishment he got from repairing a roof or strengthening a windmill.

But he couldn't stay here. Esther deserved someone better than him, and when she found out the baby she was caring for was the son of the rustler who ruined her father and caused his death, she'd be so upset—and rightly so—she wouldn't have Thomas if he was hung from top to toe with diamonds. His stomach muscles tightened. Hurting her was the last thing he wanted, but in the end, he knew he would.

"Do you still ride?" He eased his holster on his hip, stretching his legs out. Rip flopped down and put his head in Thomas's lap. He stroked the floppy ears.

Esther feathered her fingers through Johnny's dark hair, smiling down at the baby. "I haven't ridden in years. All the saddle horses were sold off along with the cattle to settle debts. And my sidesaddle was in the barn." She let out a heavy sigh.

"I've got an extra horse. Johnny's mama's. And if you don't mind riding astride, I have all the tack in the bunkhouse."

"What about Johnny?"

"Put him in that sling you wear when you're doing clothes. He'll love it."

A smile spread her lips, and her eyes took on a spark of life. "I'd like that. When?"

"First thing tomorrow? Before it gets too hot?"

As he went to clean his tools near the windmill, Thomas watched the high ground for movement. He wanted to scout out the property, but he didn't want to leave Esther unprotected. Taking her along would be the best of both worlds.

Chapter Eight

Esther tipped her face up to the sunshine, basking in the warmth, the wind on her cheeks and the smell of the hot earth. Johnny seemed content enough, rocking to the sway of her body as she rode beside Thomas.

"Where are we going?" she asked.

"Let's start up at the ridge and circle around to the north."

"There's a lot of brush up there. Don't you want to ride where it's more open?"

"Sure, but I'm curious about something." He put his horse to the slope, and Esther followed. Once they reached the top, they both turned to look down on the ranch buildings.

"I haven't been up here for years, but you can't beat the view." She crossed her wrists on the saddle horn.

Thomas nodded. "Stay here for a few minutes." He snapped his fingers to Rip, motioned flat with his hand, and the dog plopped his rump down. "Stay, boy."

He disappeared into the brush, snapping twigs and clattering branches. "Where are you going?"

"I'll be right back."

She blushed, thinking maybe he was answering the call of nature, and turned back to the view. The large black square where her barn had once stood looked pitiful. Would it ever be rebuilt?

Her horse cropped grass, making the bit jingle, and the breeze rustled through the brush, redolent of sage and summer.

After what seemed a long time, Thomas returned. "Where is your property line?"

"Just south of here." She waved behind them. "That's the Newton ranch, the Circle Bar 5. Their property borders mine on the entire south boundary. Why?"

"Just wondered. Is it possible that some of those cowboys have been cutting through here instead of using the road?"

She shrugged. "It's possible, but why? The road is mostly level and wide open, and as you can see, the brush is thick here, and it's hilly. I can't imagine anyone preferring this route."

"That makes sense." He lifted his reins and nudged his horse's flanks. "I found some tracks, but maybe it was somebody who got lost."

"That's easy enough to do out here. I remember once, when we had lived here only a couple of months, that I got lost in the brush. My father was frantic and sent every ranch hand from three ranches out to find me." She chuckled. "He was so relieved and so angry when I was found, he didn't know whether to cry or shout."

"When was that?" Thomas asked over his shoulder as he led the way along the ridge.

"I think I was twelve. It was the first summer after we moved here from Tennessee. The year after my mama died."

She patted Johnny. The baby had lost his mama, too, but unlike Esther, he wouldn't remember her at all. Esther at least had memories to cherish of her gentle mother, laughter that sounded like bells, lemon verbena perfume, rustling skirts and soft hands. A hard lump formed in her throat, and tears prickled the backs of her eyes, both for herself and for this sweet baby boy.

Rip darted and zigzagged, nose down, tail wagging, obviously happy to be free to roam. Esther watched Thomas's back as she rode behind him. His shirt, a new one he'd brought back from town to replace the ones Daisylu had chewed on, fit his broad shoulders perfectly. He was as tapered as a turnip, and his hips rocked easily to the movements of his horse. He'd been to the barber in town, and his hair now barely brushed his collar under his tan hat.

He turned in the saddle, and she blushed to have been caught staring. "The brush ends up ahead, here, doesn't it?"

"Yes. At least it used to. The best grazing land on the Double J is along Silar Creek."

They emerged from the cover, and a meadow opened before them. Thomas pulled up. "What's this?"

Esther brought her mount to a stop beside him.

A wooden corral, falling apart now, sat in the center of a wide basin, and two long fences angled out from the gate, acting as a funnel. She put her hand on Johnny's back. "This was where the rustlers were penning the cattle they stole before they took them up to Fort Davis."

"So the heart of the operation was right here on the Double J?"

She nodded. "I think that, as much as anything, was what devastated my father. Some of his hands had to know about it, and he felt betrayed. He must've felt foolish, because he wasn't a hands-on rancher. He trusted his men, especially Bark, his foreman, to run everything. And they did. They ran it right into the ground."

Thomas reached over and put his hand on hers. "I'm sorry, Esther."

Drawing comfort from his gesture, she gave a weak smile. Johnny squirmed and snuffled, and she released her hand from Thomas's touch. "I think someone might be waking up."

"Let's head back toward the house along the creek, and if he gets wound up, we can always stop."

They rode for another quarter of an hour, and Esther felt her muscles tensing as they drew near the spot on the ranch she found hardest to visit, though she forced herself to from time to time.

Johnny subsided for a while, but finally, he fussed, butting his head against her shoulder, squirming, slurping on his fist.

"Let's pull in here." Thomas reined to the left, toward the water.

Cottonwoods lined the banks of Silar Creek, and the temperature dropped several degrees when they entered the shade. Sunlight dappled through the branches and scattered diamond glints on the water. Rip went right into the water to his belly, lapping with his huge tongue, cooling off.

Thomas swung out of the saddle and rounded his horse to help Esther dismount. He reached up and spanned her waist, pausing, looking up at her with a grin. He hadn't shaved that morning, and stubble darkened his cheeks. "Put your hands on my shoulders and swing your leg over."

She did as he asked, and he lowered her to stand before him. The horse shifted, warm and bulky at her back, and Thomas loomed over her, his hands still on her waist. Her palms rested on his chest, feeling the thud of his heart, the heat and masculinity and musk that was *him*.

Leaves fluttered in the breeze overhead, a bird twittered, and somewhere a branch rubbed against another with a dull squeak. Time slowed, and she found herself staring at his mouth, at the slight bow of his upper lip and the fullness of the lower. Her breath went shallow, and her heart tripped.

Johnny snuffled, his mouth opening against the skin on her neck, and squawked.

Esther blinked and stepped back, bumping into her horse. She patted the baby.

"I'll water the horses." Thomas's voice was deep and gruff, and his brown eyes had darkened. "You tend to the little fellow."

Slipping out of the sling, she unwrapped Johnny, but her mind wasn't on the baby. Had Thomas been going to kiss her? And had she been about to let him?

If the disappointment pinging through her was any indication, not just let him, but kiss him back?

She found a grassy spot and laid Johnny on the sling. He stretched and yawned and blinked, staring at the canopy of branches and leaves overhead. His hair stood up in an adorable quiff atop his head, and his tiny fingers opened like flower petals.

"He all right?" Thomas squatted on his heels, holding his hat in his hands, twirling the brim through his fingers. Rip bounded out of the creek with a bark, shaking, scattering droplets, but thankfully far enough away not to shower anyone. Esther laughed.

"Yes, he's just tired of being cooped up, I think." Esther strove for a normal tone of voice, as if her heart hadn't tumbled around her chest like a leaf in a high wind. "I brought the bottle along, which is a good thing, because he's hungry again." She went to dig in the saddlebag she'd packed with the bottle and extra diapers. Gathering up Johnny, she offered him the bottle, and he greedily latched on and began to suck.

"Seems mostly all he does is eat and sleep." Thomas grinned. "And make more laundry for you to do."

A fish flopped in the water, drawing her gaze away from his warm, brown eyes.

Thomas tugged a bandanna from his pocket and wiped the sweatband on his hat. "It's so peaceful. Hard to believe that there was ever an upset here, much less that this ranch was the center of a rustling operation. When I talked to the sheriff, he said the rustlers made off with more than three thousand head in less than a year."

Esther nodded. "They were forging bills of sale,

stealing a couple hundred head at a time, driving them west to the forts. Most of the ranchers around here didn't realize there was anything going on until the spring roundup when tallies were much too short. The rustlers took steers and breeding stock and youngsters alike." She gripped the grass, anger spearing through her. "But they took more than that. They took my father from me. If I ever meet Jase Swindell or one of his gang face-to-face…" The bottled-up anger and pain tried to force themselves through her carefully constructed self-control, and she had to breathe deeply before she could continue.

"Let's just say, when he went to prison, it was a relief. Hearing he broke out brought it all back again. I might not like what bounty hunters do, but I can appreciate the need for them. Why don't you put your skills to work tracking him? He's been out for a year now. It isn't fair that Jase Swindell is running loose and free to do whatever he wants when my father is in his grave, when I'm all alone here and in danger of losing my home. I know we're supposed to forgive, and we're not supposed to hate, but I hate Jase Swindell. I hate everything about him." She glanced up from the baby and was surprised to see an odd expression on Thomas's face before he looked away.

She expected censure or commiseration and understanding, but what she saw was…guilt? But why? What did he have to feel guilty about?

Perhaps he had tried to track Swindell since the escape and hadn't been able to catch him? Knowing how relentless he was, how efficient and capable, the fact that he hadn't apprehended the most famous bounty in the state must chafe.

Johnny grasped her finger on the bottle, squeezing it. His hazy blue eyes locked on hers, and her heart swelled with warmth. A new life, a reminder that there was more to this world than pain and grief. There was love, and though she had tried to steel her heart against him, this little boy had snuck past all her defenses.

What was she going to do when Thomas took him away?

Thomas skipped a rock across the surface of Silar Creek while Esther changed the baby's diaper and wrapped him in the sling once more. He flung a second rock, this time with more force.

She hated Jase Swindell, and she had good reason. But what would she do if she found out the baby he'd brought her was Jase's son?

If only he'd been able to capture Swindell at that shack. He'd hesitated, stunned to find the woman in the cabin with him, and pregnant, to boot.

In his defense, when he'd brought the baby to Esther, he hadn't known her father had killed himself because he couldn't live with what Jase had done to him.

And now it had gone from what might be construed as an oversight to a blatant lie of omission.

But if he told her now, she'd have him and Johnny off the property and out of her life in a brace of shakes. He glanced over his shoulder. Wisps of hair teased her temples and cheeks, and the knot she'd fashioned at the back of her head seemed too heavy for her slender neck. She took a moment to cuddle the baby, crooning to him and smoothing his unruly hair gently. Rip snuffled the boy and flopped to the grass, putting his head on his paws, staring at them with his mismatched eyes. The dog was clearly a goner.

And if Thomas was truthful, so was he. When he'd helped Esther from her horse, when she'd stood there with her hands on his chest, her face just inches from his, heat had shot through him like a branding iron. The way she'd stared at his mouth had his heart clanging like a hammer on an anvil, and he'd wanted so badly to kiss her, he could hardly breathe.

"You are the best baby in the whole world." She nuzzled Johnny's nose with her own, brushing a kiss on his head.

Guilt took another stab at his chest. How could he tell her?

"Time to go." He brought the horses over, held the baby while she climbed into the saddle and handed the boy up to her to nestle into the sling. He mounted Smitty and headed along the creek, staying under the trees to keep the sun off Esther and Johnny. The trip would be longer this way, but easier on them now that the sun was high and the temperature rising.

They had gone less than a quarter of a mile when they came upon a big cottonwood with spreading branches that towered over a small, iron fence. A white headstone rose up from the ground.

Esther pulled up several yards away, and Thomas knew in an instant whose name he would read on the stone.

Elihu Jensen.

Esther gathered herself and nudged her mount forward. Thomas followed until they sat their horses before the gate.

Grass grew thickly inside the plot. No one had tended the grave for a while. Esther's hands whitened on the reins, and she brushed the hair off her forehead.

"I buried him here because it was his favorite place on the ranch. You can't tell now, but in the spring, this hillside is covered in bluebonnets." Her voice sounded thick. "He would bring me out here, and we'd stroll through thousands of flowers. He said he felt closest to my mother here because she would've loved this place best of any on the ranch."

He imagined Esther, knee-deep in bluebonnets, the sunlight gleaming off her hair. "I missed bluebonnet time when I was here before."

He'd missed a lot of things when he was here before. And a lot since.

So many experiences that normal men had of home and family. Owning a place, putting down roots, making it better than when you started. Finding someone to spend the rest of your life with, a companion, a wife and mother for your kids.

That life had never been for him in the past. Could it ever be? Probably not, but he could enjoy the here and now and take the memories away with him when he had to leave.

"When I was in town, I noticed posters everywhere. The Founders Day Celebration? I think you and I should go. Take Johnny. What do you say?"

She took her eyes from the headstone. "The celebration? I haven't been to that in years."

"Then you ought to go. You need a break, something fun. You've been stuck out here with Johnny and your washtubs, working hard. What is it they say about all work and no play? Anyway, it would give you a chance to wear that new dress."

Esther was already shaking her head, but he reached over and put his hand over hers on her saddle horn. "Please. I want to take the baby to town to have him looked over by the doctor, and I'd like you to go with me. While we're there, we might as well take in the sights."

Studying his hand on hers, she raised her eyebrows. "So what you're saying is, this is for the baby?"

Grateful that she hadn't pulled away from his touch, he grinned. "Yeah, it's for the baby."

"Then I guess I can't say no." She gifted him with a smile and placed her other hand on Johnny's small back. For a moment, the three of them were linked by touch, and he had to remind himself that it couldn't last.

Chapter Nine

"Whatever you're doing, keep on doing it." Dr. Preston quickly wrapped up a fussing Johnny and handed him to Esther. She patted and rocked the baby, who immediately settled down against her shoulder. "He sure prefers you, doesn't he?"

Esther nodded, glad to have the examination over. Not that the doctor had hurt Johnny, but the baby had cried at being unwrapped and having someone look in his ears and up his nose and bending his legs this way and that. It had been all she could do not to snatch him up off the examination table and run out the door.

Thomas had hooked his hat over his gun butt at his hip, and stood with his back to the window, arms crossed, feet apart. "So he's fine?"

"Fine as frog's hairs." The doctor put his instruments on a tray and set them on the counter. "You did a good job delivering him."

"His mama did all the work. I was shaking so bad, I almost dropped him." Thomas shifted his weight. "I wish I could've done something for her."

Dr. Preston washed his hands at the stand in the corner. "From what you say, the coughing, the weakness and pallor, I don't think anyone could've saved her." He leaned against the examination table and dried his hands with a white towel. "Childbirth is a risky business for a healthy woman. A consumptive as far gone as she sounds, it would've been remarkable if she survived. It's amazing that she was able to carry the baby to term as it was."

Esther swayed gently, pressing her cheek into Johnny's hair. "He didn't seem to do too well on canned milk, so we switched to goat milk instead. He's filled out and put on a little weight since."

"That's exactly what I would've recommended. You're a natural, Miss Jensen." Dr. Preston went to the door and opened it, inviting them into the hallway. Boisterous noise spilled from the back of the house, and he smiled. "My sons are eager to head over to the celebration. Their springs have been twanging all day."

The swinging door at the back of the hall burst open, and three stair-step boys tumbled out. "Is it time, Pa?" the middle one asked.

"Did you misplace your manners, son?" Shrugging out of his white coat, Dr. Preston plucked a gray suit coat from the hall tree. "This is Mr. Beaufort and Miss Jensen, and this little gentleman is Johnny."

The boys lined up, tallest to shortest. "Pleased to meet you, sir, ma'am," the eldest said, sticking out his hand. "I'm Matthew Preston."

"I'm Mark," said number two.

"I'm Luke," said number three, and grinned, showing a gap where his upper front teeth should be.

Each boy was dark-haired and blue-eyed like their father. As Esther greeted them, a beautiful woman came from the back of the house, tugging on her gloves. Her blond hair was swept up under a lovely straw bonnet with a flowered brim. "Hello." She smiled at them. "You're Esther, are you not? So nice to meet you. I'm Eliza Preston." Her dress, a pretty pink lawn, stretched to accommodate her obvious pregnancy.

Esther shared a glance with Thomas and knew he was thinking the same thing as she. If this baby was a boy, would they name him John to complete the set? She smothered a smile and looked away.

Mrs. Preston checked her appearance in the hall mirror. "Have you finished your examination? Everything is well?" Receiving a nod from her husband, she put her hands on the heads of her youngest sons. "I hate to bustle off, but Gareth, you're judging the pie contest, remember? Mrs. Clements will be anxious if you don't arrive soon."

"I don't know how I let myself be roped into this. I'm liable to start a feud." Dr. Preston held open the front door and showed everyone out. "Perhaps I should diagnose myself with some illness and stay in bed."

Rip rose from where he'd been waiting on the porch, tongue lolling, tail wagging. The little boys made much of him with hugs and pats.

"Pa, you can't thtay in bed. You promithed to let us try the gameth and buy uth thome candy." Luke lisped his way down the porch steps. Esther couldn't quell her smile then, wondering what Johnny would sound like when he grew up a bit and lost his front teeth.

Which sobered her. She wouldn't see that. She

wouldn't see his first steps or hear his first words or be the first to cut his hair or dress him in pants. All those would go to another woman, someone from his family or some woman who would adopt him.

Her arms ached as if they were already empty, though she held the baby close. Maybe it wasn't her arms that were empty, but rather her heart. She would be lonely for sure when Thomas and Johnny left.

Once they reached the main street, the Preston family went one way, and Thomas and Esther the other. People crowded the sidewalks, banners and bunting hung everywhere, and the town smelled of popcorn, candy and cooking meat.

"Let me tote him for a while." Thomas reached for the baby, cradling him in one arm while offering his other to Esther. "I have to say, Miss Jensen, you make that dress look mighty nice. I'll be the envy of every man in town."

Esther smoothed her hand down the beautiful blue fabric. She had taken such care dressing this morning, and she'd fussed over putting her hair up, using her curling iron for the first time in ages. Usually she left her hair hanging in a braid down her back or coiled it up out of her way, but today, she'd decided upon a proper hairstyle.

All the work had been worth it to see the expression in Thomas's eyes when he'd driven the buckboard to the front door this morning.

"What do you want to do first?" Thomas stopped as a pack of children raced by, chasing a hoop over the rutted dirt. "There's food, the bazaar booths, livestock, games." He reached down and patted Rip's head. "I probably should've left you at home, boy. Stick close."

She couldn't get over the bustle and noise and how happy everyone seemed. And for the first time in a very long time, she felt a part of the community. She had Thomas to thank for that, because if he wasn't here, she wouldn't have thought to come into town for the celebration.

"Let's stroll through the bazaar booths. I'd love to see what people are selling, even if I'm not buying."

He led her to one of the side streets that had been blocked off to horse traffic. Lining both sides of the street were tables and flags and banners. Esther stopped at the first booth where the Ladies' Sewing Circle had linens and laces and quilts for sale, as well as a large raffle quilt displayed at the back. A double-wedding-ring pattern of soft pastels and scalloped edges.

"It's beautiful."

Trudy Clements grinned and came around the laden table. "Esther, so good to see you. Let me get a gander at that boy." She moved back the blanket from Johnny's face, standing on tiptoe until Thomas obligingly bent so she could get a better view. "Why, he's positively blooming with health. And growing like a well-watered weed."

Esther tried to ignore the burst of pride that shot through her at Trudy's praise. The doctor's report had bolstered her confidence, but Trudy's affirmation that she was taking good care of the baby meant so much.

Thomas led Esther down the street and back up the far side as if he had nothing better to do in the world and all day to do it. He waited patiently while she examined all the baked goods, the metalwork, the sewed, crocheted or needlepoint items. Every time a lady passed, he tipped his hat, but he kept close to Esther, clearly her escort.

Johnny slept, and Rip followed at Thomas's side, alert and watchful.

"Now it's your turn." Esther took Johnny, resting him against her shoulder, making sure his bonnet covered his head against too much sun. "What do you want to do?"

"Are you hungry?"

"I'm not, but if you are, lead the way."

"Not yet, then. How about we check out the games?"

They had to pass the rows of animals on display in the field behind the livery, and paused to watch a class of cows being judged.

"There's your milk cows, Esther. Maybe we should see if one's for sale." He grinned. "How about that little brown-and-white one? If you had a cow, you could get rid of that horror, Daisylu."

"Never. Daisylu is like family." She squeezed his arm.

"If that's true, then she's the crazy, unpredictable third cousin nobody talks about. Did you see what she did yesterday? There I was, painting the tool shed, and out of nowhere, she comes charging in, butts into the ladder I'm standing on and knocks me clean off. Paint went everywhere. Except on her, the menace."

Esther laughed. She'd come running when she heard the ruckus and then had been helpless to do anything to aid Thomas. Daisylu had stood off to the side, chewing her cud and blinking in the sunlight, while Thomas had sprawled in a puddle of dirty whitewash, his face a thundercloud.

"I don't need a cow. Johnny likes Daisylu's milk, and anyway, I couldn't take care of a milk cow by myself. Daisylu I can manage, and she's actually very good at keeping the grass and weeds down. A cow would be too much for me to manage once you leave."

Thomas stopped walking. He started to say something, tugged on his earlobe and then nodded. "I suppose you're right."

Mentioning his departure hurt, but it was a good reminder. This interlude would come to an end, and she needed to remember that.

Nearby there were pens of geese, crates of chickens, horses, sheep, pigs. Thomas leaned down to whisper against her ear, "You'll notice there aren't any goats. People know better than to try to bring goats to town. Or anywhere else they don't want to go."

She was still laughing as they moved away from the animals toward the game booths. Bobbing for apples, ring toss, dart throwing, arm wrestling, three-legged and wheelbarrow races. Thomas found her a spot on a bench in the shade where she could watch the races, both human and horse. "I see the sheriff over there." Thomas scanned the crowd near the barbecue pit. "He was looking into something for me. Will you be all right here for a while?"

"We'll be fine. Go ahead."

"I'll leave Rip here with you." He hesitated.

"Go on. If we're not here when you get back, it means I went to the buckboard to get Johnny a bottle or clean britches. You don't have to hover. Go mingle with the men."

He nodded and sauntered away, and Esther found herself watching him, the easy way he moved, the breadth of his shoulders, the length of his stride. Thomas was powerfully built, but he gave the impression of agility more than sheer muscle, though she knew he was strong. Every time she touched him, she was aware of his strength.

Her cheeks heated, and she looked away. What if someone caught her watching him? She turned her attention to the baby. Rip leaned against her leg, content to be near his beloved Johnny.

"I don't know who is going to be saddest when Thomas finds a home for this little guy, me or you." She patted the dog, stroking his rough-yet-soft coat. Rip put his head on her lap.

Thomas and the sheriff stepped off to the side for what appeared to be a serious conversation. He had asked for Sheriff Granville's help in finding the baby's family. Had the lawman been successful? What if, even now, he was telling Thomas that some of Johnny's people were on their way to Silar Falls to get him?

Her heart contracted, and Johnny squirmed, causing her to realize she was holding him too tightly. She forced herself to relax. "Sorry, sweetie." She kissed his face, inhaling his milky, soapy, darling scent.

"Esther!"

She turned and found herself enveloped in the motherly embrace of Sarah Granville, Johnny pressed between them. "Sarah. How are you?" she asked when she could breathe.

"Look, look." Sarah waved her hand toward the blue ribbon pinned to her blouse. "First place for my pecan pie." She beamed, a dew of perspiration on her temples and upper lip. Her iron-gray hair was pulled up into a bun atop her head, and her cheeks were pink. "I was praying you'd come to town for the festivities, but I hardly dared hope. You haven't come for years. But introduce me to your little fellow. Trudy told me all about him, but I want to hear it from you."

"This is Johnny." Esther folded back the blanket. She gave a brief retelling of how she came to be caring for him.

Sarah took the baby, cuddling him close. "Charlie tells me that Thomas is staying out at your place."

Esther twined an escaped curl around her finger. "He's staying in the bunkhouse, just for a few more days." She dropped her hand to rest on Rip's back. The dog was watching Sarah intently, making sure she took good care of the baby.

Taking a seat on the bench, Sarah sent her a skeptical look. "That man is far too handsome for you not to have noticed. What are you going to do when he finds a home for this baby and leaves? I'm no fool. I remember how heartbroken you were the last time he left. Did you ever tell him how you felt?"

"No. And that was a long time ago. So I had a bit of a girlish crush on him once upon a time. I'm over all that now." Esther loved Sarah, but she didn't want to face these questions. Sarah's knowing eyes challenged her.

"Really? You're so over him that the minute he rides in needing a helping hand with a *baby*, you invite him to stay?"

"What should I have done? Tossed them both out on their ears? I'm doing it more for the baby than for him. Johnny needed someone to care for him."

"But for how long?" She touched the boy's cheek, and his lips puckered. "If you're not careful, you're going to get your heart broken again. And how can you be careful with a precious baby like this?"

I know. I already love him. When the time comes to give him up... "I'll be fine. It's just for a few more days, until Thomas finds some of his kin or another family to adopt him. He's got Charlie working on it already."

Trudy bustled by with a wave, and several of Sarah's friends stopped when they saw her holding the baby. Esther was grateful for the interruption. Sarah's questions and assessments had come uncomfortably close to a lot of truths she didn't want to examine.

"My, what a handsome little fellow."

"Where did he come from?"

"Esther, it's so good to see you again."

"Is this the baby Trudy was talking about? The one the bounty hunter found?"

They were all so friendly and talkative, Esther barely had time to answer their questions before more were launched. They were a bit overwhelming, but it felt so nice to be sociable again.

The ladies took turns passing Johnny around, and he seemed not to mind.

"He didn't care for canned milk too much, but the

doctor says he's doing well on goat milk." She told of the running feud between Daisylu and Thomas, and they all laughed.

"How long will Mr. Beaufort be in town? My husband says he's the best bounty hunter in the state. Surely he'll be back on some bandit's trail before too long?" Vivian, the wife of the newspaper owner, asked.

"He'll be gone in a few days." Esther tried to answer blithely, as if Thomas's departure meant nothing to her.

When the ladies moved on, Sarah smiled. "You've been missed here in town. Maybe after this you won't be such a stranger."

Esther had to wonder at the difference time had made. When her father died, the people of Silar Falls had been scandalized, shocked and standoffish. But now they were generous with their friendship, returning to the way she had been received when her father had been a local rancher.

"I hardly expected this kind of reception. Is it me, or is it the town that's different?"

"Both, I would say. Time heals, not just for you, but for others, too."

In the first, blinding, crushing weeks after her father's passing, Esther hadn't wanted consolation. She vaguely remembered a few people stopping by with meals and words of condolence, but she had stayed in her bedroom, silent and aching. Sarah Granville had come out to stay with her in the early days, she and Trudy Clements alternating, until in the end, Esther sent them away, too, so she could grieve in private.

Had Esther been in such a fog of sorrow and shock that by the time she emerged, people had moved on with their lives and assumed she was doing the same? Was it her own shame at her father's actions and her fall in status that made her brand the people of Silar Falls as cold and judgmental?

Sarah continued. "I don't think people meant to hold you at arm's length. It's just that when someone dies under the circumstances that took your father's life, people don't always know what to say. An accident or illness, people can sympathize, and they have lots of practice knowing how to act. I think people didn't know what was appropriate, or what would hurt you more, so they said nothing." Sarah returned Johnny to Esther's arms. "Bring yourself into town to see me soon, girl. I've missed you. I worry about you. With Thomas staying out in your bunkhouse fixing some things up around your place, I'm not sure if I'm relieved or more anxious for you. That man is handsome enough to turn any girl's head, not to mention kind, and I don't want to see you hurt again. Take care of yourself." She gave Esther a one-armed hug before bustling through the crowd.

Take care of yourself. But how could she do that when she was half in love with him already?

Forcing herself to concentrate on the festivities, she was pleased to watch several of her cowboy customers line up for the horse race. Danny Newton was among them on a large gray horse with a dark mane and tail. When the starter's pistol went off, Esther jumped, and the crowd cheered the surging horses.

They thundered around the open field, passing by

the staked flags that marked the course. A dozen horses and riders plunging and digging for all they were worth, sending clods of dirt into the air and hats flying. The cowboys rode low over their horses' necks, their faces half-obscured by blowing manes. As they rounded the last curve, they jostled and jockeyed for position. Danny's gray was easy to spot, heading a wedge of horses that neared the finish line to the screams of the crowd.

Esther's heart lodged in her throat as they swept past and under the wire. People crowded forward, cutting off her view, but when the noise died away, it was Danny's gray being led to the trophy area. He beamed, patting his sweaty horse, laughing and calling out to his friends.

"Is that your baby?" A girl of maybe ten or eleven tugged on Esther's sleeve.

Esther turned from the horses and sat on the bench once more. "I'm taking care of him."

"What's his name?"

"I call him Johnny." She lowered him from her shoulder to her arms so the girl could see.

"I love babies. Can I hold him?"

Though Esther was reluctant to give him up, she caught the wistfulness in the girl's big, green eyes. There was no harm in it, surely. Just for a few minutes. "Have a seat here." She patted the bench beside her. "Hold out your arms, and I'll put him in them. Be sure to keep his head supported. He's too little yet to hold it up himself." She transferred Johnny into the girl's arms, smiling at the rapt expression on her face. "What's your name?"

Rip gave a little whine and sidled close, nosing the

blanket. The girl giggled and pushed him away a bit, clearly not afraid of the dog.

"Katie May Buckland. My pa's the blacksmith here in Silar Falls." She never took her eyes off Johnny's sleeping face. "I'm the youngest of six girls, and all my sisters got to hold babies all the time growing up, but there weren't any more after me, so I missed out."

"I'm an only child, so I missed out on younger siblings, too." Esther searched the crowd for Thomas. She'd lost track of him during the horse race. Was he still talking with the sheriff?

"The next event," a man with a barker's megaphone shouted from a bunting-festooned stand, "is the shooting competition. I have it on good authority that the field of shooters is top-notch. The winner of the rifle shoot gets this fine new saddle scabbard as a prize." He held a shiny, tooled-leather scabbard over his head to the applause of the crowd.

"I should go." Esther certainly didn't want to watch a shooting contest.

"All right." Katie May reluctantly relinquished Johnny and stood. "I saw you and your man earlier today, walking by the bazaar booths. My ma said he was a famous bounty hunter. I reckon he'll win easy."

Looking up from the baby, Esther asked, "Win what?" She didn't correct the girl's notion that Thomas was her man.

"The shooting contest. Look." She pointed to where several men were lining up, facing away from the crowd. Out on the wide pasture, men were setting up targets at various distances. Fourth in line along the row of contestants was a silhouette she recognized.

Thomas. With his pistol drawn, checking the chambers.

Her heart stopped in her chest, and her knees weakened. She wanted to run away, but something held her fast to the spot.

Thomas stood back as the rifle shoot got underway. He had been set to bring his rifle to town, but she'd asked him not to. If she could've, she would've asked him to leave his sidearm at the ranch, too.

The rifles cracked, the smell of gunpowder drifted toward her on the breeze, and a winner was announced. Through it all, Esther fought to control the trembling of her limbs.

Then it was time for the pistol shoot. As the men lined up one after the other to fire their six shots, she flinched at every burst of sound. By the time they got to Thomas, her field of vision had narrowed and black spots swam before her face.

Thomas couldn't remember a day he'd enjoyed more. The weather had been perfect, the doctor had pronounced the baby healthy and he got to stroll through town with Esther on his arm.

He had approached Sheriff Granville, waiting until he finished his conversation with a man Thomas recognized as the blacksmith he'd taken Esther's harness horses to last week. When Mr. Buckland clapped the sheriff on the shoulder and walked away, Thomas had intercepted Charlie before someone else could.

The sheriff had grinned. "Just the man I hoped to see. I meant to ride out to Esther's place yesterday, but I got sidetracked setting up for the festivities. Did you hear my wife won the pie contest? Best pecan pie you ever ate. Doc Preston had it down to Millie White and Sarah, and for a minute, I thought he might be leaning toward the dried apple, but by sugar, he gave the ribbon to Sarah. I was so proud, I thought I might bust."

"Congratulations." Thomas hoped Doc Preston wasn't being vilified by the dried apple fans. He had drawn the sheriff away from the crowd and into the lee of the livery stable. "Did you get a chance to check on Regina Swindell?"

"I did. I'm sorry, Thomas, but you can't take the baby to her. She can't even take care of herself. Squalor would be too kind a word for what she's living in. I talked to the sheriff over in Spillville, and they're working on getting a judge to sign a custody order to have her sent to an asylum down on the coast. She hears voices and wanders around talking to herself. She's filthy and her clothes are a mess. No way she can take care of a child."

He shouldn't have felt relieved. This was Johnny's aunt, after all. But he couldn't deny a loosening of his neck muscles when he heard she couldn't take the baby.

"Any news on Swindell's location?"

"Wires have been silent. I sent out some feelers to a couple of sheriffs that I know, but nothing's turned up. I'll keep checking, but if I was Swindell, I'd have been neck deep in the Rio Grande before the sound of your gunfire at that shack had faded." Sheriff Granville had plucked a toothpick from his hatband and jammed it into the corner of his mouth. "Never could figure out why he kept hanging around central Texas when every lawman and bounty hunter in the state would like to have stretched his hide on the barn wall."

"I think it was the woman. He didn't want to leave her. Maybe she wouldn't go to Mexico with him when he asked, and by the time she finally gave in, she was too far gone with the baby to make any kind of time."

"Hard to imagine an outlaw falling in love, ain't it?" The sheriff swapped the toothpick to the other side of his mouth. "Still, love will make a man do funny things, won't it? I figured you'd be hot on Swindell's trail, now that you got the baby settled in at Esther's place for a while, but here you are, enjoying the town celebration, escorting Miss Esther around, acting for all the world like you have nothing but time to spend here in Silar Falls." His gray eyebrows waggled. "You thinking on sticking around?"

He wasn't.

He couldn't.

And yet, his eyes sought out Esther under the trees. She had been sitting with a group of women, and they were passing Johnny around, chattering and laughing. Making friends. He smiled. That was what Esther needed. To feel a part of the community again, to meet people and live a life beyond her washtubs and grieving for her father.

He was glad he had given her a new dress. It made him proud to see her in fine clothes, smiling and happy. She had looked up and their eyes met. For a moment a thread of electricity arced between them, and his chest tightened. When she brushed a curl off her cheek and looked away, he found he could breathe again.

"They're lining up for the horse race. I'm surprised you didn't enter. I've seen that horse of yours. He looks like he could cover some ground." Granville leaned against the livery stable corral fence. Thomas joined him, crossing his arms on the top rail, watching the cowboys milling with their horses, trying to get organized to start the race.

"You're right, Smitty's a goer. More than fast, he can canter all day. I think it's because he's stubborn and doesn't know when to quit." It was one of the reasons Thomas liked the animal.

"Not unlike some men I know. Don't know when to stop running." Granville had sent him a pointed look.

Thomas considered the older man's words. As a bounty hunter, he was the pursuer, not the quarry. He had nothing to run from.

And nothing to run to, if he was honest about it. He had never been in one place for more than a few months ever since the day he escaped the orphanage. He'd never wanted to stay anywhere long, except for once, five years ago.

He found Esther again. Sunlight dappled over her through the trees, and pink rode her cheekbones. She was standing, watching the cowboys. Thomas recognized Danny Newton and his friends among the race contestants. Esther's customers. His chest muscles tightened. Danny Newton was like a vulture, circling over Esther's not-quite-dead ranch, waiting for the fatal moment to swoop in.

The starter's pistol had boomed, and the horses took off. Cowboys yelled, the crowds cheered and the horses were off. All around the wide circle marked with flags, they stuck together as a pack, nobody gaining a clear advantage.

"Looks like it will be a close one this year. Last year Danny won it going away, but he's got a new horse this year, bigger and stronger, but not as fast from the look of things."

The horses had pounded around the last turn, and the gray stuck his nose out, a few inches at first, and then a neck. Danny had swept under the wire in first place by half a length.

People around Thomas and Charlie Granville had cheered, and Thomas had added a few claps. It had been a well-ridden race, but Thomas couldn't like Danny, not when he had been so rude to Esther and wanted to take her home from her.

"Now here's a contest you should enter." Charlie pointed to where men were setting up targets out on the open field. "Rifle, skeet and pistol competitions."

Thomas's interest piqued. He enjoyed a good target shoot. "You going to enter?"

Charlie gave the toothpick another mauling. "Nope. Truth is, I'm not that great a shot, and I don't care to advertise the fact. I'm better at keeping the peace by talking folks out of doing something stupid. I've used my pistol as a bludgeon a time or two, but I've never had to shoot anyone."

Thomas's fingers went to his sidearm. He'd had to shoot people before. It went with the job, since he was often tracking down violent offenders who would shoot to kill rather than face going to prison.

"Go on. Unless you're like me, only a fair shot." Charlie nudged him.

"Is there an entry fee? Some place to sign up?"

"Nope, just walk on over and tell Phil Crenshaw you want to shoot." The sheriff pointed to a portly man in a tall hat and black frock coat. "He's the mayor. Also the undertaker."

Thomas chuckled and headed over to put his name on the list.

"You gonna shoot?"

He turned to see Danny Newton behind him, scowling.

"I thought I'd give it a try." Thomas looked down at the shorter man. Danny reminded him of a bantam rooster, strutting and flashy.

"I wouldn't get my hopes up if I was you." Patting his two-gun rig, he grinned at his boys. "I'm the fastest gun in the county."

"Is that so?" Thomas turned to the mayor. "Thomas Beaufort. Pistol." He wished he had brought his rifle into town, since he was better with a long gun than his sidearm, but Esther had been adamant that he leave it behind, and she would've had him completely unarmed if she'd had her way.

Thomas didn't understand her aversion to guns. They were everywhere, and she'd never been squeamish about them before.

He checked the angle of the sun, the direction and force of the breeze, and the chambers of his Colt. Good thing he'd cleaned and oiled it just last night, sitting in the doorway of the bunkhouse listening to the cicadas and crickets, watching for the square of light from Esther's window to go out as he did every night, never retiring before she was in bed.

One by one, the contestants lined up, joshing one another. The first contest was for rifles, and several men took part, lying, kneeling and standing; best score won. To the surprise of the crowd, a youngster of about fifteen took the prize, a handsome saddle scabbard, for hitting the most bull's-eyes.

His pa beamed, tucking his thumbs under his braces and rocking on his feet. "I taught him everything he knows. Always had a steady eye, did Teddy here. Let's go celebrate with some of that lemonade, shall we, boy?" He patted his son on the shoulder and threw his arm around him, leading him toward the refreshment tables.

Thomas watched them go. He'd missed that, having a father to teach him things. Most everything he'd learned, he'd gained through experience. The orphanage had seen to it that he got some book learning, to read and write and cipher enough to get by, but mostly he'd watched and learned from the men he had worked with and ridden for. He liked to say he hadn't been so much raised as he'd scrambled up on his own.

Was that the fate that awaited little Johnny? No father in his life to teach him how to ride and hunt and fish and build things? No mother to see that he bathed and ate and learned his manners and knew how to treat a lady?

"Men in the pistol competition, there are two phases to this one." The mayor held up his clipboard. "First is the target shoot. Top two scores move on. The second part is new this year. It's the speed round. We'll use a launcher to toss a can into the air. Most hits before it strikes the ground wins. We'll keep going until a clear winner is declared. Everybody understand?"

The six contestants nodded. Seemed straightforward enough to Thomas. As each man stepped up to the line, he watched their technique. He'd been blessed to be able to work for a man down in Galveston for a time who was an excellent marksman, and Duncan had taught him all he knew.

When it came Thomas's turn, he unholstered his sidearm, letting it rest beside his thigh for a moment as a new target was set up. Black rings on white paper, maybe a foot across, the bull's-eye the size of a silver dollar. Twenty yards downrange.

He rolled his shoulders to loosen any tension. This was a doddle, really, since the target wasn't shooting back at him. He took his time, raised the gun and squeezed off a single shot.

The gun recoiled, the motion absorbed by his wrist and arm. Smoke wisped from the barrel, and he waited, counting to three, keeping his stance the same, one booted foot slightly ahead of the other, shoulder-width apart.

He followed the same procedure for the next five shots, taking his time, unlike some of the other contestants who had snapped off shots like they were in a gunfight on the streets of Abilene or Dodge City.

The scorekeepers ran out to get his target, but he knew what they would find. As they ran back, Thomas opened his cylinder and removed the spent shells, reloading the chambers with bullets from his belt. Another thing Duncan had taught him. Always reload right away, because an empty gun was useless.

"Thomas Beaufort has a perfect score! Every bullet in the bull's-eye!" Mr. Crenshaw shouted. A smattering of applause went through the crowd, and Thomas nodded.

"Pretty good, Beaufort." Danny swaggered up to him, the last contestant to shoot in this round. "But that was as slow as an old woman with the rheumatism. Get ready to be beaten." He drew the shiny pistols with the ivory grips and twirled them.

Stepping aside, Thomas waved to the new target out on the range. "Go to work."

Danny reholstered his pistols, stepped to the line and shook out his hands, setting his feet.

The crowd hushed, and in a blur, Danny drew, firing the pistols alternately with barely a breath between the shots until he'd sent six bullets down the range.

No doubt about it, he was fast. With a practiced flip, he reversed his guns and slid them into his holsters, grinning. "Looks like you and me will be moving on, Beaufort."

The scorekeepers jogged back with his target. "Four bull's-eyes, and two more in the next ring," Mayor Crenshaw called out. "Beaufort and Newton advance to the next round."

Sheriff Granville stepped to the makeshift launcher they had used for the rifle shoot and put a tin can into the spring-loaded holder.

"Beaufort, since you had the better score, you can choose to go first or last."

"I believe I'll go second." Thomas tucked his thumbs into his gun belt. He was a pursuer by nature, so he wanted to know what kind of a score he had to beat in order to win.

Danny's grin broadened. "Won't matter." He patted his guns. "It's two against one. No way you can beat me. I'm faster."

"We'll see."

The sheriff steepened the angle on the launcher so the can would go as high as possible and turned to Danny. "You ready?"

He drew his pistols and held them ready. "Go ahead."

With a clank, the launcher flung the can high into the air. Almost right away, Danny snapped off a shot and missed, then connected with his next shot and the one after that, sending the can jerking through the sky. He shot five more times, the last pair exiting his pistols at the same time.

Grinning, he holstered his guns. "Hit it three times all told. Not bad. It's harder than it looks."

Three out of eight shots. Now Thomas knew what he needed to do.

Feeling the expectations of the crowd, Thomas tried to see where Esther was. Too many people ringed the shooting area. He hoped she could see. He wanted to do well, to make her proud of him.

Thomas checked his loads, squared his shoulders and took a deep breath, letting it out slowly. Finally, he nodded to Granville.

Bang! Bang! Bang! Bang!

In perfect rhythm he fired off four shots, tracking the can as it kicked after each bullet hit it. His final shot sent it tumbling over the grass, just inches from the ground. Two little boys, waiting eagerly for the signal, raced out to pick it up, the taller of the two reaching it first and holding it aloft as he scampered back.

"Four out of four!" Mayor Crenshaw took the can, examining the holes.

Sheriff Granville clapped Thomas on the shoulder as a shout went up. "Nice shooting, son."

Thomas grinned. "Thanks."

Danny stomped up. "How'd you do that? You were so slow at the target shooting. I had two guns to your one. You can't be that fast."

He looked up from reloading. "You ever hear of Wyatt Earp?"

"Course I have. I read the papers, same as everybody else," Danny spit out. "What's that got to do with anything?"

"I had a friend who knew Wyatt when he was a lawman in Kansas. He said Wyatt had a saying that he always ascribed to, and I've taken it to heart myself. Wyatt said, 'Fast is fine, but accuracy is final. You must learn to be slow in a hurry.'"

"Sound advice," the sheriff said. "I do know this. If I have to get a posse together, I want you to be on it. That was some tall shooting."

"And here is your prize." Mayor Crenshaw handed him a stiff new gun belt, all tooled leather and silver conchos. "Made right here in Silar Falls by our saddler and harness maker, Mr. Pillar."

"Thank you." Thomas took the rig, hearing the leather squeak, running his hand over the glossy tooling. It was far more ornate than anything he would wear in his job, but it was nice workmanship, nonetheless. Making his way through the crowd, he accepted congratulations along the way. When he reached the bench under the tree, Esther wasn't there.

Initial disappointment speared through him. She must have needed to tend to Johnny.

The young girl he'd seen with Esther earlier came up to him. "Mr. Beaufort? I saw you win. I'm so glad. I was hoping you would."

"The lady who was here before, with the baby? Did you see where she went?" Thomas looked over her head toward the main street.

"Oh, she wasn't feeling too good. She got real pale and gave me the baby to hold, and she sat right down and put her head down. Musta been all the heat and excitement. It gets to my ma that way, too. The lady was pale as milk, but when she sat up, she said she felt better, and she took the baby with her thataway." She pointed toward the east end of town.

Guilt speared him. Here he was having fun, and Esther was feeling poorly. "Thanks, miss." He tipped his hat, tucked the new gun belt under his arm and headed for the shady spot by the church where they'd left the buckboard and team. If she was still ailing, he'd take her home, and if she'd recovered, she could help him celebrate his win by sharing a meal before the fireworks.

Chapter Ten

"Sure, I saw her." Trudy paused from dishing up bowls of ice cream. "She and the doc's wife were headed toward the doc's house not more than ten minutes ago."

The doctor? How badly was she feeling? Thomas's heart scudded. "Thanks." He took off at a jog. He'd been to the buckboard and left his prize there, and he'd visited the food stalls and the street where the bazaar booths were being dismantled, searching for her. Low booms of the shotgun shooting contest punctuated his steps.

Rounding the corner, he spied her on the porch, rocking with Johnny in her arms. Rip lay at her feet, his paws hanging over the edge of the porch, tongue lolling. Relief slowed his steps. Rip had a keen sense for the people around him, and if Esther was really ill, he wouldn't be looking so relaxed. She looked fine. Better than fine, actually. The doc's wife sat in another rocker beside her, and there was a pitcher and glasses on a low table between them. Shade from several trees in the yard would make it a nice, cool place.

He sauntered up the path, trying to hide the fact that he'd been a bit panicked just moments before. "Afternoon, ladies."

Rip yawned, showing all his teeth, and snapping his jaw shut, lowering his head to rest on his paws.

Mrs. Preston smiled, but Esther barely acknowledged him.

"Mr. Beaufort," Mrs. Preston said. "Won't you join us? I was finding all the heat and noise to be a bit much." She rested her hand on her unborn child. "Esther was feeling the same, so I persuaded her to come sit for a while."

Thomas removed his hat, running his fingers through his hair to straighten it. "That's kind of you, ma'am." He came up the steps and knelt by Esther's chair. "I heard you were feeling poorly."

He didn't mistake her leaning away from him, and her nose wrinkled. "You smell like gunpowder."

Blinking, he sat back on his heels. "I've been shooting. I won the pistol competition."

"Congratulations." A cold wind blew through her voice, and she turned her face away. "You must be very proud." More than a fair helping of sarcasm accompanied her statement.

Mrs. Preston looked from Thomas to Esther. "I believe I'll refresh this pitcher." She levered herself up and took the earthenware jug into the house.

"What's wrong? Are you sick or not?" Thomas straightened and went to lean against the porch railing.

"I'm fine."

"I heard a fellow say once that if a woman says she's fine, you better believe she's madder than a caged bobcat about something. What's got you peeved? Are you mad because I left you alone for a while? I needed to talk to the sheriff, and you were surrounded by ladies. I did check on you." He put his hat on again, crossing his arms.

"You took part in the shooting." Her brown eyes accused him.

"Yes."

"I *hate* guns. You know that. Especially pistols." She sounded suspiciously close to tears.

"Why? It's just some metal and wood. You see them all the time. Every man who rode for your father carried a pistol or rifle or both. Your dad carried a gun every day." Thomas rubbed the back of his neck. He did smell of gunpowder, but he didn't find the scent unpleasant. It was part of who he was and what he did for a living. As normal as leather or horse or dog or gun oil.

The color drained out of her face, and her eyes grew enormous. "Esther?" He moved to take the baby, afraid she might faint and drop him. "Esther?" Placing his hand on her forehead, he tested for a fever. Instead of heat, she felt cold and clammy. "What is it? Talk to me."

She covered her face with her hands, leaning forward, rocking slightly. "My father *did* carry a pistol. He used that pistol to shoot himself." Her voice was muffled behind her hands, but he heard every word as it collided with his chest. "I heard the shot, but I didn't think anything of it at the time. It wasn't close to the house. When the men brought him home, his clothes stank of gunpowder. Every time I hear a shot, every time I smell gunpowder, every time I see a handgun, I get queasy."

He wanted to go to her, but he reeked of the very thing that sent her back to her worst memories. Patting Johnny, he stood, helpless to comfort her. He'd assumed her fears were typical women's reactions to guns, not considering there might be a deeper cause behind her aversion to hand guns.

"I'm sorry, Esther. I didn't know my shooting in the pistol contest would upset you so."

Her hands dropped to her lap, and she leaned her head against the back of the rocker. Her eyes were dulled with her inner pain, and she stared at him. "How could you know? You weren't here. You left, and he killed himself, and I had nobody." Her voice was flat and lifeless, infinitely more painful to him than if she had raged. She braced her hands on the rocker and surged to her feet. "I still have nobody."

She hugged herself, as if cold on this warm day. "I don't want to talk about this anymore. I want to go home. You can stay in town if you wish. It's not more than a half-mile walk if you want to stay for the dancing and fireworks."

He couldn't let her leave, not alone, not like this.

"Please, stay. You haven't had anything to eat, and like you said, there's going to be music and fireworks. I don't want your day ruined." If he'd only come back to her after speaking with the sheriff instead of entering that contest. He hadn't needed to prove to anyone he could shoot. It was a pure indulgence on his part.

Mrs. Preston returned to the porch, the screen door

slapping behind her. "Are you thinking of leaving? Oh, do stay. We have these festive days so rarely." She set the pitcher back on the table. "Can I pour you a glass of lemonade, Mr. Beaufort?"

"Thank you, ma'am." Thomas had barely acknowledged to himself how much he had been looking forward to the dance and the fireworks and the drive home under the stars with Esther. If she left now, he'd go with her, because there would be no party without her. "Would you mind if I washed up first?"

"Of course not. Let me hold that beautiful boy. There's a washstand in Gareth's office. You saw it earlier, didn't you?" Mrs. Preston took Johnny. "And I'll prevail upon Esther to stay awhile longer."

Thomas went into the doctor's office and poured water from the pitcher on the washstand into the bowl. Pressing his hands flat into the basin, he leaned forward, staring into the mirror on the wall.

Elihu had shot himself with a pistol. The smell of gunpowder made Esther sick.

He was a bounty hunter. He carried a gun. He felt exposed without his gun.

Wherever he went, he was alert to the possibility that he might run into someone he had hauled off to jail who might now be out, who might bear a grudge and who might seek some sort of revenge. When he went into a restaurant or railroad station, he sat with his back to the wall where he could see the door. When he went into a store, he kept an eye on all the patrons. For that matter, when he went to church, he stood along the back wall or sat in the very back pew so he could see everyone who entered.

And he always wore his gun. Even in church.

He would never leave it at home. Not because he was some bloodthirsty killer, but because his gun was for protection, his and others'.

Grabbing the bar of soap, he lathered his hands. The soap smelled of carbolic and lye, and he hoped it cut some of the gunpowder smell, though there wasn't much he could do about the acrid aroma clinging to his clothes. It would dissipate soon.

A rumpus sounded outside the open examination-room door, and three boys tumbled into the house, all high-pitched voices and nonstop movement. Thomas rinsed his hands and toweled them dry.

"Pa, he's in here." The eldest, Matthew, stuck his head into the room. "I saw you shoot, mister. You were so fast. My friend Darby says you're a bounty hunter and you never miss." He hopped from one foot to the other, his forelock bouncing against his head. "I reckon you could even beat Jase Swindell or Sam Bass."

Thomas ruffled the boy's hair as he went by. "Thanks, buddy."

"When I grow up, I want to be a bounty hunter and shoot good like you." Matthew followed him out onto the porch. "Bam! Bam! Bam!" He pointed his finger like a gun and mimicked shooting a can out of the air.

Esther's skin paled to alabaster, and her mouth set in a hard line.

"That's enough, Matthew." His mother gave him a serious look. "We'll have no more talk of guns and shooting."

The youngest, Luke, had his arms wrapped around Rip's neck, who appeared not to mind, though he had little experience with affectionate little boys. "But why can't we have a dog? Why can't we have thith one? I like thith one. And he liketh me. Look." He gave Rip another fierce hug.

"Of course he likes you. Everybody likes you. But that dog belongs to Mr. Beaufort, Luke." Mrs. Preston sat in her rocker and picked up her fan, fluttering it until the curls at her temples blew back. "He needs him for his work. We'll get a dog someday."

"You promith?"

"I promith." She gave him a loving smile. "For now, enjoy this fine animal's company."

The middle boy had taken up residence on the porch swing and had the seat swaying alarmingly fast. Doc Preston, who was just mounting the front steps called to them, "Slow it down, Mark, before it bucks you off." He removed his hat, kissed his wife on the cheek and grinned at Esther.

"See what you have to look forward to with Johnny here? It's noise and dirt and motion from dawn till dark." He patted Matthew on the shoulder. "But we wouldn't trade it, would we, dear?"

Mrs. Preston laughed and placed her hand on her rounded belly. "Just as well, since we're adding to the chaos soon."

Thomas watched Esther. She had recovered her color a bit, and she met his eyes briefly when the doctor spoke of looking forward to Johnny being a boisterous lad someday.

Was that hope in her eyes? Wistfulness? Or was he imagining things? He'd asked for her help with the baby until he could find a suitable home for him…

not that he'd given the task his whole attention in the ten days since he'd come back to Silar Falls. Esther keeping the baby wasn't sensible, though. She had a hard enough time keeping herself, and her future on the ranch was by no means secure. And she was a single woman. Johnny needed a family, with two parents, and security and love.

Still, leaving Johnny with Esther would make riding away from them both easier when the time came.

"So, it's agreed?" Doc Preston rubbed his hands, looking pleased. "Mrs. Miller is going to watch the boys tonight, and she'll take Johnny, too. That way you can enjoy yourselves."

It was agreed? Thomas had missed the conversation with his inattention. Esther sent him a pleading look, but Mrs. Preston was beaming.

"Oh, please say yes. I can't dance, not in my current condition, but I would love to watch fireworks with you both. And you could use a break from child care, Esther. Mrs. Miller is our housekeeper, and she helps with the boys all the time. I'm sure one more won't bother her a bit."

At that moment Mrs. Miller turned in at the gate, a comfortable looking woman with a large bag over her arm. "Evening, Doctor. Missus." She set her bag on the steps and opened her arms as the youngest Preston, Luke, launched himself off the porch. "Och, child, you're a tear, aren't you?" She hugged him. "I brought a new game for us to play tonight."

Esther came to Thomas and whispered, "What do we do?" Her breath tickled his ear and sent his nerves tingling. "I don't want to be rude."

He turned, and they were inches apart. She backed up a pace, eyes blinking. "Mrs. Preston," he spoke over the chatter of the boys. "We'd be delighted. Esther could use a break this evening. We'll try to make sure she has a good time."

Reaching out, he took her hand, as small as a bird's in his larger one. He leaned down, keeping his voice low. "Just enjoy tonight, Esther. No pressures, no work, no worries, no chores or cares. Nothing pulling from the past or pressing from the future."

She looked up at him with those big, brown eyes, and his heart thumped hard. Her hand stirred in his, and he thought she was going to pull away, but at the last moment, she squeezed his fingers and nodded.

But the burdens of her everyday life and her past lingered in her eyes. Would they ever be dispelled? Would he be able to help her, or was his presence a constant reminder of things she preferred to forget?

Esther accepted the laden plate Thomas handed her, leaning to the side as he stepped over the bench and put his own plate on the table. All down the main street of Silar Falls, tables, sawhorses and doors, planks and crates had been set up to form one long dining surface. Overhead, lanterns hung on ropes suspended across the street, and people laughed and talked and ate.

Thomas reached into his shirt pocket and withdrew a napkin-wrapped bundle of silverware. "Here you go." He put his hand over hers when she reached for it, and she glanced up into his eyes.

"Shall we say grace?" Without waiting for her response, he bowed his head near hers and said a simple prayer of thanks for the food and the company before releasing her fingers.

"I'm famished." He grinned and tucked into his supper. Across from them, Dr. and Mrs. Preston, now Doc and Eliza at their insistence, found their seats.

"Oh, good, you took some of my cucumber salad. I know it's silly, but I always have a fear of bringing a dish to a supper like this and no one taking any. I'm sure I would walk in the shame of it for weeks." Eliza unfolded her napkin, tried to spread it in her lap, then laughed. "I don't have much of a lap these days."

Esther took a bite of the creamed cucumbers. "Delicious. I didn't plan on staying for the dinner, so I didn't prepare anything to contribute."

Doc buttered a slab of corn bread. "Don't you worry. There's enough to feed a town this size twice over. Say, I ran into Sheriff Granville when I was standing in line for the food, and he tells me if you can't find any of Johnny's relatives to take him, you might be looking for a family to adopt him. He thought I might be able to help you out, since I know most of the families in the county. Shouldn't be too hard to place a healthy baby boy."

Eliza paused, her fork suspended between her mouth and her plate, and she looked from Esther to Thomas and back again. "You're going to adopt him out? But I thought…that is… I wish…" She floundered to a stop.

Doc chuckled and put his arm around her. "Now, dear, I know you love babies, but don't you think your hands are pretty full now?" He looked at her middle and smiled. "Soon to be even more so?"

She shook her head. "Of course. Our four will keep me quite busy, it's just that I was surprised. I guess I assumed Esther would keep Johnny herself."

Esther's chest squeezed, and she put her fork down, appetite gone. With the sheriff and the doctor and Thomas on a mission to find a family for Johnny, it wouldn't be long before he was taken from her forever.

Her hands clenched in her lap. Which would be for the best, since she couldn't provide for him alone.

And she was alone. She needed to remember that.

And yet, for the first time in years, she had spent a significant amount of time in town with other people. People had been warm and cordial, and she sensed she might have found a new friend in Eliza Preston. Perhaps, though she had been on her own for such a long time, and she soon would be again, she wouldn't be so very alone.

Doc asked Thomas about his work. "A job like that must be pretty exciting. All those chases and tracking and such."

Thomas shook his head, but he leaned forward, eyes intent. "Actually, it's fairly boring most of the time. Lots of riding, lots of sleeping out. Lots of trying to sneak up on someone who is looking out for pursuers."

"But how do you do it? Do you lie in wait, or do you chase after fugitives?"

Esther turned away, but she couldn't help overhearing. And part of her wanted to know, wanted to know what was so appealing about the life of a bounty hunter that he'd chosen it over staying on the Double J.

"Mostly I use my head. Criminals are creatures of habit, same as most folks. I try to learn as much as I can about my quarry before I set out." He gestured with his fork. "Any family or friends he might have, any patterns he's established. Some men who break out of jail head right home. I've even been there to meet a couple of them when they step off the stage or ride into the barn."

"You're kidding."

"Nope. Those are the easiest jobs. The ones where they ride right in." He laughed. "You wouldn't believe it. They look shocked and then defeated. One fellow even held his hands out for the shackles without saying a word."

"But surely you have had some hair-raising encounters? It can't be all dull."

"I've been in a tight spot a time or two. But mostly it's just using my head and trying to outthink the other man. Rip helps. He's great on the trail. And he's good at watching a prisoner once I have him in custody." Pride colored his voice. "I trained him myself from a pup."

"How do you decide who to go after? The size of the bounty?" someone asked from down the way.

Esther noticed Thomas had gathered quite an audience. Sheriff Granville and Sarah, Trudy and Frank, and even Mayor Crenshaw had stopped by their table.

Thomas shrugged, grinning. "Depends on the circumstances. It's always easier to catch someone right after a crime or after they've broken out of jail, but it doesn't always work that way. Sometimes it's a warrant or bail jumper, and you have to wait until they don't show up for court before they're in violation. Whenever I turn in a bounty to a sheriff or a prison, I check the new wanted posters. Once I showed up at Huntsville to deliver a prisoner, and they'd had an escape just the night before. I was able to put Rip on the scent right away, and we tracked him down in less than forty-eight hours." He grinned. "That was a pretty tidy bounty, even though there hadn't been time to swear out a warrant or get a reward posted. The governor himself sent me a letter and a bank check for that one."

"So who were you chasing when you found Johnny and his mother? A bandit or bail jumper or prison escapee?" Doc tucked his last bite of corn bread into his mouth.

"An escapee. But Johnny's arrival threw me off the trail for a bit. I'll get back to it soon."

The sound of an accordion and a fiddle drifted from the end of the street where a temporary dance floor had been set up. The band tuning up. A cheer went up from the crowd, and people began stacking plates and moving toward the music.

Thomas reached for Esther's plate. He frowned. "Are you still feeling poorly? You didn't eat much."

"I'm fine." She hadn't missed how his eyes had sparkled or his mouth had stretched in a smile while talking about his life as a bounty hunter. He was good at his job, sounding as if he loved it and would never consider doing anything else. And she had no right to ask him to, even if she wanted to.

"I haven't danced with a pretty lady since 'Hector

was a pup.' I'm no great shakes at it, but I'm itching to shuffle my boots. Are you game?" He held out his hand.

"You two go along." Doc stood and helped Eliza to her feet. "I'll take your plates."

Esther hesitated. "Maybe I should offer to help with the dishes."

Sarah Granville shook her head. "No, you don't. Trudy and I are on dish duty along with most of the Ladies' Aid. You young folks go have a good time." She picked up Thomas's and Esther's plates and motioned Esther to move along. "Don't show your face around a washtub today. You get enough scrubbing through the week. Thomas, take her away from here before she's tempted."

Thomas offered his arm, smiling so that the creases beside his mouth deepened. "You heard the lady."

Esther put her hand through his elbow, and he covered it with his other hand. "Remember," he murmured. "No worries, no cares."

The music was quick and lively, and boots rang out on the dance floor, skirts belled and the crowd clapped. Thomas took her into his arms and swung her into the melee. His hand was firm on her back and strong, holding her close, but not too close.

"It's been a while, hasn't it?" He bent his head to speak into her ear, sending flutters through her middle. "Ferguson's barn dance?"

Five summers ago. Thomas hadn't been her escort. Nobody had, since her father didn't think her old enough for courting. But she'd danced three times with Thomas that night, something surely noted by everyone who attended.

Dancing with him that night, her heart had threatened to burst through her stays. The world had been perfect that evening, and full of promise.

And three days later, he'd ridden away.

She missed a step, and his arms tightened, supporting her. Trying to recover, she shrugged. "Was it? I don't remember."

He pivoted, drawing her in. "You're a liar, Esther Jensen." His voice was kind and even conspiratorial. "I think you remember that night very well. I sure do."

Thankfully, the song came to an end at that moment. She stepped back. Before she could move, Sheriff Granville was there. "Miss Esther, can I have this next dance?"

A hard lump had formed in her throat. Thomas remembered that night, but obviously it hadn't meant anything special to him.

"I'm sorry, Sheriff. It's time I was heading home. We left Johnny with the Prestons' housekeeper, and we can't impose any longer."

"It has been a big day, hasn't it? Still, I think the founders would be proud, don't you?" He turned to Thomas. "I'll send out a few more wires tomorrow, see if there's any word about Johnny's relatives. Should have some news soon."

Time was racing much too quickly toward that moment when Thomas and Johnny would be gone from her life. A chill went through her in spite of the warm night.

Chapter Eleven

"How on earth can a clothes wringer be for the baby?" Esther put her dripping hands on her hips. For the past two days, she'd kept her feelings rigorously under control, focusing on the work of each day, caring for Johnny, who was fractious and out of sorts, cooking meals, and washing clothes, deliberately not thinking of the wonderful time she had at the Founders Day Celebration, the shock and fear of seeing Thomas shooting his pistol, or the feeling of being in his arms on the dance floor.

Definitely *not* thinking of any of those things.

Thomas appeared not to think of them, either. From dawn until dark, he worked as if racing some deadline he'd set. He'd finished whitewashing the outbuildings, repaired the porch boards on the house and rebuilt the corral fence where the barn fire had damaged it. He had even replaced the glass in the windows on the west side of the house, windows that had been boarded up for years, ever since the hailstorm had broken them. And every repair and rebuild and replacement had been justified as somehow being "for the baby."

He'd also ridden over the ranch several times. She'd seen him silhouetted against the sky up on the ridge where he said he'd seen evidence of someone stopping. In the evening, when he returned, he would tell her about some new discovery, a spring back in the hills, a new meadow or swale perfect for grazing, his eyes bright as he told her of the potential her place had to be the finest ranch in the county.

And last night, she'd found him doodling on a scrap of paper.

"What's that?" She set his plate of roasted chicken and vegetables in front of him, sliding the fresh biscuits closer.

He'd glanced up. "Thank you. That smells great. I was just sketching out plans for a new barn." He folded the paper and tucked it into his shirt pocket. "How I would build it if it was mine."

"That's wasted time. I don't have the money for a barn, even if I needed one. Daisylu is content enough with the shed you built in the corral."

"I still can't believe I built anything for that cranky goat." He waited for her to take her seat at the table before saying grace. "I give her shade and shelter, and she isn't even grateful, still stamping her feet and bleating at me every time I come near. Anyway, the plans are just for fun. I don't have a place to put a barn. I don't own enough ground to spread my bedroll, much less enough to build a barn."

Now he stood beside the buckboard, rolling the tarp off a shiny new clothes wringer and galvanized tub on a stand. Pushing his hat back, he shrugged. "Johnny was telling me just this morning that he wanted one."

"Right." She blew a strand of hair off her forehead. "And what else did he say?"

"That you work too hard, that a wringer would make things easier for you, and that then you could spend more time rocking him on the porch and singing lullabies, since that's his favorite thing to do."

She couldn't deny that the wringer would make her life much easier, but she had priced them in the catalog at Clements' store and knew they came dear. She frowned. "Frank and Trudy don't keep these in stock. Where did this one come from?"

He shrugged again and lifted the tub and wringer off the buckboard. It sat on a metal table base, and he strode over and placed it before her. "Frank ordered it for me the first night, when we went to the store to get things for the baby."

"Why didn't you tell me?"

"Would you have let me buy it if you knew in advance?" He gave the handle a crank, spinning the rollers. "Now it's here, and I can't take it back. I can't take it with me. Smitty wouldn't care to tote around a washtub." He smiled, and Esther smiled too at the notion of his rangy horse carrying a washtub and wringer behind the saddle.

A cry came from the porch. "See, Johnny will be sad if you don't accept." Thomas headed toward the house, and Esther wiped her hands on her apron as she followed him, shaking her head at how he managed to outmaneuver her each time…and how she let him.

"He's sad anyway, today. Restless, like he can't get comfortable. He barely gets to sleep before he's awake and crying." She bent over the basket and lifted the baby out, holding him to her shoulder, rocking him. Rip, who hadn't left Johnny's side all day, whined and raised himself up a bit on his hind legs, trying to snuffle the baby.

"Is he off his feed like before?" Thomas's brows bunched. "Daisylu giving sour milk?"

"No, it's not like that. No throwing up, just restless. He doesn't want to eat at all." She kissed the baby's forehead and drew back. "I think he might be sick. Do you think he has a fever?" The niggling unease she'd been fighting all day rippled through her.

Thomas cupped the back of Johnny's head and ran his hand down over the boy's arm to surround his tiny fist. "He feels warm to me, but it's a warm day. I guess I'm more bothered by the fact that he isn't hungry. He's been hungry since he first drew a breath."

"I can't point to any one thing. And I don't know anything about sick babies except that things can go from bad to worse quickly. I'm just uneasy, is all." She pressed another kiss to Johnny's head, sure that he felt warmer than usual.

Thomas rubbed the back of his neck, his brow bunched. "I don't know anything about sick babies either, but I'm a big believer in being safe rather than sorry. I'll go get the doc. Do what you can to make the little fellow comfortable, and try not to worry. It's probably nothing."

He bounded off the porch, and she couldn't help but be thankful he was so capable and steady. Nothing seemed to get him into a flap. He was right. Dr. Preston would come, and he'd probably laugh at her fears and tell her that babies had off days the same as everyone else, and that Johnny was just out of sorts.

The baby cried, his head bobbing against her shoulder like a baby bird's. She shifted him to lie in her arms, swaying and shushing him. Two tiny tears formed in the corners of his eyes and rolled toward his ears. Poor baby.

Rip growled and began pacing the length of the porch, pausing at the north end to stare after the buckboard before turning to pace back, for all the world like a nervous father. His presence comforted Esther, even though his pacing drove her to distraction.

She stayed on the porch since it was cooler than in the house where there was no breeze. The dust cloud from the buckboard showed Thomas's progress into town, and she followed it with her eyes.

Please, Lord, let this be nothing. Let this be me overreacting. Johnny's too little to be sick.

Esther wet a cloth and wiped the baby's red face, crooning to him. His sobs diminished, and he dropped into a fitful sleep once more. She sat in the rocker and held him, staring out at her washtubs and the shining new wringer. She couldn't deny that having Johnny to care for made getting her work done harder, and the wringer would certainly help, but…she tried to tally how much Thomas must've spent since he rode into her yard two weeks ago. Food, supplies for Johnny, a new dress for her, window glass, water piping, whitewash, even a goat. He made up excuses about all of it being for the baby, but she knew better. His generosity made her feel cherished, but frustrated her, too. Before long, he would leave, and she would have to get by on her own once more. He'd stayed well beyond the few days of his original plan. Surely he would be packing up his scant belongings and clearing out of the bunkhouse any day.

The baby stirred and whimpered. His hand opened, and she put her finger into his little palm, feeling as he closed his tiny fingers as if he were grasping her very heart.

Thomas returned within the hour, driving past the house and up to the corral to care for the team. That was another change he'd made, currying and brushing the horses, taking them to the blacksmith for a hoof trimming and new shoes, oiling the harness and tightening the hardware on the buckboard. Everywhere she turned, he'd made a difference somehow.

"How is he?" Thomas bounded onto the porch, a bundle under one arm and a box under the other.

"The same, I guess. Where's the doctor?"

"He'll come as soon as he can. Seems like there's some bug going through the small fry in town, his own boys included. Fever, no appetite, headaches, chills. Doc Preston's got his hands full making the rounds. Mrs. Preston said she'll send him along as soon as he comes home. Until then, she gave me a list of things to do." He tugged it from his pocket. "And I stopped by the mercantile and picked up the supplies she recommended. Trudy sent along some bread and fresh butter when she heard Johnny was ailing. Figured you wouldn't want to do much cooking with a sick baby in the house. Said to call on her if we need to, but Frank said she was headed to the neighbor's to help care for their sick kids."

Real sickness, going through the children in Silar Falls. Esther held the baby closer, her heart tumbling.

"Is it bad?"

"Mrs. Preston says it's too soon to tell, that kids can get sick in a hurry and you think they're in a terrible way, then the fever breaks and they're up and running around like nothing ever happened," Thomas said, his eyes grave, as if he wanted to believe what he was saying but wasn't sure.

"What are we supposed to do for Johnny?"

Thomas unfolded the note. "Try to get him to drink. If he won't take milk, try water. Dribble some into his mouth from a rag or spoon if he won't suck. Mrs. Preston said it was important not to let him get dehydrated."

"What about fever?"

"He's too little for medicine, but she said to dress him lightly, not bundle him up too much, and if the fever gets too high, give him a bath in barely warm water. She said to lay him back and pour the water over the top of his head. If that doesn't work, then we should use this." He unwrapped a bottle of surgical alcohol. "She said dip some cotton wadding into the alcohol and run it over his skin. As it evaporates, it's supposed to help cool him off. Just be careful not to get it near his eyes or mouth."

Esther feathered her fingers through the baby's hair. "How many children are sick?"

"I don't know. From what Frank said, a lot of them. It spread pretty fast, so they're hoping it burns out pretty fast, too. Mrs. Preston says she feels awful about it, since Johnny probably picked it up from her boys." Thomas set his parcels on the table and tucked his thumbs into his gun belt, his feet braced apart.

Esther shook her head. "It could've been from anyone. Several ladies passed him around at the festival, and there were people everywhere."

"That's what I told her. Her housekeeper was there to help her. They had the boys on palettes on the floor of the front room so Mrs. Preston didn't have to climb the stairs too much in her delicate condition. The little one, Luke, saw me and asked if I had brought Rip with me." He smiled. "So he can't be too bad off."

Rip had quirked his head at the sound of his name, but he resumed his pacing.

"Have any adults come down with it?" What would she do if she got sick? Or Thomas? Who would care for Johnny? And if she was laid up, how would she do her work? She needed every last dollar before her taxes came due.

"Not that I heard, but I imagine it won't be long if this thing is as catching as they say. But maybe kids are more susceptible to it? We can't worry about that right now." He set the bottle back into the box. "What can I do to help?"

"I have so much work to do. Can you hold him for a while? He seems to sleep better if someone's holding him. Then I can get a few more tubs of laundry done." If she at least got them washed and on the line, she could sprinkle and roll them tonight and iron them tomorrow before her customers came to pick them up.

Thomas took the precaution of putting a clean diaper on his shoulder before letting her put Johnny into his arms. "That way you won't have to rest against my rough old work shirt, right, buddy?"

Esther pushed the straggling hair off her forehead. "I'll get you a bottle of milk and a cup of water and a spoon. If he rouses, you can try to get him to drink."

Thomas glanced up at her before returning his attention to the baby, and that look somehow made her feel better. Being alone with a sick baby terrified her, but Thomas's presence comforted.

Looking back at him sitting in the rocker with a vulnerable infant sheltered in his protective arms warmed a place in her heart that she had kept carefully hidden and guarded for such a long time, she'd almost forgotten it existed.

Thomas rocked the baby, but Johnny didn't settle. He squirmed and snuffled and grimaced, his face flushed. He began to cry, and nothing Thomas did consoled him. Rocking, patting, pacing, nothing.

Rip looked at Thomas with reproachful eyes as the baby's distress increased.

"I'm doing the best I can." Thomas reached for the bottle, but when he tried to get Johnny to take it, the boy cried harder.

Esther quit scrubbing clothes and trotted back to the porch, wiping her hands on her apron. "What's wrong?"

"I don't know." The notion that the little fellow was

hurting and neither of the adults in his life could do anything about it made Thomas want to punch something. "I don't know what to do."

"Let me try." Esther took the sobbing infant, nestling him under her chin, swaying gently. "Shh, it's all right. Don't cry. I'm here."

Johnny immediately subsided, hiccupping and sniffling, but quieting.

"Well, would you look at that? Guess he knows what he wants…or rather *who* he wants." Thomas shrugged. "Can't fault his logic."

"Maybe I should put him in the sling so I can hold him and work, too?" She cuddled Johnny, her cheek against his hair.

"How about you let me do the washing and you just hold him? It's too hot out in the sunshine for him right now." Thomas had never done more than scrubbed his shirts out beside a creek before, but he'd rather wash every stitch on the place than helplessly hold Johnny while he cried.

"I can't let you do that."

"Sure you can." Thomas was already rolling up his sleeves. "If I run into trouble, I'll ask for help."

He filled buckets at the spigot and poured them into the iron kettle, poking the coals underneath and throwing on a few mesquite logs. Several baskets sat in a row ready to go through the boiling process, and another batch was already in the washtub. Light clothes first, then the heavier, darker clothes.

That made sense. The boiling water would be freshest first and keep the light clothes light. Using a paddle, he stirred the items in the kettle and then turned to what was in the soapy washtub.

"This thing is a knuckle buster." He rubbed a white shirt on the scrub board, banging his fingers the first time until he got enough fabric bunched between his knuckles and the corrugated metal to cushion them.

He took the time to fill the rinse tub on the new wringer setup, plopping each clean shirt into it. One after another until he had twelve shirts clean. His lower back ached from bending over the washtub, which had been set to Esther's shorter height. No wonder she was so trim and fit. He felt as if he'd been chopping wood for a week.

"You'll need to add bluing to those white shirts."

He turned. Esther had come down from the porch, her arms empty. "He's sleeping?"

"For now. It's cooler for him when I'm not holding him. I thought I could give you a hand until he woke again. You have to add bluing to that batch of shirts or they won't look clean."

"Bluing?"

A small bucket stood off to the side holding cakes of soap and other items, and from it, she withdrew a bottle. "Add a bit of this." She held up the bottle which read Mrs. Stewart's Liquid Bluing.

"It gives the white clothes a bluish gray cast instead of a yellow one, which makes them look whiter."

He raised his eyebrow. "You make clothes blue so they look white?"

"It's a bit of an optical illusion, I suppose, but normal wear on white linen yellows it, and using bluing masks that yellow tint." She tipped two capfuls into the rinse water. "Trust me."

"You're the expert."

Johnny cried from his basket on the porch. "That didn't last long."

"Go on up. I can manage here."

Thomas set to work, running the clothes through the wringer, pegging them out on the clotheslines, replenishing the fire. All afternoon, his hands were never dry, his arms never still, his mind roiling and tumbling like the boiling garments in the kettle.

For five years Esther had made her living this way as the ranch crumbled around her ears. Why hadn't she sold out and moved to town? Surely she could've gotten a fair price for the property and lived a mite easier. She would have close neighbors and friends, access to the stores and community doings. And no tax money to try to raise each year.

It hadn't been right of her father to shackle her to this place with his last wishes. Of course, it hadn't been right for him to leave her by his own hand either.

From time to time, Thomas went to the house to check on the baby. Each time, Esther was more concerned. The little fellow seemed to have shrunk, and his skin was paper dry. The only place he seemed to get any rest at all was snuggled up on Esther's chest.

Late afternoon, the doctor finally arrived. He looked as tired as Thomas felt, dark circles under his eyes, lines of strain beside his mouth. Pulling into the yard in his buggy, the doctor slowly climbed from the rig.

Thomas stepped off the porch to meet him. "Doc. You look like you were ridden hard and put up wet."

"I feel like it, too. How is the baby doing? Are either of you feeling poorly?" He reached into the buggy for his bag. Thomas took the rope and weight from the buggy and clipped the end of the rope to the horse's bridle, dropping the weight onto the ground.

"Johnny's feeling pretty puny. Hot and uncomfortable." Thomas followed the doctor into the house.

Esther stood at the table, Johnny in her arm, a basin of cool water next to her. She wrung out a cloth, letting it drip over the baby's head. Johnny squawked and fussed, not liking the dousing at all.

"Hush, now. It's for your own good." Esther sponged his neck and chest. She'd stripped him to just his diaper for his bath, and his spindly legs jerked and his arms flailed.

Doc Preston set his bag on the table and picked up a towel. "Let's see him."

Esther placed Johnny in the doctor's hands on the towel, biting her lower lip. "He's so feverish. I got a little water into him, but he won't take milk at all."

The doctor took a seat and laid the baby in his lap. He took an instrument from his bag. "We'll just have a listen to his heart and lungs." The doc popped two bits of the thing into his ears and placed the bell end on Johnny's chest.

He seemed to listen forever. Finally, he took the earpieces out. "No congestion, which is good. His heart rate is a bit fast because of the fever. Has he been coughing or throwing up?"

"No, just feverish and fussy."

"Adults in town are starting to come down with it now, but it's hitting the children the hardest. Are either of you feeling ill?"

Thomas shook his head, but looked closely at Esther. Her face was flushed, but it had been a warm day.

"I feel fine," she said. "Just worried about the baby."

Doc dug in his bag. "Johnny's too young for medicine. I've never treated a baby this small for an illness. There's some speculation that a baby who is nursed by his mother doesn't get sick as easily, that the mother's milk somehow protects the child. I don't know if that's true or not, but Johnny doesn't have the benefit of mother's milk." He set an envelope on the table. "This isn't for him. This is in case either of you starts feeling sick. They're powders that will help with headaches and fever. Stir one packet into a cup of water and drink it."

"What about the boy?" Thomas asked.

"As I said, I've never tried to medicate a child this young. Anything I do could do more harm than good. We have to let the illness run its course and hope he's strong enough to take it. Most fevers rise in the night, so don't be surprised if that happens. And fevers in children can rise especially high. Do what you can to keep him cool and comfortable, and above all else, keep him hydrated. Watch the clock, drizzle some water into his mouth every fifteen minutes, offer him water in the bottle. Dip the nipple in sugar if you have to, to get him to take it." He rubbed his hands down his cheeks. "I'd tell you to bring him into town, but you'd come into even more contact with sick folks. It seems our Founders Day Celebration spread more than good cheer."

"How many are ailing?" Esther took Johnny back from the doctor, shushing and snuggling him. Amazingly, the baby settled in with a whimper, sucking on his fist. Thomas smiled at the boy's continued preference for Esther.

"Two dozen at least, most of them children."

"How are your own boys?" Thomas went to the stove and poked in some kindling. "You look like you could use some coffee, and don't say you don't have time. You'll probably be up all night."

"Thank you. I've been going nonstop since before dawn. The boys are holding their own, cranky and tired, mostly. It's Eliza I worry about. She's wearing herself out and won't rest."

"Don't forget to serve some of Trudy's bread and butter, Thomas." Esther went to the rocker and sat, and Rip leaned into her legs, putting his head in her lap, staring up at the baby. "I don't blame Eliza. I wouldn't sleep, either, if my children were sick."

Thomas sliced the bread and set it by the doc's elbow and then filled the coffeepot with water. "How long do you think this will last? The sickness, I mean?"

Doc shook his head. "Too soon to tell, though something like this that springs up quickly can disappear just as fast. Especially in children. I'm not really worried, just yet, not about most of the cases. It's not typhus or yellow fever or cholera or the like, so we've dodged a bullet there. But I won't lie. Johnny's very young, and he isn't big enough to fight off much illness. These things tend to hit the very young and the very old the hardest."

Thomas's gut tightened. What would he do if Johnny didn't make it? He'd delivered the baby, had done everything he could to ensure the boy's safety and well-being, and he'd come to care for him in a way he hadn't expected. If anything happened to him, he didn't know what he'd do.

The coffee boiled, and he poured a cup for the doc. "Careful. It's strong enough to stand a spoon in, just the way I brew it on the trail."

Blowing across the top of the steaming cup, Doc smiled. "If it's that strong, it should carry me through the night with no trouble." He took a sip and grimaced. "You weren't joking."

He stayed a few more minutes, helping himself to a slice of buttered bread and finishing his coffee. "I'll be at home tonight unless there's a crisis. Most folks will ride this out without too much drama. But if the baby stops wetting his diapers or if his fever gets too high, come and fetch me. Sometimes high fevers in children can cause seizures. I'm praying that won't happen in this case, but I want you to be prepared. I'm going to relieve my wife of nursing duties and see that she gets some rest." He put on his hat, squeezed Esther's shoulder and nodded to Thomas before heading to his buggy.

Esther kissed the top of Johnny's head, her eyes clouded with worry. Thomas realized that she wouldn't escape unscathed from his bringing the baby to her doorstep. When Johnny recovered from this ailment—Thomas would consider no other option—there was still the matter of finding a family to place him with. The sheriff said he had a line on a couple of local families who might be interested, and Thomas was still waiting on a telegram he'd sent to the sheriff where he'd first picked up the news that Swindell had taken up with a local woman. Perhaps that sheriff would know of some of the woman's family, though she'd claimed to have none.

And there was Swindell himself. Outlaw he might be, but once he was captured, he should have a say in what happened to his son.

In any event, Thomas would be taking Johnny away from Esther, breaking her heart.

When did life get so complicated? For the past five years, he'd known exactly what he would do every day. He knew who and what he was after, and he took steps to make sure he got his quarry. Now he couldn't even make up his mind when he should leave, where he should look next for Jase Swindell, or what was best to do for a baby not even a month old.

And he didn't know what to do about Esther. Everything he'd felt for her as a boy had come back and stronger, more mature. But nothing had changed. He'd ridden away from her, knowing that what her father said was true. He wasn't good enough for her, not a foundling drifter who didn't even know who his parents were. Granted, her situation had changed, from ranch heiress to laundress, but she was still too good for him. She deserved better.

He was a bounty hunter, a legalized gunman, basically, and she hated guns and all they had cost her.

She would no more consider his suit than she would become a sharpshooter for a traveling show.

Thomas owed it to her to keep his feelings for her under wraps and leave her as heart-whole as he could.

"I wish the little fellow would rest if I held him. You're in for a long night if the only place he'll sleep is in your arms." He scooted out a chair, straddled it and rested his arms on the back.

"I don't mind. If I wasn't holding him, I'd be pacing and worrying." She rubbed small circles on Johnny's back. "He's so helpless. He can't even tell us where he hurts."

Thomas rested his chin on his stacked wrists. "Would you mind if I prayed? Out loud? I've been praying all day, but in little snatches. I find if I pray out loud, I can organize my thoughts a bit better." Heat crept up his neck. He'd never prayed aloud in front of anyone before…well, except Rip, unless it was to say grace before a meal. He'd never let anyone close enough to hear him talk to God about anything but a brief premeal thank you. But he felt the need pressing on his heart.

"I'd like that. I've been sending up 'arrow prayers' today, too."

Thomas took off his hat, hooked it over the corner of his chair and bowed his head. His mind blanked until he remembered he was talking to God, not to impress Esther.

"Dear Father, we're worried about Johnny. He's so little, and he's so sick. We know that You care for him, and that You hold his future in Your hands. We know You can heal him if it is Your will. We're asking for strength to care for him, and we thank You for bringing him into our lives. We thank You for sending Doc Preston to Silar Falls, and we pray that You'll give him strength and wisdom as he treats the folks who are sick. And we pray for the sick folks in town, that You will heal and comfort them. We know what we want, Lord, but we're asking for the grace to accept Your will. Amen."

He looked up, surprised to see tears on Esther's face.

"Thank you, Thomas. It's been a long time since anyone did any praying aloud in this house." She sighed. "For a long time after my father died, I felt like God was far away. That He didn't really see me. It's so difficult to see Him at work when things are so hard. And it's not easy to pray when you aren't sure you're being heard."

Thomas's heart hurt for Esther, for all she had been through. He wanted to put his arms around her and assure her that God was good regardless of circumstances. And to assure her that he, Thomas, would also be here to help her through these tough times… but he couldn't make that kind of promise. At least, not right now.

Chapter Twelve

Esther leaned her head back against the rocker, closing her eyes. Her blouse was damp with sweat, and a trickle of perspiration raced down her temple. Holding a feverish baby on a hot Texas night was similar to what she imagined a Comanche sweat lodge must be like. But he cried when she laid him down or passed him to Thomas.

"It's time to try some more water." Thomas poured some from a glass into the feeding bottle. His watch lay on the table, and he'd scrounged a piece of store paper and pencil to make a chart. He'd kept careful track of every diaper change, every bath to reduce the fever, every administration of water.

She shifted the baby until he was lying in her arms and took the bottle, pressing it against his mouth. His tongue darted out, and a few drops dribbled onto his tiny lips.

"Is he taking it?" Thomas leaned against the table, crossing his arms on his chest.

The baby's eyes opened, and he sucked a few

times, before letting go. "A little, but it's like he's too tired to take much." She tried again, but he wasn't interested.

"Try the spoon again?"

"All right." Because there was nothing else to do. Dark had fallen hours ago, and Johnny's fever had risen. His little eyes burned like hot coals in his face, and his skin looked parched. Bright fever-spots burned in his cheeks. Esther spooned water into his mouth a few drops at a time.

She blew across his head, lifting his dark hair. If only he would sleep in his basket for a while, but every time she put him down or passed him to Thomas, he cried inconsolably. He wanted only her.

Poor baby.

"What's going to happen to him?"

"He's going to get better." Thomas took the spoon and cup.

Esther wanted to believe him. She *had* to believe him. Any other option was unthinkable. "But what happens after that? Where will he go? What if you can't find any of his family, or what if you can't find someone to take him in? Will you put him in the orphanage in San Antonio?" She didn't know why she needed to know right now. She'd been ignoring the truth for two weeks, not wanting to think about Johnny's future, living day by day and not looking ahead. But the baby's obvious preference for her stirred her suppressed worries into a tempest in her heart. What if he went to someone else, and he cried for her all the time?

"Not the orphanage. I would never do that to a kid.

I remember too much what it was like." He paced the small space, stopping at the open door to look out at the darkness.

"You never talked about that part of your life much." She noted the tenseness in his back muscles, the grip of his hand on the doorjamb.

"It was a long time ago."

"But you haven't forgotten." She shifted Johnny, laying him in her lap and picking up her fan to stir the heavy air over them both.

"I was a foundling. I don't even know who my parents were. My name isn't even my own. The matron gave it to me. The baby before me was given a last name that started with *A*, and the one after a last name that started with *C*. She said she picked Beaufort out of the newspaper. And Thomas came from a Union general who distinguished himself at the Battle of Chickamauga. The matron was a lady from up north." He chuckled, but there was no humor in his tone. "So I'm named after a Yankee and some random newspaper clipping."

Her heart went out to him. There had been no one to love him, to lavish attention on him, to make him feel as if he was important to anyone, that anyone cared.

He stared over her shoulder, looking in the direction of the black square of window behind her, but with what her father used to call a "thousand-yard stare." Looking but not seeing. Staring into the past. "Did you know there's a pecking order in an orphanage? Though 'pecking order' sounds too mild for how things really were. It's almost like one of those caste systems, like they have over in India. Kids whose parents had died were the highest tier, and then kids who had been taken away from their parents by the county or the state. Because they at least knew who their folks were, where they came from. Kids like me were at the bottom."

He rubbed his hands down his thighs. "In an orphanage, you learn not to form attachments to people, because they would be there one day and gone the next. We had plenty to eat, and we were warm at night, but there was no sense of family, of belonging to anyone or any place. You learned to look out for yourself."

"Is that why you never stay in one place long? And why you're so capable and self-sufficient?"

He shook himself slightly, as if casting off old memories, and shrugged. "I suppose. When you don't belong anywhere, it's hard to find a place to settle down."

What about here? What about with me? Hearing him talk about his life at the orphanage, when he was so young and vulnerable, broke her heart, and for the first time, she began to understand why he might have needed to leave five years ago. And why he would need to leave again.

Thomas leaned against the doorjamb, staring out into the night. "You know how earlier you were talking about God seeming far away?"

"Yes."

"One thing I'll say for the orphanage, they made sure we had schooling, and they made sure we learned about God. One of the first things I learned to read was a sampler someone had stitched that hung on the wall in the boys' dormitory. It was from Psalm nine, verse ten. 'And they that know thy name will put their trust in thee: for thou, Lord, hast not forsaken them that seek thee.'

"That verse had brought me a lot of comfort over the years. I learned early on that people may come and go in your life, you may not have a place to call your own, but God never forsakes you, not when you belong to Him."

He shrugged and continued to look out into the night. Esther pondered his words and the Bible verse. He was right. God hadn't forsaken him as an orphan, and He hadn't forsaken her, either. As Sarah Granville liked to say, "If God seems far away, it isn't Him that moved." It was just that sometimes she was so overwhelmed by life and worries that she forgot.

Johnny whimpered, his hand flailing weakly, and Thomas turned. "How's he doing?"

"I think his fever is getting worse."

"Doc said it probably would during the night."

He uncorked the bottle of rubbing alcohol and soaked a ball of cotton wadding. Gently, he stroked it down Johnny's arm, blowing on the wet trail. Swiping a few more times across the baby's tummy and legs, he sat back on his heels.

"Do you think it's helping?" she asked.

"I think it helps for a little while, but it doesn't last long." Thomas cupped the baby's head.

For hours Esther rocked and sponged and dripped water into Johnny's mouth. Thomas never left her side, bringing fresh water, clean towels and encouragement. Sometime around three, the infant began shivering, racked by chills. She bundled him up, tucking him in close to her body. Thomas prayed and paced, refusing to go get some sleep, even when she urged him to.

"I'm going to go get the doc." He reached for his hat. "There has to be something else we can do."

"We're doing everything he told us to. There's no medicine he can give." Esther blinked back the tears burning her eyes. "He said we'd just have to wait it out and pray Johnny is strong enough."

Thomas slapped his hat onto the peg by the door. "Normally, I'm a fair hand at waiting, but not in this case."

Mind numb, heart breaking, Esther clung to hope, whispering prayers, humming hymns that seemed to soothe Johnny. They bathed and cooled him, drizzled water into his mouth and prayed some more. His breath was short and shallow, and his fever soared. He writhed and wriggled, crying at times, whimpering at others. Just when she was wondering how much more he could take, he went limp in her arms. She let out a little shriek.

"What is it?" Thomas stopped pacing, and Rip's ears went back as he let out a whine.

She lowered Johnny from her shoulder, afraid to look, afraid of what she might find.

"He's…" She blinked.

"What?" Thomas skidded to his knees beside the rocker.

"He's sweating." She wet her dry lips. "Do you think his fever's broken?" Her arms felt weak, and her chest felt empty.

She didn't miss the tremble in Thomas's hand as he reached out to touch Johnny's face.

"He's cooler. Thank You, Lord." He closed his eyes, resting his forehead on the arm of the rocker.

Esther let her hand caress Thomas's hair for a moment, so thankful that she hadn't been alone tonight.

Johnny didn't stir.

His fever *had* broken.

For another hour, she rocked and held him, watching his face, relaxed and peaceful for the first time in more than a day. Thomas sat at the table, his head pillowed on his arms, dozing.

"Thank You, Lord. Thank You, Lord." She whispered her gratitude against Johnny's temple again and again. The longest night of her life was nearly over.

Her eyes were gritty with lack of sleep, and her back and shoulders and arms ached from holding the baby, but she was reluctant to let him go.

"He's sleeping so hard now you could probably put him in his basket and get a little rest yourself." Thomas stirred and stretched.

"Poor mite's exhausted." She laid Johnny in the basket and covered him with a light blanket.

"I know how he feels." Thomas stood with his hand on her shoulder, looking down at the baby. "I think he's going to be all right now."

At his affirmation of her hopes, something inside Esther crumpled, and she turned into him, burying her face in his neck. Thomas's arms came around her, holding her tight, smoothing her hair, whispering comforting words.

"I was so scared." Tears leaked out of her eyes, dampening his shirt.

"I know. Me too." His voice was raspy and deep.

It felt so good to be in his arms, so safe. His heart thudded reassuringly under her cheek, and his broad chest felt like a bulwark against anything that might harm her. She raised her head to look into his eyes. Her hand came up to cup his cheek, feeling the prickle of his unshaven face.

She hadn't intended to kiss him, but the need to propelled her to draw his mouth down to hers. He didn't object and bent his head. His lips were warm and firm as they moved over hers. Spreading his hand on her back, he held her close as the fingers of his other hand tunneled into her hair. She clung to his shirtfront, her knees turning to wash water. How could she be held so tightly and yet be flying?

This, her first kiss, was better than her dreams. And in this moment, held in his arms, giving and receiving this kiss, her dreams expanded, exploded into all the glorious possibilities.

And he would leave her.

Reality crashed in, and she pushed against his chest, stepping back. Her breath came fast, and her heart ricocheted in her chest.

"Esther?" His eyes were dark as he whispered her name.

"No." She shook her head, her hair tumbling down where his hand had dislodged the pins. "We can't. I can't." Her hand shook as she touched her lips, still tingling from his kiss.

He tucked his thumbs into his back pockets, standing with his weight on one hip, waiting. With narrowed eyes he studied her, and Esther feared he looked right into her heart.

She smoothed back her hair, trying to steady her breathing. "I'm sorry. I shouldn't have done that. I suppose we're both just tired. Reaction set in because the baby's feeling better."

"Reaction?" His right eyebrow went high. "Is that what that was?"

She laced her fingers at her waist. "That's all that was. That's all that can be."

"I see." The skin on his cheekbones stretched as he tightened his jaw. His chest expanded on a long breath.

She could not allow herself to care for him, not again. Not when she knew he had no intention of staying.

She would not care about him. She would not.

And she knew she lied to herself.

Thomas stood on the porch, facing the rising sun, weary down to his boot heels. His heart still kicked in his chest from that kiss, and his head spun. He pressed his hand to his stomach, feeling sucker punched at the way she'd looked at him. Stricken, mortified, angry, all three? He wasn't sure. He just knew he had never wanted the kiss to end, and she'd bolted from his arms like a frightened deer.

Had that kiss been prompted only by relief that Johnny's fever had broken? Maybe on her part, but certainly not on his. He'd been thinking of kissing her for hours. Who was he kidding? He'd been thinking of kissing her since the moment he showed up in her yard with a newborn. Maybe since the first time he ever clapped eyes on her as a twenty-year-old.

Overreaching again. Why would she want a drifter like him, a man who didn't even have a claim to the name he bore? He was of some use to her right now, and she was doing him a favor taking care of the baby, because she was kind and giving, but that was all it was. By her own admission, it was all it could ever be.

She'd taken Johnny's basket with her into her bedroom and closed the door, shutting him out. Rip sprawled on the porch on his side, snoring, clearly tuckered out from his all-night vigil. Thomas rolled his shoulders. Dawn crept across the yard, moving up and over the clotheslines heavy with the garments he'd washed and hung out. The shirts and pants would be damp with overnight dew, but the sun would dry them quickly.

A light flashed to his right, and though he wanted to turn toward it, he forced himself to stay still. Someone was on the ridge watching the ranch again, and he was using a spyglass. The glint could only be the dawn on glass. Who was it, and what did he want? What could possibly be so interesting about the Double J?

Thomas stretched once more and stepped off the porch, deliberately not looking toward the ridge. He strolled around the house and up the rise. He would play it casual, go about his chores, and wait for his chance to slip away and get around behind the watcher.

Daisylu bleated at him through the corral fence,

and he scowled. She needed to be milked, and Esther was getting a much-deserved nap.

He made a quick trip to the bunkhouse, returned to the corral and plucked the milking bucket off its peg. "All right, girl. You and I are going to have to come to some sort of understanding." He vaulted the corral fence and put his hands on his hips.

Daisylu let out a squall, stamped her foot, lowering her head and shaking her neck until her ears flopped.

"So you think that's how it's going to be, huh? Well, not this time. I have enough females disappointed in me right now." He reached for the thin rope coiled on the post where Esther tethered the goat when she milked her.

Daisylu bleated and backed up, clearly seeing what this encounter was to be about, but Thomas stopped her from escaping. He latched the rope to the ring on her collar and nudged her against the corral fence.

"Easy, girl. It's time you and I buried the hatchet." Stroking her warm side, he ignored her bleating. "I'm glad I don't speak goat, or I'd have to wash your mouth out with soap."

After a minute, she stopped squawking nonstop and began bleating intermittently about the injustice and indignity of her life. Thomas continued petting her, talking softly, waiting. When she finally quieted, he dug into his shirt pocket and withdrew an Arbuckle's peppermint stick. Breaking off a small piece, he held it flat on his hand. Casually, he glanced around, letting his eyes drift up toward the ridge.

Whoever it was had chosen a good spot. Even if the watcher stood, he would be hard to pick out at this distance, since the heavy brush that grew nearly to the edge of the rise would mask a silhouette.

"A peace offering." He held the candy in front of Daisylu. Horses liked peppermints, so he assumed goats did, too. Weren't goats supposed to eat about anything?

She sniffed, eyeing the candy suspiciously. He almost laughed at her distrust.

"I know. A week ago, I might've poisoned you, but you're keeping Johnny going, and Esther likes you, so you have nothing to fear from me."

Her soft upper lip brushed his palm, and the red-and-white candy disappeared with a grinding sound. Daisylu grunted and looked at him hopefully.

He grinned. "I guess I've found the way to your heart, haven't I?" He offered her another piece of the candy.

It took the entire stick, but Daisylu condescended to allow him to milk her eventually. He carried the pail to the house, careful not to wake Esther or Johnny. Once outside again, he headed for the horse trap. Thankfully, the trap was out of sight of the ridge. If Thomas went to the bunkhouse for his saddle, whoever was watching would know he intended to ride out, so he'd have to ride Smitty bareback if he hoped to surprise his quarry.

He wished he had his rifle with him, but he would make do with his sidearm. Smitty came when Thomas whistled, trotting up, snorting and shaking his head. Threading Daisylu's tethering rope through the halter ring under Smitty's chin, Thomas grabbed a handful of mane and jumped onto the horse's back. "Good thing you're not any taller, boy."

Legging the sorrel into a canter—easier on both of them—Thomas headed south, well west of the ridge. "We'll come up on them from behind."

The morning smelled fresh, with a hint of the heat to come. Sage and mesquite and rabbitbrush grew denser. He wished he had Rip with him, but also took comfort that he hadn't left Esther and Johnny unguarded.

She didn't even have a gun in the house for protection. She was completely vulnerable out here alone. And she wouldn't leave because this was her home, the place she felt she belonged, the place she had promised her father she would stay. He could appreciate that. If he had a home of his own, he'd die fighting to keep it.

But he hated to think of Esther alone here on the Double J, scraping out a living, dealing with rough cowboy customers or the smarmy likes of men like Danny Newton.

He pulled Smitty to a stop and dismounted, tying him to a mesquite branch. He'd have to go the rest of the way on foot.

Slinking through the brush reminded him of coming up on the cabin where Johnny had been born. He slipped his gun from its holster. At that cabin, he hadn't been prepared for what he'd encountered. This time, he determined to be ready.

Crouching, he made his way toward the place he had seen the reflected light. The brush thinned out as he got to the edges. He heard a horse stamp and the chink of a bridle bit and the creak of leather. His fingers flexed on the butt of his pistol, and he paused to steady his heart and breathing, readying himself.

Some movement ahead, again the creak of leather. Thomas crept forward, gun ready. As he leaped into the open, a bullet whizzed past his head. He whipped his gun to the right and got off a shot, crouching just as the horse bolted toward him. In two bounds it was on him, barreling into his shoulder as the rider hunkered over the animal's neck. On the way past, the man swung his handgun, connecting with Thomas's hat crown, sending stars and sparks shooting through his vision as he reeled into a clump of twisted brush and thorns.

It all happened so fast. Head ringing, vision blurred, he went to train his gun on the gap in the brush where the rider had disappeared, then realized he'd somehow lost it in the collision. Desperately, he searched the ground around himself, sweeping through the grass until his hand closed over the barrel.

How had he given his position away? How had the man known he was there?

Thomas staggered to his feet, broken branches falling about him. His shoulder screamed where the horse had hit him, and his head throbbed. Whoever it was, he was long gone. Thomas put his hand to his head. It felt like a steam engine pounding away in there.

This was humiliating. He must be losing his touch. He was a *good* bounty hunter, but twice in the last two attempts to apprehend someone, he'd been landed on his backside. He was slipping.

Slipping could get him killed.

Taking deep breaths to stop the horizon from rocking, he put his hands on his knees and slammed his eyes shut. Shot at, trampled and pistol-whipped in the space of a second or two. He really was losing it.

When the worst of the pounding in his head subsided, he opened his eyes, hanging on to a tree trunk, blinking and rubbing his shoulder. The area looked much the same as it had when he'd ridden up here previously. The same small hollow of pressed grass where the watcher had lain, looking down on the ranch complex below.

A flutter caught his eye. A paper. He plucked it from the tall grass...part of a newspaper. Thomas turned it over in his hands. Yellowed a bit, brittle. Part of an advertisement? Liver pills? Then he turned it over. It was a notice of a reward. For Jase Swindell. Five thousand dollars for his capture, dead or alive.

Thomas's gut clenched. Had a fellow bounty hunter learned that Thomas had Jase's son? Was he hoping the baby would lead to the father's capture?

His was a dangerous business. Hard men hunted hard men. Some bounty hunters were not above sabotaging another's plans if it meant collecting a bounty.

It made sense. Someone had gotten wind that Thomas had been close to capturing Jase Swindell. Someone had probably followed the same trail, learning of Swindell's hooking up with a woman, making a run for Mexico. That person had probably also learned the woman was pregnant. If whoever it was had spent any time at all in that cabin, he'd know she'd delivered a baby, and he'd see the grave. A small matter to track Thomas to Silar Falls.

He probed the edges of the sore spot on the top of his head. It was a greenhorn move getting dry-gulched like that. He'd have to be more vigilant, and he'd have to get Johnny to a permanent home soon. The longer he stayed, the more danger Esther was in. Some bounty hunter might think she knew something about where Jase Swindell was hiding and accost her in the house.

She knew nothing, of course, not even that Johnny was Jase's son. And what would she do when she found that out?

He had to tell her so she would be on her guard, but the minute he did, she would send him and Johnny packing.

Chapter Thirteen

Esther woke, hot and prickly, with sunlight streaming across her bed and the day heating up. How long had she slept? She rolled over, her limbs leaden.

Johnny.

She checked the basket. The infant slept on his tummy with his diapered rump in the air, his hands relaxed and open, and his lips pursed. His dark lashes fanned his cheeks, and when she placed her hand on his back it was cool, rising and falling with his quick breaths.

"Thank You, Jesus," she whispered.

Dressing quickly, she braided and coiled her hair, her stomach rumbling. She glanced at the clock when she stepped into the main room. Ten o'clock. Not much of a lie-in, considering she had been up all night, but she didn't remember the last time she stayed in bed this late.

The stove was cold to her touch, and the coffeepot held only sludgy grounds. Munching on a slice of Trudy's bread, she began cleaning up the kitchen.

Johnny slept on. *Please, Lord, let him be hungry when he wakes up.*

Rip, coming in from the front porch, shook himself from nose to tail, and looked up at her.

"He's better. No, you can't go see him. He's sleeping." She shook her head to be talking to the dog like he was a person, but she filled a bowl with fresh water and set it down for him, and buttered a slice of bread for him, too.

She found the fresh pail of milk, carefully covered with a cloth. Oh, my, poor Daisylu! Esther had forgotten all about her. Thomas must've milked her, but how had he managed it without getting kicked or butted or bleated at?

Where *was* Thomas? Asleep in the bunkhouse? If he had any sense, he was. Her fingers went to her lips, remembering his kiss. His arms had felt as strong as oak beams, and his masculinity had overwhelmed her carefully guarded defenses.

But she had herself firmly in hand now. Daylight brought a return to her senses.

The clatter of horses' hooves outside had her checking her mental calendar for who would be picking up laundry today. Was it even ready? Thomas had helped wash several loads, but they'd been left drying on the line.

She checked outside and then relaxed. Stepping onto the porch, she shaded her eyes against the morning sunshine.

"Dr. Preston."

"How is he?" The doctor didn't bother with pleasantries, vaulting out of his buggy, bag in hand.

"He's sleeping. His fever broke early this morning."

Lines of tension smoothed out of Doc's face, and he smiled, his shoulders easing. "I had hoped that would be the case. The children in town are following much the same schedule. This illness hit hard and fast, but it appears to leave almost as quickly."

"Come inside. I was just going to make myself some coffee."

He followed her in, and when she motioned to the bedroom doorway, he went in to check on Johnny. She busied herself with the coffeepot and some kindling. Johnny cried, but before she could hurry to him, the doctor emerged with the baby in his arms.

"He was beginning to wake up when I got to him. And he needs a change, which is a very good sign." Doc held the squalling baby like a seasoned professional. "Show me where the diapers are, and I think you'd better get him a meal started before he starts gnawing on my finger."

With amazing speed and proficiency, the doctor got Johnny rediapered. He managed a quick examination in the process before bundling the baby up in a light blanket and handing him to Esther. "I'll pour myself some coffee. You get some food into this strapping young man."

She backed into the rocker, already putting the bottle to Johnny's open mouth. He rooted for a moment before latching on, staring up at her as he concentrated on his breakfast.

"That is a sign a doctor loves to see, a patient on the mend and stowing away his chow." Doc lifted the lid on the coffeepot. "You don't brew this as strongly as Thomas, do you? I think I rasped off a layer of my tongue with the stuff he served me last night."

"What should we do for Johnny now that his fever has broken?" She rocked, not taking her eyes from the baby's. "He gave us quite a scare yesterday."

"You were right to be concerned. I've never had a patient so young catch an illness like this." He blew across his coffee cup. "For now, feed him as much as he wants, keep him cool and comfortable, and if you can, get him to take some water between feedings. He's liable to sleep a lot over the next few days. And, Esther—" he leaned forward, and she looked up at him "—you've done a wonderful job with this baby. He couldn't have better care if you were his own mother."

Bittersweet emotion filled her. Happiness at his praise, and sadness that she *wasn't* Johnny's mother.

The doctor finished his coffee and stood. "If you need me, or if anything's worrying you about Johnny's recovery, send Thomas to fetch me. My boys were ravenous this morning, too, though they all fell asleep after breakfast. The house is oddly quiet." He smiled. "They'll have the place in an uproar in a day or so, I have no doubt."

He had no sooner gone than another buggy pulled in, this time with the Granvilles. Charlie helped Sarah down and reached back for a basket.

"Come in," Esther called from her chair.

"We passed Doc on the way back to town. He said the baby's feeling better?" Sarah bustled over to check for herself.

"Yes, after giving us quite a fright. His fever was so high, but it broke, and the doctor said he's on the mend."

Sheriff Granville set the basket on the table. "Where's Thomas?"

Esther shook her head. "I'm not sure. He hasn't come in yet. We were up all night with this little fellow." She took the bottle from him, holding it up. He needed to burp, but he fussed at having his meal interrupted.

"Let me have him, the precious boy." Sarah laid a dish towel on her shoulder and reached for him, bouncing lightly as she patted his back. "What's the idea, scaring the two people who care the most for you in the whole wide world?" She spoke against the baby's temple.

"I think I'll go scout out Thomas. He had a couple of telegrams come in." The sheriff patted his pocket. "Might be able to shed some light on this little guy's future." He smiled and headed outside.

Esther leaned her head back against the rocker, worrying her lower lip. With Johnny's future settled, Thomas would have no reason left to stay.

"You love him, don't you?" Sarah asked, her eyes kind. "I don't blame you. I would, too."

Heat charged into her cheeks. "What?"

"Johnny. Who wouldn't fall in love with this handsome boy?" Having brought up the baby's wind, she picked up the bottle and settled into a kitchen chair to feed him.

"Of course." Relief shot through her. "I think I fell in love the first time I looked into his eyes and realized he needed me." She smoothed her hair back with both hands.

"It's going to be hard on you to let him go." Sarah

turned her bright blue eyes toward Esther. "Have you thought about that?"

She nodded.

"And not just Johnny."

Esther laced her fingers in her lap.

"What are you going to do about Thomas?" Sarah's voice was gentle, but insistent. "You loved him once. Do you still?"

She pressed her lips together, staring at her hands. "Even if I did, it won't change anything. He won't stay. He can't stay. It isn't in his nature. As soon as he can, he'll find a place for Johnny and then be off to hunt the next fugitive or bank robber or rustler."

Sarah snorted. "Who says?"

"He does."

"He sure doesn't seem to be in any hurry to get this boy settled, does he? If he was so set on dumping him and leaving, why didn't he take him over to the orphanage in San Antonio, or leave him with the doc, or even Charlie and me? Why bring him to you, and then stay here, cleaning up and making repairs? It's been what, a couple of weeks, at least."

Johnny finished the bottle, and she set it on the table, bringing him to her shoulder once more.

"Honey," she said to Esther, "you know I love you like a daughter. And I like Thomas, I really do, but I don't want to see you get hurt. Just promise me you'll be careful. If he's bound to leave, like you say, then maybe you should hurry him along."

Thomas rode out of the brush in time to see Charlie Granville step out of the house and onto the porch.

Just the man he wanted to see. He slid from Smitty's back, dropping to the ground with a jolt that set up the pounding in his head again. His entire side where the horse had knocked into him felt stiff and sore.

"What happened to you?" Charlie greeted him in the yard behind the house.

Thomas glanced down. His shirtsleeve had ripped at the shoulder, and his arm was scratched up.

"Did you know you are bleeding?" Charlie pointed to Thomas's face.

He touched his temple and came away with a smear of blood. His noggin had been cracked harder than he thought. "Ran into a little trouble this morning. Whoever has been watching the ranch. I tried to sneak up on him, but he got the jump on me, plowed me over with his horse and whacked me with his pistol for good measure."

Pulling the paper from his shirt pocket, he handed it to the sheriff. "I think it might be some of my competition. Somebody after the Swindell bounty. Maybe thinking they can get to him through the baby?"

"How would they know who the kid belonged to?" Charlie scanned the scrap. "This notice was in every paper from the Red River to the Rio Grande. The governor wants Swindell bad."

"And there were a lot of bounty hunters who jumped on the trail at first, but that's been whittled down over the last year as leads dried up and sightings dwindled. Whoever this is probably followed the same trail as I did, tracked me here and is getting the lay of the land. He's patient, I'll give him that. He's probably waiting for me to get back on the trail so he can follow me to Swindell and hopefully beat me to the bounty."

"Or let you arrest Swindell and then kill you so he can get credit for the capture." Charlie shifted his weight. "Either way, I don't like it."

"I don't cotton to it, either." His head throbbed. "I just want Esther and Johnny to be safe, and for Swindell to be behind bars where he belongs."

"Which reminds me, there were a couple of answers to the telegrams we sent out. That sheriff where you first tracked Swindell's woman says the baby's mother didn't have any kin that he's aware of. She was one of the working girls at a saloon, though she had to quit when she got the consumption. Sounds like Swindell traveled through there often, and she was always his favorite, and when he needed a place to hide, she helped him out. When you got too close, they hit the road, and you know the rest."

Thomas nodded. No family on the mother's side, and only a crazy aunt on the father's side. "What's the other telegram? You said there were two?"

"Yeah, not sure whether you'll think this is good news or not. When Swindell was cleaning out the ranchers around here, he used to cut over to Fort Stockton and Fort Davis to sell the cattle to the army. Rumor had it he holed up over near Sonora on his way back from the forts. I wired the marshal there to see if there had been any sign of him."

"And?" Thomas frowned. Sonora was a three-day ride from here.

"He says he saw someone matching Swindell's description in town a week ago, buying supplies at the mercantile. A rough looking fellow, well-heeled, riding a line-back dun."

A jolt went through Thomas, the kind that he got when a trail warmed up. He flexed his fingers and rested them on his pistol grip. "Swindell was riding a dun when I last saw him."

"So it might be him. Marshal says there are some caves west of town where outlaws have been known to hide out. He says he wouldn't be surprised if Swindell is holed up in one of them."

"Did you send a reply?"

"I did. I told him if he thought Jase Swindell was in his county, he'd better keep an eye out for trouble."

"So Swindell's probably near Sonora."

"That's what my friend the marshal thinks."

"Will the marshal go after him?"

"No, not this fellow. He's good at keeping the peace in Sonora, but he's a bit long in the tooth to be chasing outlaws."

Thomas rubbed his sore shoulder. "Maybe I should head over there and check it out. Even if Swindell's not there anymore, I could probably pick up his trail again. It's as good a place to start as any, and better than most."

"You'd leave the baby here with Esther when there's someone watching her place?"

"I should've gone right away, before anyone else showed up. If I had left the baby here and gone right after Swindell, I might've caught him and collected the reward before another bounty hunter got this close."

"Why didn't you?"

Because she has beautiful brown eyes, and because she needed me. It had been a long time since anyone needed him. "I was worried about the baby, and I wanted to make sure he'd be all right."

Charlie's white mustache bristled as he pursed his lips. "Riiight. I think you best get that head seen to."

Thomas wasn't sure if he was referring to his injury, or the fact that he hadn't been the least bit logical when it came to the Swindells, father or son. They walked down to the house.

As they entered, Esther took one look at him and shot out of her chair. "What happened? Are you hurt?"

He had to admit, having her fussing over him was gratifying. Especially since she'd run out of his arms this morning after they kissed.

He might've limped to a chair a bit more dramatically than strictly necessary. This certainly wasn't the first time he'd been injured, but most of the time he tended to himself alone in a hotel or boardinghouse room, or out on the trail where cold creek water was his only remedy.

"A fellow up on the ridge didn't appreciate my trying to have a word with him." He winced as he sat down. Esther took his hat off gently, but it still hurt.

"Put your chin down." She parted his hair and looked at the sore spot. "You've got a goose egg and a cut, but I don't think it's too bad." She fetched a basin of water and used the corner of her apron to dab at the dried blood. "We're out of dish towels and washcloths. Johnny used them all up last night."

Charlie took a turn holding Johnny. "Glad the boy's on the mend."

Sarah began unpacking the basket she brought, while Esther worked on Thomas.

Esther held back the ripped edge of his sleeve to assess the damage. "Who did this? Danny Newton?"

He grimaced. "I didn't get a chance to see. He bushwhacked me. But it wasn't Danny Newton. This guy was bigger than Danny." When he reached for the sore spot on his head, Esther pushed his hand away. "It all happened pretty fast, and his face was in shadow, and I feel like a fool letting him take me down so easily."

"Do you have any idea who it was?" Sarah Granville asked. She rummaged through the cupboard that blocked the back door, coming out with a jar of salve. "This should help."

He didn't want to say, not here in front of Esther. If he told her that another bounty hunter was watching the place in order to try to capture Jase Swindell, she'd want to know why, and he'd have to tell her Johnny's parentage.

Thomas shot a glance at Charlie Granville and then shrugged. "Hard to say. Now that he knows I'm aware of him here, he might clear out. I'll keep a good watch."

Esther dabbed salve on his cuts and said nothing.

"Oh." Sarah brightened. "I can't believe I almost forgot. The search committee has finally found us a preacher. At least they hope they have. A man and his family will be arriving this afternoon, and there will be a church service and picnic to welcome them tomorrow. You two will be there, right?"

He wouldn't. He needed to stop dithering and get back on the trail. The lead in Sonora was a strong one.

Esther's brown eyes glowed. "Real preaching? It's been so long." She rested her hand on Thomas's shoulder, sending warmth spiraling through him, though she appeared unaware of what she was doing. "We'll go, right?" She picked up the basin of water with her other hand.

He shouldn't. He should gear up and get over to Sonora. Too many loose ends needed tying up, and he was kicking his heels here in Silar Falls.

"You should come." Sheriff Granville patted Johnny. "I'll wire the marshal we talked about, and he can try to get some specific information on the man you're looking for. And you can keep a close watch around here."

Torn, Thomas rotated his hat in his hands. He felt the pull to get after Jase Swindell, and yet, he wanted to stay. For the first time in his life, he had put down roots someplace. The boyish feelings he had once had for Esther had grown into the feelings a man had for a woman. He wanted to stay with her. Her and Johnny.

"Church and a picnic sound nice." He made his decision. Or rather he put off the decision he knew he had to make.

Esther donned her new blue dress, smoothing the navy lace on the polonaise. Attending church for the first time in she couldn't remember how long. And a picnic.

Johnny had bounced back quickly from being ill. He was his normal, hungry, happy self. Dr. Preston said that was the nature of children, and his own boys were up and terrorizing the house again as if nothing had happened.

She heard Thomas's boots on the porch. Right on time. Esther hadn't admitted to herself that something had changed between them since the night Johnny had been so sick. Since the night they had kissed.

Her fingertips went to her lips as she studied her reflection in the mirror. That kiss had rocked her right down to her heels. And in spite of all her warnings to herself, warnings to guard her heart, warnings about him leaving in the near future, warnings that she couldn't rely on anyone but herself, her heart had gone traitorous, flying out of her chest and his for the keeping once more.

And he had stayed. For three weeks now he had stayed.

"You're a foolish girl, Esther Jensen." She studied her flushed cheeks and her bright eyes and shook her head. "Hopeless, that's what you are."

She went into the front room, tying the ribbons on her straw bonnet, eager for the sight of him. Thomas stood in the open doorway, broad-shouldered and masculine, making her heart bump. He wore a clean, white shirt, one that she'd pressed for him last night, and dark pants.

And his gun belt, slung low about his hips. She stopped, feeling the familiar dread and revulsion sweep over her.

"Buckboard's ready when you are." He carried his

hat, twirling it on his finger. "Do you have everything packed for Johnny? Seems like the smaller they are, the more supplies they need." He hefted the basket of diapers and bottles and extra blankets. "I don't take this much gear on a three-week hunt."

"Thomas."

He paused, looking back over his shoulder as he went out to load the buckboard. Silhouetted against the morning sun in the doorway, his pistol stood out in clear relief.

"Thomas, would you do a favor for me, please? Would you leave your sidearm here today?" She laced her fingers together, arms straight down in front of her. "Church is no place for weapons."

He was already shaking his head. "I always wear it, Esther."

"I know, but just this once. For me? This day feels special. The first time to hear preaching in the church in months, a picnic afterward where we can have fellowship with friends. I'm finally starting to feel part of the community again, to feel like my old self, and I don't want anything to mar the day. Every time I see your gun, it takes me back to what my father did. I don't want to look back today. I want to look forward." A tremor went through her, and she closed her eyes, wanting this so much, though she didn't even know how to put into words why. "Please. This one time, can you leave the gun at home?"

He walked outside and set the basket of baby things on the buckboard, and her heart sank. If he couldn't do this one thing for her, was there any possibility that they could ever be more than they were?

When he returned, he put his hands on his hips. "I can't believe I'm doing this." He reached for his gun belt, unbuckling it and wrapping it around the holster and gun.

Hope surged through her.

He put the gun on the table, slowly, as if against his better judgment. "I want you to be happy, Esther."

"Thank you."

They rode into town, the day already warming up. Johnny lay in Esther's arms, looking up at her. Buggies and wagons and buckboards stood around the church, and several families from town walked together toward the white, steepled building.

"Looks like it's going to be a good crowd to get a gander at the new preacher." Thomas guided the horses to a spot in the shade of a big cottonwood. "The whole county is here." He hopped down and helped Esther alight. "How much of this stuff do you want to take in?"

"Just my Bible. If Johnny needs anything, I'll bring him out here." She reached into the basket she'd been using as Johnny's crib and got her Bible. The small book had belonged to her mother, and Esther treasured it.

Thomas took her elbow and escorted her up the steps and into the church. He led her into the back row, though she would've preferred to sit farther toward the front. Still, it was probably best with the baby. If he got fractious, she could easily slip outside.

When Thomas took his seat, she noticed his hand went to his thigh as if to adjust the pistol that wasn't there. He wore a slight frown, easing back and crossing his arms.

Katie May Buckland, her twin braids tied together with an enormous bow, followed her sisters and their blacksmith father up the aisle, turning to grin at Esther as she went. Sarah Granville chatted with the woman next to her, not knowing that her husband behind her had to lean away to avoid the feathers on her wide-brimmed hat.

Trudy Clements stepped to the small pump organ in the front, sat on the upholstered stool and set to work. Music swelled out and the crowd settled.

A young man in a dark suit stepped through the doorway at the front of the church that led to the pastor's study. Trudy finished the prelude with a flourish, and the young man stepped into the pulpit.

Esther exchanged a glance with Thomas. This was the preacher? He looked about sixteen.

"Good morning. Let's pray." His voice, at least, sounded grown up.

Johnny was as good as could be, wide awake during the singing and the passing of the collection plate, but falling sweetly asleep when the preaching started.

"I am Pastor Ness, and I assure you, I am older than I look." He grinned boyishly. "My wife, Greer, is here in the front row with our daughters. Beulah is four and Sharon is six months. We're looking forward to getting to meet you all and fitting into the community here. Let's open God's Word."

The preaching and worship fell on Esther's heart like rain into a parched desert, washing away hurts that had piled up in the corners of her spirit like tumbleweeds. She didn't realize she was crying until Thomas reached out and took her hand, concern clouding his brown eyes. Giving him a watery smile, she used the corner of Johnny's blanket to wipe her cheeks.

"When I felt God's call to come to Texas, I believed—and I still do—that it was right and good," Pastor Ness said. "And my wife was behind the move, one hundred percent." He smiled at her. "But when we informed Beulah that we would be leaving Indiana, she wasn't so sure. She asked me, 'How can we leave? God lives here. I don't want to go without God.' You see, we had taught her that the church was God's house. She was afraid that if we left there, we would leave God behind."

A chuckle went through the congregation.

"We explained to her that God not only would go with us to Texas, but that He was already there. And I shared with her this verse from Hebrews thirteen. 'Let your conversation be without covetousness; and be content with such things as ye have: for he hath said, I will never leave thee, nor forsake thee.'" He paused. "Beulah's fears were understandable, because she is a child. And yet, don't we, as adults, also have fears that keep us from experiencing the joy and contentment and peace that God has for us? Do you fear being forsaken? Perhaps you already feel this way, as if God has somehow abandoned you to your circumstances. I would say to you, preach the truth to yourself as often as you need it. God has promised in His Word that no matter what, He will never leave us or forsake us."

Esther didn't hear the rest of the sermon. The verse from Hebrews echoed in her head. *I will never leave thee, nor forsake thee. I will never leave thee, nor forsake thee. I will never leave thee, nor forsake thee.*

Before she knew it, Trudy was playing the closing hymn and people were standing to sing. Johnny stirred at the sudden noise, and Esther raised him to her shoulder. They stood for the closing prayer and were soon outside in the sunshine, greeting people they knew. Pastor Ness and his family were surrounded, and Johnny was getting fractious.

"Let's get him into the shade." Thomas put his hand on Esther's back and guided her through the crowd to the buckboard.

"He's hungry. I can't believe how well he slept through the service, though."

Thomas spread a quilt on the opposite side of the tree from the horses. Esther laid Johnny down and changed his diaper, then tucked him into her arms to feed him. She'd wrapped an earthenware jug of milk in wet clothes to keep it cool, and Thomas filled the bottle expertly for her.

"Hard to believe he's going to be a month old next week." Thomas set their picnic basket on the blanket. Others were doing the same around the church building. Children ran and laughed, adults talked and sorted out food, and the sky blazed with sunshine, the distances shimmering. Thankfully, a slight breeze stirred the leaves, and in the shade the heat wasn't unbearable.

Johnny stared at her as he ate, his eyes such a dark,

hazy blue she was sure they would turn brown soon. Lighter brown like hers? Or a dark like Thomas's?

"They're setting up a lemonade table by the church steps. How about I go get us some?" Thomas asked. He'd put his hat on as soon as they had gotten outside, and the brim shaded his face. At her nod, he strode across the grass, and she studied him. Without his gun, he looked slimmer than normal, and sort of out of balance. She'd gotten used to seeing him wear it, she supposed.

Doc Preston had brought one of his front porch rockers down the street, and he helped Eliza into it, laughing with her. She surely had to be close to delivering her baby any day now. Esther smiled at the tender look the doctor gave his wife.

The clatter of a horse's hooves drew her attention, and she looked up, lifting Johnny to her shoulder to burp him. He would be ready to nap soon, already yawning and blinking slowly.

A tall man on a dusty horse rode straight into the crowd. He wore a long, brown coat, a wide-brimmed hat, and bandoliers crossed his chest, bristling with bullets. Most menacing of all, he brandished a shotgun. Children ran, mothers shrieked and men shouted. The rider ignored them all, wheeling his horse, scanning faces until they lit upon Esther and Johnny.

"You. Get up." He motioned with the shotgun.

Esther froze, her arms tightening on Johnny. What did the man want? Why had he singled her out?

"Get up and give me my son."

Chapter Fourteen

Her heart lurched and began a rapid gallop that filled her ears with thunderous noise. Esther stood, though she had no intention of handing Johnny over to this man. Who was he? What did he want with the baby? He raised the barrel of his shotgun, and the black opening yawned like a cannon's mouth. The familiar sick feeling swarmed over her.

Guns. Always guns.

But surely, if he wanted the baby, he wouldn't use a shotgun from this range.

Her knees trembled anyway.

People around her scrambled, pulling their children to safety, hurrying to get out of the line of fire. She heard glass breaking and footsteps. The peace of the afternoon had been shattered.

Thomas started forward from the lemonade table, and the rider turned the shotgun on him. "Hold it right there, Beaufort." Thomas halted, hands held out and low, palms down. "You move, and I'll blow you clear to Santone."

This man knew Thomas. Was it someone Thomas had put in jail once? Was it someone he had been chasing? Was this some sort of revenge? But why would he want Johnny? Esther's mind whirled, trying to make sense of what was happening.

The rider kept the shotgun trained on Thomas but glanced at Esther. "Get over here and hand me that baby."

"There's no call for this." Thomas inched toward her, as if to get between Esther and Johnny and that terrible gun.

"I said don't move." The rider thumbed the hammers back on the shotgun with an ominous double click. Thomas froze.

Esther could barely make out the man's features under the brim of his hat. He had a shaggy beard, and his clothes were filthy and worn. His horse sidled, and he brought the animal back into line with a firm hand. Every inch of him looked hard and ruthless, and he seemed to miss nothing, not a person or object or single movement from the townsfolk all around him.

Her breath staggered in her throat, and she pressed her hand to the back of Johnny's head, bringing it down to her shoulder, covering as much of him as she could with her hands and arms.

Sheriff Granville edged off the church steps. "You say this boy belongs to you? Why don't you put the shotgun down so we can talk about this like civilized folks?"

"Civilized?" he barked. "What makes you think I'm civilized? You there." He flicked his hand toward Esther. "Bring me that boy, or I'm going to start blasting."

She shook her head. Was he mad? "This is ridiculous. You can't just ride in here and demand someone give up a child to you. I don't even know who you are."

"I'm his pa, that's all you need to know."

His pa?

Why didn't Thomas do something? She risked a glance at him, and she remembered that she had insisted he leave his gun at home. Not even the sheriff had his sidearm, not on a peaceful Sunday afternoon at a church picnic.

If Esther didn't give the baby to this man, someone would get hurt. Thomas, Sheriff Granville, one of the townsfolk? A child perhaps? Yet, how could she turn over Johnny to a stranger with a gun?

She couldn't.

The rider jerked the shotgun skyward.

BOOM!

He fired one barrel and had the gun trained on Thomas before anyone could move. "Anybody think I won't do it, go ahead, move. I am taking my son with me. How many bodies I leave behind depends on you-all." His dark eyes glittered above his beard.

Esther trembled from head to foot, waves of weakness and terror coursing through her. Her mouth was as dry as pillow ticking, and her vision narrowed.

"You can have him, but I'm going with you."

"Esther, no." Thomas shook his head.

"Yes." She sent him a pleading look. She couldn't allow anyone to be shot. And she couldn't let someone take Johnny away from her.

The rider looked from her to Thomas, his eyes narrow, calculating. "You!" He jerked his chin toward Frank Clements who stood in front of Trudy against the church wall. "Bring a horse. And it better be a good one, or I'll plug you full of holes."

"Esther, please don't do this," Thomas said, his voice low.

"I have to." *And please, God, let him come after me.*

Frank jerked the reins of a chestnut horse away from the hitching post in front of his store and tugged it over to where Esther stood on the picnic blanket.

"I'll help you, Miss Esther. And don't you worry. A posse will be after you before you reach the county line."

She barely heard his whisper as he put his hands on her waist to boost her into the saddle. Mounting, even with help, while holding a baby, proved an awkward and muscle-straining endeavor, but finally, she was aboard. Her skirts drew up, revealing her stockings and boots, but that was the least of her worries.

The rider edged his horse alongside hers and took the reins from around the saddle horn where Frank had wrapped them. He also rested the shotgun barrel on her shoulder beneath her right ear. She sat as still as a stone, concentrating on drawing air into her lungs and not dropping the baby.

"Y'all listen up!"

She flinched as he shouted to the onlookers, and Johnny let out a cry.

"Any of you get the bright notion to follow us, and I'll kill her, understand? When we get to Mexico, I'll turn her loose. I see so much as a shadow of somebody following us, and she's dead."

Though the day was hot, Esther's fingers were numb with cold as she shifted Johnny, anchoring him low in her arms. She braced herself, but even so, she was unprepared when the rider used the ends of his reins to swat her horse on the rump. He spurred his mount, and the horses leaped forward, racing down the main street of Silar Falls.

Esther gripped the saddle with her knees and leaned into the wind, trying to cushion the jarring for the baby. By the time they reached the edge of town, her hat had blown off and her hair tumbled from its pins.

In a blur, they galloped south, passing the turnoff to her ranch, and she caught sight of her little stone house, the windmill and the blackened rectangle where her barn had once stood. A gray streak shot off the front porch.

Rip.

He barked furiously and raced toward them. The rider hauled back on his reins, skidding his horse to a halt, jerking Esther's mount to a stop so suddenly she was almost thrown from the saddle. He raised his shotgun toward the dog.

Esther's heart lodged in her throat, and before she could think, she raised her leg and kicked, hitting the man in the elbow just as he pulled the trigger. Rip stopped cold in the space of two bounds, and Esther cried out.

Then the dog lowered his head, his mismatched eyes burning hot, growling.

She let out a breath. The shot had gone wide. He wasn't hurt.

The rider rounded on her. "What are you doing?"

"I'm keeping you from shooting that dog."

She called to Rip. "Stay, boy. Stay." She motioned, her hand parallel to the ground, palm down, as she had seen Thomas do. "Stay."

"Lady, you do that again, and I'll beat you from here to the Rio Grande." He cracked the shotgun open, levering out the two spent shells and reloading from the loops on one of the bandoliers crossing his chest.

Rip had dropped to the ground, eyes on Johnny and Esther, waiting for the signal to attack. Esther shook her head and repeated her motion for him to stay put.

The rider snapped the shotgun shut and spurred the horses into a run again. Johnny began to cry, and she held him tighter. They pounded down the road, and she risked a glance behind her. Rip had disappeared from the ranch gate.

Johnny continued to cry, and Esther wanted to join him. Who was this man? He had known Thomas, and Thomas had clearly known him. Was he really Johnny's father? Where was he taking them? They were more than a hundred miles from the Mexican border.

As they passed the entrance to the Circle Bar 5, Danny Newton and a pair of riders rode out onto the road.

"Esther?" Danny shouted as they swerved their mounts to avoid a collision. "Wait! Stop!"

Before she could blink, the rider drew his pistol

and fired. He goaded the horses to run faster and continued firing over his shoulder. Esther crouched in the saddle, clutching Johnny. When she dared a look behind them, Danny had fallen to the road. His fellow riders had their guns out, but didn't return fire, probably afraid of hitting her or the baby.

Tears streamed down her face, whipped dry by the wind. South of the Circle Bar 5, they veered off the road and into the brush. At last they were no longer racing, but the thickets closed in around them like sinister ranks of soldiers, cutting off the view and any hope of being spotted.

Thomas was in motion before Esther and Johnny were halfway down the street. He turned to Charlie Granville. "Give me a gun."

"Son, let's get a posse together and think this one through." Charlie put his hand on Thomas's arm. "You heard what he said. If anyone follows, he'll kill Esther."

"I never should've let her talk me into leaving my gun at home." Thomas pounded his fist into his other hand. "Give me a gun and a horse. You organize the posse and follow, but I'm heading out now…alone."

Charlie studied him for a moment and then nodded. "All right." He marched toward the jail in the middle of the block, and Thomas fell into step beside him. "Take what you need from the gun cabinet in my office."

As they walked, Charlie motioned Frank Clements to follow. "Frank, gather some men, and have Trudy pull some provisions together for Thomas, and more for the posse. Tell Buckland down at the livery to saddle his fastest horses."

Thomas felt surprisingly calm, considering that the woman he loved had been kidnapped by the most dangerous outlaw he'd ever tracked. He couldn't panic now. Not with so much at stake. Emotion dropped away, replaced by clear-headed, cold hard thinking.

"Tell Trudy not to bother with anything for me, and forget about the gun. I need my own horse, my own gear. I'll stop by Esther's place and get them. Can somebody bring Esther's team out to the ranch later?"

"Mr. Beaufort." A skinny kid with a mop of white-blond hair jumped off the boardwalk. "Take my horse. I'll bring your buckboard and team out to the ranch for you and keep an eye on the place until you get back."

It was the boy who had won the rifle-shooting competition at the Founders Day Celebration. Teddy?

"Thanks, son. I'll leave your horse in the corral at the Double J." He took the reins of a sleek little bay that looked as if he'd been curried within an inch of his life, his coat was so shiny. Clearly he was Teddy's pride and joy.

Thomas swung into the saddle and put his heels to the bay, which raced through town as if he had no other purpose in life but to go fast. Teddy had a winner here.

Soon Thomas was riding under the crossbar of the Double J gate, galloping past the house and up the slope to the corral. He turned Teddy's horse into the pen and led Smitty to the bunkhouse.

"Time to get on the trail, old son." Ducking inside

the bunkhouse, he grabbed his tack, heading out into the sunshine to saddle up. When the saddle blanket was smooth, the bridle in place with no twists in the leather, and the girth tight, he went inside once more for the rest of his gear. His rifle slid into the scabbard easily, and he flung the saddlebags he always kept packed over the cantle, tying them down firmly. Every movement was practiced and familiar.

Leading Smitty down the slope to the house, he put two fingers to his lips and let out a piercing whistle. Rip had not been pleased to be left behind this morning, and now Thomas regretted keeping the dog at home.

He whistled again when Rip failed to come. Where was he?

Thomas entered the house, grabbed his gun belt from the table where he'd left it this morning against his better judgment, and buckled it on. He checked the gun, opening the cylinder and snapping it shut. He was ready to go. At the last minute, he spied the stacks of clean laundry on the table and grabbed a couple of diapers and a gown for the baby. Esther had left the rest of Johnny's things behind at the picnic.

With one more quick thought, he reached into the hamper where Esther put dirty clothes and pulled out one of the baby's gowns. He wadded it up and stuffed it into his saddlebags with the clean clothes.

Where was Rip? Thomas mounted up, sent out another loud whistle and headed toward the road to pick up Swindell's trail.

Lots of Rip's tracks were there, and a bunch of chewed up ground right by the gatepost. Buckshot made holes and grooves in the hard-packed dirt, and several splinters stuck out from the old gate. Swindell had taken a shot here. Probably at the dog.

Thomas's gut tightened, and he searched the ground all around the gate. He found no blood and exhaled. Had the shot scared Rip and driven him off, even if it hadn't wounded him?

"I could sure use you right now, boy."

He whistled again, but heard no answering bark. He had never been on a more crucial hunt, and he was going to have to do it without his partner.

Lord, help me track Swindell down before he hurts anyone else.

Deep in the thickets, no air moved. Esther felt as if she rode through an oven...a sage-scented oven. Sweat trickled down her back and sides, dampening her shirt. Her hair stuck to her temples and neck. Lather formed on her mount's withers in foaming ridges.

"Can't you shut him up?" The rider whirled in the saddle as Johnny continued to sob.

"Don't you think I would if I could?" Esther snapped back. "He's hot and thirsty and not used to being jounced around like a quarter in a tin can. He needs a diaper change and a cool bath and a nap." *And so do I.*

The man turned back to the front, holding his arm up and forcing his horse to plunge through the brush. Esther followed because she had no choice, all her efforts on keeping Johnny from being whipped by a limb or poked by a branch. She got scratched and poked many times herself, hearing her dress rip and feeling the sting of thorns and twigs.

"Where are we going?" She looked up at the sky. The sun was ahead, so they clearly weren't heading south toward Mexico. They'd veered west.

"Never you mind."

He didn't speak again for what seemed like hours. They wove through the trees and brush, up and down hills, around ridges. Always west. Her thirst grew, and Johnny alternated between fretting and sleeping.

"The baby needs water. I need water. You do at least have a canteen, don't you?" she finally asked.

"There's a creek not too far ahead. We'll get water there. Until then, keep your mouth shut."

Her legs and back ached from gripping the saddle and holding Johnny. If they didn't stop soon, she was afraid she might drop him.

Surely Thomas was already on their trail. The rider didn't seem to be making any effort to hide their passage through the brush. His method of escape seemed to rely mostly on speed to outrun any pursuit.

With nothing better to do, her mind hopped from one question to another, interspersed with quick prayers and pleadings that God would protect and rescue her and the baby.

Where had Rip gone when she'd ordered him to stay?

Was Danny Newton dead? Esther had never been fond of Danny, but she didn't want him killed. His ranch hands hadn't pursued them, which was just as well, since her captor seemed all too willing to shoot his way to freedom rather than risk recapture.

Dear Jesus, You know where we are, and You have promised not to forsake us. Help us, Lord.

The way opened up ahead of them, sunshine beating down on an open grassy area. At the bottom of the slope, small trees grew in a winding path that indicated a stream or creek.

When they reached the water, Esther sagged from her saddle and stumbled forward with Johnny in her arms. She knelt by the water, cupping a handful at a time into her mouth and dribbling some onto Johnny's lips in between.

"Slow down. You'll founder." The man shoved her shoulder.

Scowling at him, she let water drip off her fingertips into Johnny's mouth. He stuck out his tongue, swallowing over and over. His face was red and his hair damp with perspiration. She dipped the corner of his blanket into the creek and wiped his cheeks and forehead and under his chin.

Which suddenly seemed like a good idea for her, too. She let the water trickle down her face and neck and the front of her dress, sighing at the relative coolness. If only she could submerge herself in the water and let it soak into all her pores.

She spread Johnny's blanket in the thin shade and laid him down. He kicked and squirmed, happy to be free of her arms and the confining blanket. She wished she could carry him without the covering, but the sun was too hot, and he would burn. Her own face felt tight and hot, and she wished she still had her straw bonnet. She would be as red as an apple by evening.

Evening. Would Thomas find them before nightfall?

She studied her captor. He had dark hair, long, hanging on his shoulders, and a beard that looked to be maybe a week or so old. His boots were worn and scuffed, and his hands large and suntanned. He dipped his hat into the water and filled it, offering it to his horse, a dun with a roman nose. The horse drained the contents and looked for more, but when the man refilled his hat, he held it out to Esther's horse.

At least he had enough care to keep the horses from drinking too much before they were properly cooled out. She cupped another handful of water for herself before drizzling more into Johnny's mouth. Water wasn't going to hold him long. He would need milk.

"Can I at least know your name? Who are you?" she asked, bending to rip a strip of cloth from her petticoat. She winced as it tore all too easily, testament to its threadbare condition. Dragging her fingers through her hair, she pulled out leaves and twigs. When she had as many tangles as possible out, she gathered her hair into a bunch at her nape, fashioned a hasty, lumpy braid and tied it with the scrap of fabric. Maybe that would keep it from snagging on every bush and branch between here and the Brazos River.

"Didn't Beaufort tell you?" He leered over his shoulder as he scooped up another hatful of water. "I'm Jase Swindell."

She sucked in a breath and forgot to let it out. Jase Swindell, the man who had rustled her father's cattle and sent him to an early grave. The man she had hated for five years.

And Johnny was his son?

Johnny... Johnny Swindell.

She had been caring for the son of the man who had, in effect, killed her father?

And Thomas had known the whole time?

Betrayal hit low in her abdomen, and she sank to the creek bank, drawing her knees up and wrapping her arms around them. Her head whirled, and she thought she might be ill.

"I thought I was a goner when Beaufort busted into that shack last month. He's like a bloodhound on a scent, but he'd never gotten that close before. Thanks to Anna, I got away that time, and thanks to you, I'll get away this time." He dunked his bandanna into the water and wiped the back of his neck. "And Beaufort's coming. I have no doubt about that."

Her heart thrilled to that statement, then plunged when she thought of the way Thomas had deceived her. He had brought her the offspring of the man who she blamed for her father's ruin and death. Hot tears prickled behind her eyes and inside her nose, but she sniffed and scrubbed the heels of her hands on her eyelids. She'd never felt so alone.

Men were untrustworthy, every one of them. They lied and used and abandoned the people they were supposed to care about. If she had her way, she'd never clap eyes on another male for the rest of her life.

The baby cried, sucking on his fist, kicking his legs, drawing her attention. And yet, this little male had stolen her heart. He was innocent in all of this. Johnny hadn't chosen his parents. He hadn't known Thomas was lying to her about his parentage.

"He's going to be hungry soon. And he needs a new diaper."

"He'll have to wait. We need to make tracks." Swindell—she hated the sound of his name—checked his mount's girth. "Mount up."

"Babies don't wait very well. You hustled us out of town so quickly there wasn't time to grab any of his things. He needs milk. And a feeding bottle. And clean britches. And his basket." She drew the blanket, now looking dingy and limp around Johnny, and picked him up.

"He's my son. He's tough."

The man was either in denial or an idiot or both. Did he think he could will the child not to cry, not to be hungry, not to need anything?

She went to her horse, but with Johnny in her arms, she couldn't mount. "You'll have to hold him. Which means you'll have to put down your gun."

Swindell leaned the shotgun against a tree and wiped his hands down his thighs. His Adam's apple lurched, and the skin around his eyes tightened. She didn't miss the way his hands trembled. "He's so small." There was a tinge of awe in his voice. Was it possible for this hardened outlaw and killer to actually care for his child?

"I didn't know what to call him, so I named him Johnny." She put the baby into his large hands.

"My pa's name was John." He held the baby away from his body, one hand under his diaper, the other under his head. "I didn't realize he would be so tiny."

"He's bigger now than a month ago, but he was sick, too, so that set him back some."

"I saw the doc come to the house." He didn't take his eyes off Johnny's face.

"You what?"

"I was watching your place from up on the ridge. Waiting for the right time to come get my son. When I saw Beaufort leave the house this morning without his gun, I knew I could snatch the boy up if I followed you into town. Hadn't planned on bringing you along, but I reckon you're going to come in handy."

And she was the one who had insisted Thomas leave his gun behind. "You were watching my house?"

"You should be thanking me that watch was all I did. I could've shot you both and taken the boy anytime I wanted. I had a bead on Beaufort at least twice a day. I even burned down the barn as a distraction, but when I tried to get in through the back door on the house, it was bolted. I went around the front, but the dog was there. I decided to bide my time then."

So it wasn't Thomas's boot prints in the dirt behind her house the morning after the barn burned. It had been Swindell, trying to get in and abduct Johnny. And for the past few weeks he had been watching and waiting, holding their lives in his hands as he spied on them down the barrel of his rifle. A chill raced up her back in spite of the sweltering heat.

The baby squirmed and let out a squawk, and Swindell roused, as if remembering where they were. "Enough palavering. Get on your horse."

Esther dragged herself into the saddle, her muscles aching. Though she was used to hard work as a laundress, her legs and back protested getting astride again, and when Swindell handed Johnny up, her arms burned. If she only had the sling she wore while doing laundry, he could snuggle in there and leave her arms mostly free.

Swindell grabbed his shotgun, swung onto his horse and settled the firearm across his thighs. He leaned over and grabbed the reins of Esther's mount and set off.

They splashed through the creek and up the other side of the swale, heading west once more.

By Esther's reckoning, they had at least another four or five hours until dark.

Would Thomas find them before sunset, or would she be trapped overnight with Jase Swindell?

Chapter Fifteen

Thomas met the Circle Bar 5 riders on the road just south of Esther's place. They had Danny Newton propped in the saddle between them, headed to town.

"What happened?"

Danny's face glistened with sweat, and blood darkened his right arm and dripped down his hand. "He shot me." His lips were pale and his face ashen.

"Big fellow on a dun horse," the cowhand on Danny's left said. "He was dragging Miss Jensen and the baby along behind on another horse. When Danny recognized her, the man pulled a pistol and shot him."

"Yeah," the other one said. "We didn't shoot back, not wanting to hit Miss Jensen."

Thomas reached into his saddlebag and pulled out one of the clean diapers. "Tie this tight around that arm and get him to the doc's. Sheriff Granville's forming a posse. Let him know what happened."

"Beaufort." Danny gripped the saddle horn with his good hand. "Get her back. I know you might not think so, but I do care what happens to her."

Thomas nodded, lifted his reins and put his heels to Smitty. The big sorrel's stride ate up the ground, but Thomas was careful not to press him too hard. They might have a long, arduous chase ahead, and he didn't want his horse to give out on him before the end.

He nearly rode past the place where Swindell had turned off into the brush. The tracks led straight into the wall of living green. Reaching behind him, Thomas untied his brush jacket and slid it on in spite of the heat. He anchored his hat and forced Smitty into the thicket.

Thomas put away all thoughts of Esther and Johnny, focusing solely on Swindell, trying to outthink and thus outmaneuver him. If Thomas allowed himself to think of Esther or the baby and the danger they were in, emotion would cloud his judgment and they would suffer more.

Driving Smitty deeper into the brush, he became a bounty hunter once again.

The trees and bushes and vines trapped any breeze, and sounds grew distorted. It was here in the brush that Thomas missed Rip the most. The clumps of growth were so dense, he could ride past a dozen outlaws and not see them, but the dog would never pass an occupied thicket.

Seeing the trail wasn't difficult. Following it was another matter. Broken branches, the occasional hoofprint, disturbed grass, all marked the way, but Thomas constantly had to throw his arm up to shield his face, and Smitty balked at the prickly going.

Why had Swindell turned west? He had said when

he reached Mexico he would let Esther go, though Thomas planned to catch him well before the border. On Smitty he could make better time than Swindell's dun leading another horse. And Thomas wouldn't be slowed by a woman and baby.

He pushed thoughts of Esther and Johnny aside again. Instead, he focused on the trail, on keeping his wits sharp, his senses keen.

He anchored his hat again and pushed on. When he found a scrap of dark blue fabric hanging from a branch, he yanked it off. Part of Esther's new dress, ripped from her sleeve in the heavy going. Swindell wasn't choosing an easy path.

Why not? If he hoped to make it to the Mexican border, he was going the wrong direction for the closest route, and by far a more arduous one if he wanted to make time. But then again, Swindell hadn't gone to Mexico when he broke out of jail. Not for any length of time, at least. He'd stayed in south-central Texas in spite of the bounty on his head.

When he'd broken out of Huntsville, the reason he stayed was a woman. That woman was dead. Was it possible that Swindell had found someone else so soon? Not likely. So it must be the baby. He'd stayed for his son.

Guilt wrapped around Thomas's chest and squeezed. If he had left the baby with Esther and gotten right back on the trail, perhaps he could've captured Swindell before he kidnapped them both. And by now, Esther probably knew who Swindell was. Not just that he was the baby's father and an outlaw, but that he was the man who had robbed her father and led to his death.

Thomas forced down those thoughts, not wanting to get sidetracked. He had to focus on Swindell.

"So," he said to Smitty, "we can assume that Swindell has stayed in Texas for the sole purpose of getting his son. So, how did he know where Johnny was?" Thomas skirted a scrubby ironwood and wove his way around a patch of yukka. "He followed me from the shack. Which means he's probably known where Johnny was nearly the whole time."

Smitty wasn't much of a conversationalist, but it helped to talk it out. Thomas missed Rip. "Which means our watcher on the ridge probably wasn't another bounty hunter, but Swindell himself."

But what about the report from the sheriff over in Sonora?

An idea of what had happened and where Swindell was headed now began to form.

The ground finally opened up as he headed down a slope toward a creek. The trail grew fainter in the grass, but when he reached the edge of the water, he found evidence that Swindell had spent some time here. Foot and hoofprints pocked the dirt creek bank, and he found the spot where Esther had sat and an area of ground that looked like someone had smoothed it. Perhaps where she'd laid Johnny down on a blanket?

He tied Smitty well back from the creek so he wouldn't guzzle water and brought him a hatful to take the edge off his thirst until he cooled down. Crouching by the stream, Thomas plunged his bandanna into the water and wiped his face and neck and the sweatband of his hat. He drank deeply and made sure to fill both his canteens to the brim.

"You ready for some more, boy?"

Smitty stuck out his neck and shook his head, making his mane flop and bit jingle. He stamped and swished his tail. Thomas ran his hand down the horse's flank. The sweat had begun to dry on his withers.

Impatient to get back on the trail, but knowing Smitty needed a break, Thomas squatted in the shade and debated whether to try to get ahead of Swindell or keep trailing him. If he got off the trail and raced ahead, there was always the possibility that he was wrong about where Swindell was headed. But if he stayed on the trail behind them, there was the chance that Swindell would harm Esther or Johnny before Thomas could intervene.

Lord, help me make the right decision.

When Smitty was cooled out completely, Thomas led the horse to the creek and let him drink his fill before mounting and crossing to the western bank. From what he could gauge, he was an hour or so behind Swindell. And if the outlaw was headed where Thomas suspected, he would need to push Smitty hard to catch up before nightfall.

Once surrounded by brush again, he began to feel claustrophobic. And he was making a considerable racket rattling through the trees and branches. From time to time, he pulled his horse to a stop to listen. Beyond the buzzing of a few insects and the chirping of birds, silence lay over the landscape.

Distance was impossible to judge. But he had to be gaining on them. Once more he halted to listen.

Something crackled in the undergrowth to his right, and he drew his pistol. Smitty's ears swiveled, and he sidestepped, turning to face the noise. A twig snapped, and Thomas held his breath, straining to hear.

He began to think it had been a deer or coyote or something when Smitty snorted. And as casual as you please, Rip sauntered out of the brush, tongue lolling, tail wagging, eyes alight.

Thomas lowered his gun, grinning. "You rascal. You've been following them, too, huh?"

Rip stood on his hind legs, his forepaws on his master's thigh, and Thomas reached down to ruffle his ears. "Glad to see you. Glad you didn't get your fool head blown off by Swindell." Thomas dismounted to check the dog. Though dirty, he appeared unharmed, licking and lapping Thomas's hands and face, wagging his tail so hard his whole body swayed. Thomas poured a little water from his canteen into his palm and let Rip lap it up. "You set? Let's get our man."

At that phrase, Rip cocked his head. Thomas reached into his saddlebag and pulled out the baby gown he'd taken from the laundry hamper. He put it under Rip's nose. "Where's your man? Where's your man?"

Rip sniffed the garment, lifted his head to look at Thomas as if to say, "This is going to be easy," and trotted into the brush, his nose up and tail wagging.

Thomas put Smitty after him. How many times had they done this, the dog on the scent, Thomas following, zeroing in on their quarry?

Rip followed the trail unerringly at a steady trot, heading west.

Swindell had to be heading for the caves over by Sonora. The lawman there had been right. The man matching Swindell's description who bought supplies was most likely Swindell himself, laying in provisions for hiding out in his bolt-hole. He must've traveled back and forth between Sonora and Silar Falls at least once in the past month. Now he was racing to his hideout once more.

And Thomas planned to intercept him before he got there.

"Where are you taking us? If you're heading to Mexico, you're going the wrong way. You're going to wind up in California." Esther shifted Johnny to her other arm and wiped the sweat from her temples. The baby began to cry again, this time weaker. "We need to stop. He needs food and shelter."

"There's food and shelter at the end of the ride."

"And what good will that do if he doesn't survive the trip?" She wanted to scream at this man, to shake him, to make him see what he was doing. "This is your son, and yet you are putting him in danger." He ignored her and pushed on. They were heading into the setting sun, and while she didn't relish stumbling around out here in the dark, she would welcome relief from the heat.

Johnny continued to cry. "At least let me give him some water."

He whipped around and thrust the canteen at her. "Here. Now get him to be quiet."

"You're going to have to stop." She couldn't juggle the canteen and the baby while atop a moving horse.

Without a word, he pulled to a halt, reached over and uncapped the canteen. It was less than half full and the contents were lukewarm, but she tipped it carefully over Johnny, dripping water into his mouth. He stopped crying, swallowing, pushing his tongue out. She had to be careful; she didn't want him to choke. How she wished she were back at home, snuggling him in the rocker, feeding him some of Daisylu's good milk.

If Johnny didn't survive this journey, Swindell wouldn't have to worry about Thomas catching up with him. Esther would settle his hash for him.

"How much farther?"

"We're about halfway there."

"The sun's going down now. We can't ride all night." She lifted the canteen to take a small drink herself. Not too much, since it had to be saved for the baby, but enough to at least wet her mouth.

"Sure we can. I do it all the time."

"Johnny and I are not you. We can't keep going. Johnny won't make it."

Swindell glared at her and adjusted the shotgun across his lap. "Fine, we'll make camp for a while at the next water."

"How far is that?"

He didn't answer and they rode on.

Johnny hadn't eaten for six hours. He'd had only sips of water since then, and he was distinctly in need of a diaper change. Esther's body ached, and her mind was exhausted. She glared daggers at Swindell's back, but after a while, she was too tired to do any more than hang on. He'd lied to her about there being water ahead. He'd lied about them stopping for a while. He'd lied about ever letting her go.

The horses must've smelled the water ahead. They picked up the pace, and Esther grabbed the horn, swaying in the saddle, nearly dropping from fatigue. Then she heard it, the sound of water. She licked her cracked lips and tried to swallow some of the cotton in her mouth.

Here there was no open ground. The brush ran right up to the edge of the creek. When Swindell pulled up the horses several yards short of the water, Esther slipped from the saddle with Johnny in her arms and didn't stop walking until she reached the stream. Only taking time to remove her shoes and scoop Johnny up again, she walked right into the water and sat down with the baby, clothes and all.

Johnny jerked and stopped crying, his eyes wide as she lowered him into the stream. The water only came to her waist, so she raised her knees and laid him along her legs, quickly unwrapping him and removing his wet clothes. He kicked his naked little legs and waved his arms as she bathed him, cleaning him and cooling him at the same time.

"What in thunder are you doing?" Swindell squatted upstream and dunked his canteen into the water.

"I'm cooling both of us off as quickly as possible." And it felt wonderful. She cupped water on the upstream side and brought it to her mouth. Carefully, she dripped more water into Johnny's mouth. He swallowed eagerly. "Water isn't going to hold him for long. He's hours past his feeding time."

Swindell shrugged and set about unsaddling the

horses, clearing a place under the trees to make camp. When she was cooled off and Johnny's and her thirst slaked, she rose and came up out of the water, her blue dress sodden and dripping. It would dry soon enough in this heat.

"Do you have a spare shirt?"

"Why?"

"So I can wrap the baby up again."

He rummaged in his saddlebags and threw her a homespun brown shirt.

"And a bandanna?"

"Just the one I'm wearing." He pointed to his neck.

"That will do."

"For what?"

"A diaper."

"You ain't using my bandanna for a diaper."

"What kind of father are you? You claim to want your son, but you aren't willing to put his needs above your own?" She stared at him, cradling the naked baby.

He jerked off the faded red square of cloth and tossed it to her, scowling. With no suitable place to lay the baby, she sat on the grass cross-legged and held him in her lap. She quickly tied on the bandanna and wrapped him in the rough shirt. "You're right back where you started, aren't you, punkin'? I'm sorry. I wish I had some food for you, and clean clothes and your nice cozy bed."

She bent to kiss his forehead.

Lord, please help us.

The arrow prayer shot from her heart. Remembering the verse Thomas had quoted, she took comfort from the fact that the Lord had not forsaken her. *And they that know thy name will put their trust in thee: for thou, Lord, hast not forsaken them that seek thee.*

"I will trust You, Lord. Trust You to bring help, to keep Johnny safe." She whispered her prayer, raising Johnny to her shoulder and pressing her lips against his temple.

Swindell flopped the second saddle onto the ground and led his horse to the water to drink. She gathered her courage, because she had to know.

"What are your plans for Johnny?"

He tied the horse by the reins to a tree. "He's my son and he belongs with me."

"That isn't enough. He has needs. Food, shelter, schooling, love, family. Can you provide all of those things?"

Swindell glared at her. "It's no wonder you're a spinster. All you do is nag, nag, nag. I'm doing the best I can."

Stung, Esther flinched, but she persisted. "What kind of life can you give him? Hiding in Mexico? Or here in Texas always running from the law? You're a wanted man. If you're caught, you'll be hauled back to prison to stand trial for killing that guard. And you'll hang. What happens to Johnny then?"

"I ain't been caught yet."

"It only takes one time. Or, say you do succeed in staying on the run for the rest of your life. Will you raise Johnny to be like you? If he does grow up, he'll be an outlaw at best. Do you want him to die in a hail of bullets during a bank robbery or stage holdup?" The thought of this precious boy who had stolen her heart growing up to be like his father made her feel empty inside. "You're a wanted man with a price on your head. A huge price. You will never stop being hunted. If Johnny stays with you, he'll never stop being hunted, either."

Swindell scowled in the dying light. "Why don't you hush up? Nobody asked you for your opinion. He's my son, and he belongs with me. We're going to be a family like his ma wanted."

It was the first time he had mentioned Johnny's mother.

"Then why don't you hold him for a while. I'm tired." She passed him the baby. If he thought he should be Johnny's father, then he should take some responsibility for the child. He seemed to have some romantic notion about what it meant to be a parent. Trying to soothe a hungry baby might disabuse him of those ideas and give him an idea of what he was in for.

He took the baby, gingerly trying to keep the shirt wrapped around him.

Esther rolled her shoulders and rubbed the side of her neck. "Do you have a house? Somewhere for Johnny to live?"

"I have a place where I'm staying. I laid in some supplies, so I won't have to go to town for a couple months. That's where I was for a while after I burned the barn. Came back about the time the boy got sick. Figured I should wait a few days at least to let him get better before I took him."

"That was *kind* of you. Then you proceed to drag him out in the broiling sunshine with no food or clothes or clean diapers, jouncing all day on a horse, and you would've gone on through the night if I hadn't stopped you." Her stomach rumbled. Johnny wasn't the only one who was hungry. "Tell me about his mother."

"Why?" Swindell asked, easing down to sit with his back against a tree. "You never met her. Why would you care about her?" It was the second glimpse of humanity Esther had seen in him, the pain in his eyes, the roughness to his voice when he spoke of the woman who had born his child.

"Maybe I feel like you owe me, Mr. Swindell." *And maybe because you need to talk about her.*

"For taking care of my son?"

"More like for taking away my father."

He scowled. "What are you talking about?"

"You robbed my father. Five years ago you rustled his cattle. Probably with the help of the ranch foreman, Bark. My father was so devastated at the betrayal and the debts your rustling caused that he took his own life. Your actions made me an orphan, Mr. Swindell."

He dipped his head, his hat brim hiding his face, looking down at Johnny, who had fallen into a fitful sleep. After a moment, he glanced up. "Why didn't you toss my kid out the door when Beaufort brought him to the door?"

Because Thomas didn't tell me who the baby belonged to. She looked at Johnny's tiny, innocent profile. Would it have mattered? She wished Thomas hadn't kept the truth from her, but in the end, she wouldn't have turned them away. The baby had possessed her heart the moment she'd first cradled him in her arms.

"It isn't Johnny's fault who his father is or what you've done, any more than it is my fault that my father took his life. Tell me about his mother." *Because someday, Johnny will want to know, and if you aren't around to tell him, then somebody should.*

Chapter Sixteen

Rip heard them first. He was trotting ahead of Thomas when he stopped, wagged his tail one time and dropped to the ground. Thomas halted Smitty.

The dog kept his head up, ears cocked, but didn't stir, the signal that their quarry was close. Thomas's mouth quirked at one corner. Even though Rip was tracking his favorite person in the world, he hadn't broken training by barking or running to Johnny. He had followed perfectly the procedure for silent tracking.

Thomas slipped from the saddle, drawing his rifle from the scabbard and tying Smitty to a sturdy branch. He ran his hand down the white blaze on Smitty's nose and stepped quietly to crouch at Rip's side. The dog quivered, his nose twitching, eyes intent ahead.

Rising, Thomas motioned for Rip to come with him as he twisted and turned through the trees, trying not to snap any twigs or rustle any branches.

This is a lot like the last time I tried to capture

Swindell, but this time I know he has a woman and baby with him. I'm not going to let him surprise me.

Keeping an eye on Rip, Thomas moved ahead. The dog advanced, one slow step at a time, head low, eyes bright, every muscle tense.

A man's voice drifted through the trees, but with so much undergrowth distorting the words, it was difficult to tell how far away he was.

Thomas thought he heard a lighter voice answer. Esther. Relief hit him in the chest and his knees weakened. She was alive and talking. He inched closer.

"It isn't Johnny's fault who his father is or what you've done, any more than it is my fault that my father took his life. Tell me about his mother."

Thomas crouched beside Rip, peering through the branches of a rabbitbush. Water flowed a few yards away, and a horse stamped his foot. Esther sat on the grassy bank, knees tucked up, arms wrapped around them. Her brown hair had fallen from its pins, and she'd gathered it into a braid behind her head and tied it with a piece of cloth. Her shoes lay on the bank a few feet away.

Swindell sat with his back to a tree holding the baby. That was problematic. Until he put the child down, Thomas couldn't risk confronting him.

"She was a no-account by most people's standards, but I loved her. Her name was Anna." Swindell gave Esther a hard look. "You probably think a man like me isn't capable of love, but you'd be wrong."

Thomas eyed the angles. If he moved to his right, he would have a clearer view of Swindell and the baby, but he'd be blocked from seeing Esther. Bet-

ter to stay where he was and wait. He set his rifle on
the ground and drew his pistol, much better for close
work. Putting his hand on Rip's neck, he pressed and
the dog went down on his belly.

"Where did you meet her?" Esther asked.

"Uvalde, in a saloon. She was a sporting girl. I used
to stop and see her when I was coming back from selling cattle. She was from back east, but she got the consumption and headed west for the prairie cure. When
I landed in prison, she was so upset it nearly killed
her. She came to see me, and she said when I broke
out, she'd help me hide. And she did. First in a hotel
in Austin, then at a boardinghouse in San Antonio."

Johnny squawked and squirmed, stretching his little arms. What was that he was wrapped in? Looked
like a man's shirt.

This really was like the day Johnny was born.
Thomas listened, waiting for his chance to pounce.

"Things got too hot in the towns. Beaufort tracked
me to both places. And he wasn't the only one. A couple of times, we lit out in the middle of the night to get
away. Finally, we headed over toward Sonora, where
there are some caves. We hid out there together. The
lawman over that way is getting old, and he tends to
turn a blind eye to any trouble not actually inside the
city limits. Anyway, Anna seemed happy enough,
though she was coughing more every day. I wanted
to stay in the caves until after the baby came, but she
wanted to go to Mexico, said the damp in the caves
was making her consumption worse. We argued about
it, and she finally convinced me, though by the time
we set out, she was too far along with the baby for it

to be a good idea. We made it as far as a shack out in the brush about a day's ride from Silar Falls when she went into labor. That's where Beaufort found us the last time."

"Why did you leave her? Why leave your son behind?" Esther asked.

"What was I supposed to do? Beaufort got off a shot that winged me. I was wounded and on the run, I couldn't take Anna or the baby with me right then, not with a bounty hunter hot on my trail. I figured I would circle back after he left, but by the time I did, all I found was her grave. I didn't know if the baby had survived, so I tracked Beaufort. When I saw him making a beeline for Silar Falls, I figured he must have my child, otherwise he would've been on my trail instead."

"So you followed him to my place."

"And I watched from up on the ridge, waiting for my wound to get better and for a good chance to sneak in and get the baby." He rubbed his upper arm. "The wound festered, so after I burned the barn down but couldn't get into the house to get the baby, I figured I would hide out back in the caves for a couple weeks and heal up."

Thomas gripped his pistol. Swindell had been the one on the ridge, and he had burned down Esther's barn. Thomas had wounded him at the shack, which would've made him easy to follow right away, if Thomas hadn't gotten distracted by the baby's birth. He could've had Swindell back behind bars where he belonged a month ago. Yet, he couldn't have left the woman alone or abandoned the baby to get back on the trail.

"What did Anna want for her baby?" Esther fanned her skirt out. She appeared to be wet to the waist. Had she gone right into the creek? It had been hot, and she must've been eager to cool herself and Johnny off.

"Anna?" Swindell grunted. "She thought if we could make it to Mexico, we could be a real family. That's what she wanted for the boy. A home and schooling and us to be a family."

Even Thomas could hear the pain in the man's voice. All this time, he'd seen Jase Swindell as only a fugitive and bounty, a man who had robbed and rustled and escaped and killed. For the first time, he also saw that he cared in his own, rough way for the woman who had born his child and maybe even for the baby himself.

"How is kidnapping your son going to fulfill Anna's wishes? You're an outlaw and a wanted man. Not only are you wanted for murder, but now for kidnapping. Every bounty hunter and lawman in the state will be after you."

The baby began to snuffle and squirm, crying out, and Swindell held him away from his body, panic in every line of his face. "What do I do?"

At the sound of the baby's cries, Rip quivered from nose to tail, and Thomas put his hand on the dog's back to remind him to stay still and quiet.

"You're his father, as you keep pointing out to me. You feed him and change him and love him and put his needs ahead of your own until he's old enough to fend for himself. That's what being a father means."

Swindell eyed the crying baby as if he were a stick of dynamite primed to go off. "Take him."

Yes, take him. Thomas crouched, tense and ready to pounce.

"No. He's your burden now. I have loved him and fed him and prayed over him and worried about him when he was sick or when he had a tummyache for a month now, and you think you can barge in and steal him? Fine. You take care of him."

C'mon, Esther, help me out here. Help him out.

"With what? I don't know the first thing about taking care of a baby."

"Which is my point." Esther pushed herself up. "What supplies do you have in your pack?" Without waiting, she crossed the small open space to dig in Swindell's saddlebags.

Get back, girl. You're too close to him. Take the baby and get out of the way.

"Aha." Esther held up a tin can. "Peaches."

"He can eat peaches?" He shifted the baby, bouncing him lightly, his dark brows bunched as he frowned at the sobbing child.

"No. But these are packed in syrup. If I can get some of the syrup in him, that will keep him going for a while."

"Here, take him. I'll open the can." Swindell handed a squalling Johnny to Esther, but instead of moving away from the outlaw, she sat beside him. Thomas gritted his teeth.

Esther gently rocked Johnny. "Shh, soon, sweetie. I know you're hungry."

Swindell opened the can with his knife, piercing

the metal lid and working his way around the can. "Here." He thrust it at Esther.

"Do you have a spoon?"

"No, I eat peaches with a knife."

She rolled her eyes. "Fine." She took the can and set it on the ground beside her, dipped her finger into the syrup and put it into Johnny's open mouth. He wailed and then stopped, slurping away at her finger.

"Ah, surprised you, didn't I?" She smiled down at him.

Swindell squatted, forearms on his thighs, studying her. "Anna had that look."

"What look?" Esther dipped her finger again and offered it to the baby.

"When she talked about the baby. She'd rub her belly and get that same look in her eye as you have when you look at Johnny."

"That's probably because she loved him." Esther's voice thickened. She nuzzled the baby's hair. "And who could help it, right, punkin'?"

"Were you planning on raising him yourself if I hadn't come along?"

Esther offered the baby another portion of sugar syrup and shook her head. "I want to, but I can't. Not without having a secure place for him, even if the courts would award custody to a single woman. I don't know if I will still own the ranch in a month's time. The taxes will be due, and I'll be a bit short this year. I have nothing else to sell to make up the difference." She shook her head. "I promised my father I would keep his ranch, and I've let him down. Thomas plans to find a good home for the baby, one with a mother and father who will love and care for him as their own." It was going to be hard to let Johnny go, but it was the best thing for him.

"Anna would've liked you." Swindell picked up a stick and broke off a piece, tossing it into the creek. He appeared deep in thought, saying nothing for the longest time. Finally, he stirred. "I haven't done much in my life that was right, but loving Anna was one of them." He snapped off another piece of stick and flung it hard into the water. "Seems like everything before and after her has been one giant mistake." He stood and moved downstream a few feet. Thomas held his breath. *Just a little farther. Go on. A few more steps.*

"Hands up, Swindell." Thomas crashed from the brush, and Esther's heart leaped. She tightened her hold on Johnny, bringing him to her chest. Rip bounded forward, coming to touch his nose to Johnny's head and then swinging around between the baby and Swindell.

Thomas had come. Esther's heart thudded in her chest and blood swirled in her ears. He had come for them.

Jase whirled, hands reaching for his gun, then stopping halfway.

"Don't." Thomas held his pistol steady. Rip growled and lowered his head, legs stiff, back straight. Esther scarcely dared to breathe. At the sight of his gun, she shuddered, but for once she was thankful to see it in his hand.

"Beaufort." Jase spat the name. "I knew I should've shot you back there in the churchyard."

"You should have." Thomas nodded. "You would've had to kill me to keep me from coming after you."

"You're not taking me back to prison. They'll hang me." Swindell didn't move his hands, but kept them low and open.

"I don't see that you have much choice in the matter."

"Sure I do. I can shoot it out with you right here and right now."

"I wouldn't advise it. I have the drop on you. I won't miss from this range."

"Maybe I don't want you to miss."

Johnny, unhappy at having his meal interrupted, let out a wail. Esther shushed him, giving him more of the syrup. "That's ridiculous. You don't want to be shot."

"I don't want to be hanged, either." Swindell said the words to Esther but didn't look away from Thomas and the dog.

"I don't aim to let you take me in alive, Beaufort," he continued, "but if you're going to collect the bounty on me, I want your promise about something."

"I'm listening."

"I want the bounty money to go to my son." He jerked his head. "This woman here's been showing me that I can't be any kind of a good father to the boy. No home, an outlaw, always drifting from place to place, always afraid someone like you will come along. She's right. I can't give the boy what his mother wanted, not without my Anna. The best I can do is try to leave something for him."

Tears pricked Esther's eyes, and she blinked hard.

Jase Swindell seemed to have no moral compass to tell right from wrong, and yet, he wanted to provide for his son in the only way open to him.

"Swindell," Thomas said, "if you want to leave a legacy for your son, then do the right thing. Own up to your mistakes and let me take you in alive. You do that, and I promise I'll make sure the money from your bounty goes to your son." Thomas never took his eyes off Swindell, and his face was hard and intent, an expression Esther had never seen before. He looked stronger and more capable than ever, totally committed to his calling, every inch the bounty hunter. "I aim to be a part of Johnny's life somehow, and I don't want to have to tell him I shot his pa. I'd rather tell him his pa faced up to his crimes and accepted the punishment due him like a man. The money's one thing, but giving him something positive and honorable about his pa will be more important to him going forward."

Jase Swindell slowly raised his hands, his Adam's apple lurching. "You'll find him a good home, with a family to care for him? Give him proper schooling and the like?"

"I will. I promise. And I'll bank the bounty money to be used just for Johnny."

Swindell's shoulders slumped, and he bowed his head. "Take me in then."

Thomas disarmed his prisoner and snapped his fingers. Rip bounded over. "Guard."

The dog went to work, standing in front of Swindell, a low rumbling growl coming from deep in his chest.

Thomas walked to Esther's side and squatted. "Are you all right? Is Johnny? I came as soon as I could." He holstered his gun and set Swindell's on the ground, reaching up to brush the hair off her temple and look into her eyes.

"We're fine now." Relief at seeing his capable, strong self here at last made her dizzy.

"I have a few things to do, then we'll head back."

He disappeared into the brush, and Esther bowed her head over Johnny. "Thank You, Lord. Thank You, Lord."

When he returned, he had his horse and his rifle. Rip kept watch over Swindell, who stood as still as a fence post while Thomas put shackles on his wrists. When the prisoner was secure, Thomas dug in his saddlebags and brought out a clean diaper and gown for Johnny, tossing them to Esther. Then he saddled Swindell's horse, and the one Esther had ridden.

"I think it will be best to start back now. Feed Johnny as much of that sugar water as you can, then pour the rest into this." He handed her a half-full canteen. "I'll rig something to make carrying Johnny easier."

Esther nodded, frowning. Thomas seemed so remote, almost as if he was angry with her. Was this because she had insisted he leave his gun at the ranch instead of wearing it to church? Was this because she had insisted on coming with Swindell instead of just handing Johnny over to him?

Whatever it was, his mood persisted as he fashioned a sling out of the blanket in his bedroll, got his prisoner on his horse and held the baby as Esther mounted. She stifled a groan as she got into the saddle, feeling sore and battered. Thomas handed Johnny to her, and she nestled him into the sling, making sure he was secure before taking the reins.

"You'll have to bring up the rear. I have to keep Swindell close. Rip will be with you the whole way, and if you need anything, or if the baby does, sing out and we'll stop, all right? Don't get too far behind. It won't be a pleasant trip, but we need to get Johnny home." He checked her gear, not raising his head, so she only had a view of the top of his hat.

"We'll be fine."

He patted her knee and went to his horse. The sun was setting as he mounted up and led them into the dense brush.

Chapter Seventeen

Esther had never been so happy to see the dirt road that led past her house. No more branches or thorns or clinging vines to fight through. The baby slept, sustained by sugar water for the time being. The moon rose high and full, bathing the landscape with silvery light and creating deep shadows under the trees and bushes.

Thomas stopped several times on the journey to check on them, maintaining his businesslike and aloof demeanor. Esther was nearly dropping with fatigue, but for Johnny's sake she refused to complain and ask to stop. The baby needed to get home and properly fed.

A couple hours from Double J, they'd met Sheriff Granville and his posse.

"Danny Newton's going to be fine. The bullet went through his upper arm. Doc was tending to him when we left." The sheriff shifted in the saddle. "Sarah's going to be mighty happy to see you, young lady. She's waiting for you at your place."

"Let's press on then." Thomas lifted his reins.

"You want me to take the baby for you?" one of the posse men asked.

"Thank you, no." Esther peeked into the sling to check on him, reaching in to feel his breathing, making sure he wasn't too hot. She caressed his cheek with the side of her finger. How she longed to get him home.

Light shone from the front windows of her house as they turned in under the crossbar at the gate, welcoming them. Esther had to blink back tears at the sight of her home. She might not own it for much longer, but for now, it was a safe haven.

Sarah Granville stepped out onto the porch. "Thank You, Jesus!" She blinked, sniffing and wiping her eyes with the hem of her apron. "You found them. Is the baby safe?" she asked her husband.

"He's fine. Hungry and tired out, but fine as a five-cent piece." Charlie Granville swung off his horse and put his arm around his wife. "Esther's worn to a nubbin, and she'll need your help. We've got to get the prisoner back to the jail. You can stay, right?"

"Of course."

Thomas maneuvered his horse alongside Esther's and dismounted, reaching up and spanning Esther's waist to help her down. Her legs wobbled, numb from so many hours in the saddle, and she gripped his upper arms to steady herself.

"All right?" He was still distant and reserved. It was as if he had put on the persona of a bounty hunter…or had he merely put off the persona of friend? He held her firmly, but his eyes went to Jase Swindell, wrists still shackled.

A shiver went through Esther. What if this was Thomas's way of preparing himself to ride out of her life again? "Yes, I'm fine. Thank you."

"And the baby?"

"Sleeping." She let go of his arms and stepped back, cradling Johnny in his sling.

"Sounds like Sarah will help you out. I'll head into town with the posse and my prisoner."

He was leaving her.

Sarah bustled over and held out her hands. "Give me the little love. I'll take him inside out of this night air. Teddy's still here, and he'll look after Esther's horse and make sure it gets back to its owner."

Esther fished the baby out of the sling, and once Sarah had him, she dragged the heavy blanket off her shoulder and over her head. She wanted to cry, but she was too tired, too bludgeoned by everything that had happened.

Thomas took her hand and drew her away from the milling posse, turning her so her back was to them and he could see her while keeping an eye on his prisoner. He took the blanket from her and tossed it over his shoulder before taking both her hands in his.

"Esther, there are a lot of things I need to say to you, but there isn't time now. I need you to trust me. I know I've no call to ask, and you have every right to be angry with me, but I'm still going to ask you to trust me. I have to go away. I don't know for how long. But I promise you I will come back. Take care of yourself and Johnny while I'm gone." He brushed a kiss on her forehead and turned away. He quickly rolled the blanket and tied it behind his saddle and then mounted up.

In moments, the posse rode away toward town, Thomas leading Jase Swindell's horse and Rip trotting at Thomas's side.

Esther stood looking after them, watching Thomas's form for as long as she could in the last bit of moonlight until he disappeared into the darkness.

He would be back. Trust him.

Sarah Granville stepped out onto the porch and put her arm around Esther. "Come inside, child. Let's get you fed and in bed. You and Johnny both deserve a long rest."

With no desire or energy to resist, Esther let her friend mother her. Sarah heated water for a bath, and while it was heating fed Johnny a bottle of Daisylu's milk, changing and sponging him off, nestling him into his basket to sleep. Through it all she kept up a mindless prattle, talking about everything under the sun while Esther sat in the rocker and watched.

Once Johnny was settled, Sarah set in on Esther. "You poor love. A nice bath, clean clothes and your own bed. Don't you worry about tending the baby during the night. I'll take his basket into the other bedroom and look after him. It's been years since I had a little one to tend, and I look forward to it." She helped Esther wash her hair, spreading a towel on her pillow and tucking her into bed. "You sleep now. Don't worry about a thing."

Once Sarah stopped her fussing and closed the bedroom door, Esther thought she would fall asleep quickly, but her mind had other ideas. Reliving the day's events—had it all really happened in just one day?—revisiting her shock at her captor's identity, the role he played in her father's death, the stranger Thomas had turned into and Swindell's surrender, she couldn't sleep. Tears leaked from her eyes and tracked into her hairline as she watched the ceiling grow lighter, the morning sun creeping into the room.

Thomas had asked her for only one thing.

Trust.

Did he have any idea how frightening that was? It was one thing to trust the Lord, since He would never forsake her, but every time she had trusted a man, her heart had been broken.

Trusting Thomas meant letting her heart be vulnerable again. Trusting him meant letting go of the past. Trusting him meant forgiving, not just Thomas, but her father, and even Jase Swindell.

She'd thought any hope of having a happy family had disappeared five years ago when the man she loved rode out of her life, and when, a week later, her father had chosen to end his life rather than face his own ruin.

Then Thomas had returned, bringing with him a child who needed her. A child she had told herself not to fall in love with, and yet who had stolen her heart with little effort.

As had Thomas. Again. Though she'd steeled herself against ever being that vulnerable again, it hadn't done a bit of good. She loved him. And she always would. She loved his steadiness, his capability, his acts of sacrifice. She loved his sense of humor and his walk, and the way he put everyone else's needs and desires ahead of his own.

He *had* withheld the identity of Johnny's father from her, and at first, that had stung. But she could see how he was protecting her. Especially once she learned that she blamed Swindell for her father's death.

She could hold on to that hurt, piling it up with others in her past, and let those unforgiven acts keep her from happiness, or she could surrender those hurts, forgive and open herself up to...yes, being vulnerable again, but also to joy.

"Jesus, help me to forgive Thomas, my father, Jase Swindell. Help me let go of the sin of unforgiveness that has been weighing me down. Help me to trust in You, that You have a plan for Johnny, for Thomas and for me. If it is Your will that I lose the ranch, help me to be strong. And if it's Your will that I lose Johnny and Thomas, help me to bear it and trust in You. Thank You for never forsaking me." She whispered the prayer, dropping over the edge of sleep as she said, "Amen."

Esther woke hours later, stiff and sore. Sarah's voice came from the kitchen, talking to Johnny who gurgled. Esther eased out of bed with a groan, examining the scratches on her arms, wincing at the ache in her muscles.

Yet, she felt better than she had in a long time. Lighter, freer.

No longer carrying the burden of guilt and unforgiveness.

The next two days Esther did little but rest and recuperate. She ate Sarah's good cooking, held the baby and let life go on around her. But the third morning, she felt ready to cope on her own.

"Thank you, Sarah, for everything, but I can't keep you any longer. I'm fit and ready to get back to my work." Esther took a bite of fluffy pancake. "Though I am going to miss your food. I know you taught me to cook after my father died, but I'll never be as good as you."

"Are you sure, love? It's no trouble for me to stay. Or you and the boy can come stay with us in town." Sarah poured herself a cup of coffee and sat down to her own breakfast.

"I'm sure. I have customers who are counting on me, and I've been lazy enough." *And working will fill the time until Thomas comes back.* "And Charlie must be more than ready to have you back home."

"If that's what you want, I'll pack my bag. At least you still have Teddy here." She smiled at the young man who was staying in the bunkhouse and looking after the animals. He took his meals with them, putting away far more than Esther would've guessed possible by his lean frame, and was unvaryingly polite.

"Mr. Beaufort said to stay until he came back and to help out Miss Jensen any way I could." He swiped the last bit of syrup off his plate. "And to clear off the barn site. Which is what I had best get to doin'." Reaching for his hat, he bobbed his white-blond head. "Thank you for the breakfast, ma'am. Miss Jensen, if you need anything, holler. I stacked some firewood out front by your washtubs, but if you want me to fill the tubs and get the fire started, I can do that."

"I'll see to it, Teddy. Thank you."

Johnny had caught up on his feeding and sleeping, and this morning, he lay in his basket kicking and cooing. Esther leaned over and put her finger into his little hand, smiling down at him. So precious.

By the end of the first week, Teddy had cleared all the burned wood from the barn and raked over the ashes to separate any metal. Esther had caught up on the backlog of laundry, and Johnny had started holding his head up.

There was no sign of Thomas, but Hunstville was almost three hundred miles away. He would have a long journey to return Jase Swindell to the state prison and then the long trip back.

By the second week, on Trudy and Sarah's advice, Esther started Johnny on finely ground oatmeal thinned with goat milk. He slept for six hours the first night, and Esther awakened in a panic, rushing to his basket to make sure he was fine. Every day he seemed to do something different, and she longed for Thomas to be there to see it, to be able to share with him about Johnny's progress. She laundered clothes for her customers and mended and cleaned the blue dress.

At the end of the third week, Esther had to remind herself a dozen times a day that she was trusting the Lord and trusting Thomas. The days were long and empty, and Johnny was her only joy. In the evenings, she studied her calendar and her bank balance, but try as she might, she couldn't make her savings stretch to cover the taxes that were due in just four days.

Trust me.

Oh, Thomas, I miss you. I need you here.

* * *

Thomas let Smitty walk the last half mile, though he was eager to get back to Esther. His horse was spent after traveling more than six hundred miles in just over three weeks, and the midday July sun hammered the landscape. Thomas was worn out himself. Keeping constant vigil over a prisoner was hard enough, even with Rip's help, but turning Swindell over to the authorities at Huntsville had been surprisingly tough. Swindell had been nearly silent through it all. Thomas had spoken with the prison warden about finding a chaplain for Jase before it was too late.

Rip walked at Smitty's side, head down. He'd lost some weight over the past three weeks, and he had to be footsore from all the travel, but he'd get a good rest now. At least he would if things went the way Thomas hoped between himself and Esther.

He turned in under the Double J sign. Rip's ears came up, and he trotted toward the porch.

A grin split Thomas's unshaven face. Esther sat in her rocker, holding Johnny. It was an image he'd held dear for weeks, the woman and child he loved together in the place she called home.

When she caught sight of them, she rose.

His heart knocked against his ribs and tiredness fell away as he took in her face and form. Wisps of brown hair teased her temples, and her brown eyes held his. He slid from the saddle. Young Teddy appeared from around the back of the house.

"Afternoon, Mr. Beaufort. I saw you riding up. I'll take your horse."

Thomas nodded but didn't look away from Esther. "Wait. There's something I need." He yanked the leather ties fastening his saddlebags to his rig and flopped the bags over his shoulder.

Rip whined and wagged his body, rising on his hind legs, trying to touch his nose to the baby. Esther relented and placed the boy in his basket where Rip could sniff and nose to his heart's content.

Thomas mounted the stairs, dropped his saddle-bags to the porch floor and didn't stop walking until Esther was in his arms. He had no idea how she would react. All he knew was that he needed to hold her. To his gratification, she wrapped her arms around him, melting into his embrace. He tightened his grip, resting his cheek against her hair, inhaling her scent, cupping the back of her head to his shoulder, savoring her silky hair and warmth.

His own, sweet Esther. He framed her face with his hands, rubbing her cheeks with his thumbs, staring into her light brown eyes. He hardly dared hope the light shining there was love.

He lowered his head, bringing his lips to hers, lightly at first and then crushing her to him, pouring out the years of pent up love. Time stopped, and there was just Esther. She hugged him tight. How he had missed her. How he needed her.

A squawk from Johnny dragged him back to his senses. Esther broke the kiss, laughing, resting her hands against his chest. She reached up to his face, dislodging his hat to run her fingers through his hair. He closed his eyes, savoring her touch.

Thomas blew out a long breath. "A man could get used to being welcomed home this way."

Esther laughed and stepped back, fussing with her hair, color flying in her cheeks.

He steadied his breathing and went to the basket, unable to resist picking up the baby. "He's grown at least a foot since I saw him last."

"Almost two months old now. Just a couple more days. He's awake more and eating some cereal every day." She kissed Johnny's head and tried to smooth down his unruly dark curls.

"We have a lot to talk about, Esther. There's so much I need to tell you."

She nodded. "There's a lot I need to tell you, too."

"This could take a while. You might want to sit." Thomas stooped and picked up his hat, tossing it on the table, and went to the steps with Johnny. He sat on the top stair, leaning his back against a porch post. Esther took the rocker, her hands laced in her lap.

"I'm sorry it took so long to get back here. I delivered Jase to Huntsville. I had to stay there for a few days and then ride up to Austin to see the governor."

"For the reward money?" She rubbed her lower lip with her index finger, eyes clouded.

"Partly. But before I tell you about that, I need to back up about five years." Thomas lifted Johnny, inhaling his sweet, baby scent. "There's something you don't know about the day I rode away from here. I didn't tell you because I didn't want you to think badly of your father. The thing is, I wanted to stay. Me, who had never stayed in one place for more than a few weeks ever since I busted out of the orphanage." He shook his head. "I was in love with you, Esther. The ranch hands teased me a lot about having to dig post holes and string wire, but I didn't mind the work. It meant I got to stay close to the ranch house and see you every day. I used to watch for you, hoping to catch a glimpse of you headed to the barn to ride out. The times your pa told me to hitch up the buggy and drive you to town to do your shopping were the best. I remember everything about those days, what you wore, how your laugh made me happy, the way you tugged on your bottom lip when you were trying to make a decision."

She shook her head, her eyes troubled. "If you loved me, why did you leave?"

He rubbed the back of his neck with his palm. "I was just a kid, no money, nothing to offer you, not even a name that was my own. And your pa saw how I felt about you. He took me aside and laid it out for me, how I was no kind of a husband for you, how he had bigger plans. That if I really loved you and wanted what was best for you, I'd ride out and never let on to you that I was in love."

Her fingertips covered her mouth.

"The thing is, I believed him. I believed I wasn't good enough for you. I had no prospects, nothing to recommend me, just that I loved you." His heart pinged like a hammer on an anvil, those feelings of inadequacy threatening to surge back. "I did the only thing I knew how to do, which was to ride away. I headed south down to Galveston and met a man who helped me figure out what I should do with the talents God had given me. That's when I learned to shoot and track and became a bounty hunter, like I wanted."

"My father ran you off?" She sagged backward

into her chair, resting her hands on the arms of the rocker. "How could he? Especially when he didn't stick around long enough to see through any of those plans he supposedly had for me?"

"I don't want you to think badly of him, Esther. He was doing what he thought was right for you at the time. I've forgiven him. I hope you can, too."

She covered her eyes with the heels of her hands. "My father was a weak man. I know that now. He ran you off, and when he realized he was ruined by rustlers, he took his own life. And he put the burden of keeping the ranch on me, even though he wasn't brave enough or strong enough to attempt it himself." She sighed, dragging her hands down her face. "I loved him, but he was a weak man."

"About the ranch…"

"I can't hold on to it. The taxes are due, and I don't have the money. If I can arrange a sale quickly, I'll take the money and set up in town. I'm sure Danny and his father will pay me something for it rather than risk losing it to auction for back taxes."

"Esther," Thomas said, reaching for his saddlebags and unbuckling the left one. He pulled out a paper and handed it to her. "Here's the receipt for this year's taxes. I paid them at the courthouse when I rode through town."

"Thomas…"

"Now, before you scold me that you can't take charity, hear me out." He swallowed the boulder that had lodged in his throat. "Esther, I loved you five years ago, and I rode away from you because I thought it was for the best. The truth is, I never stopped loving you." Standing, he shifted Johnny to lay in one arm and held out his hand to her. "All my life I have been looking for a home, and I've found one. A place I want to stay." He gripped her fingers. "Not this ranch, not this house, but in you. You are and always will be the place my heart is at home."

Her pink lips parted, and her eyes widened. "Thomas…"

"I'm asking you to marry me, Esther. I'm asking you to let me come home." He held his breath, his entire future hanging on her response.

Her hand trembled in his, and she blinked fast, nodding. Sunshine burst in his chest as what he hoped were happy tears filled her eyes. Tugging on her fingers, he drew her close, kissing her forehead and temple, rubbing his nose on hers, grinning, laughing, wanting to throw his head back and howl.

"Say it, Esther. Say the words and put me out of my misery."

She reached up and covered his rough cheeks with her hands, smiling sweetly. "I love you, Thomas Beaufort. I have for years. I will marry you." She stood on tiptoe and brushed his lips with her own, sending a lightning bolt through him from his hairline to his heels.

Johnny gurgled and squirmed, and she stepped back, biting her lip. "What about Johnny?"

Thomas kept her hand in his, loathe to let her go. "About that. I should've told you from the first who his pa was. At first it didn't seem to matter, and then when you told me about how Jase had robbed your pa and all that followed, I was scared that you'd turn us both out if you knew the truth. I should've known better. You're a bigger person than that. I should've trusted you to do the right thing."

She squeezed his fingers. "I'll confess that it rocked me, and I was angry at first, but I forgive you, Thomas. I love Johnny, and I don't care who his parents were. Just like I love you and I don't care who your parents were."

"That's good, because Johnny and I are a package deal." He let go of her long enough to pull another paper out of his saddlebag. "That's why I detoured to Austin to see the governor. I figured I could cut through some red tape as long as the governor was in a good mood. I had just captured the most wanted man in Texas, after all. Governor Ross was kind enough to award me custody of Johnny, especially after I told him the whole story. He advised me to hotfoot it down here to Silar Falls and get you in front of a preacher pronto." Thomas grinned.

"We get to keep him?" She clasped her hands under her chin, hope gleaming in her eyes.

"Yep. You, me and Johnny. A family. Oh, and there's one more thing I need to tell you."

"I don't know if I can take much more."

"It's not a bad thing, I promise. The thing is, God has blessed me these past five years. I'm not boasting when I say I was a good bounty hunter. I'm actually pretty well-off financially right now. While I was in Huntsville, I arranged to have the money in my bank account there wired to the bank here. I want to order lumber for the new barn. As soon as that is built, I'll be heading down to the King Ranch to buy some cattle to build up the Double J herd, hire some hands and get this ranch back to making a profit." He dug out his bankbook and passed it to her. "I know you wouldn't marry me for my money, but I want to show you that I can work hard, that I can provide for you and Johnny and however many more kids God blesses us with. I'm nothing fancy, but I'm steady, and I promise you I'll always be here for you and Johnny."

She took the book and set it on the table without looking inside, her eyes shining He held out his free arm, and she went into it, including Johnny in the embrace. Rip barked and circled them, tail wagging.

Thomas closed his eyes and soaked in so much happiness, he thought he might burst. He'd set out to track down a man and had wound up finding a home and love and a family.

A place to belong.

* * * * *

If you liked this story,
pick up this other heartwarming book
from Erica Vetsch:
HIS PRAIRIE SWEETHEART

Available now from Love Inspired Historical!

Find more great reads at www.LoveInspired.com

Dear Reader,

I have so much admiration for our forefathers…and mothers! While researching for *The Bounty Hunter's Baby*, I learned about all it took just to get a load of laundry done in pioneer times, and I was humbled. In these days when doing laundry involves pouring a little detergent into a cup and pushing a few buttons, the thought of carrying and heating water, using a scrub board, wringing by hand, hanging garments on the clothesline, and pressing clothes with sad irons is daunting, to say the least. I would've perished!

But Esther, my heroine, is made of sterner stuff than I. She is resilient, and she is determined to make the best of her situation. And Thomas is a good fit for her, capable and dependable. And who can resist a man who brings you a darling newborn and a loyal, brave dog?

I hope you enjoy reading *The Bounty Hunter's Baby*. And if you're like me, you'll spend a bit of time being grateful for those who settled this country…and that some things, like doing laundry, have changed, and that the important things, like family, faithfulness and love have remained the same.

Sincerely,
Erica Vetsch

COMING NEXT MONTH FROM
Love Inspired® Historical

Available March 7, 2017

PONY EXPRESS MAIL-ORDER BRIDE
Saddles and Spurs • by Rhonda Gibson

Needing a home and a husband to help her raise her orphaned nephews, Bella Wilson heads to Wyoming in response to a mail-order bride ad. But when she discovers that Philip Young, her pony express rider groom-to-be, didn't place the ad, she must convince him to marry her for the sake of the children.

A TEMPORARY FAMILY
Prairie Courtships • by Sherri Shackelford

Stagecoach-stop station agent Nolan West's best chance to protect Tilly Hargreaves and her three nieces from the outlaws threatening his town is by pretending Tilly is his wife. And soon his temporary family is chipping away at his guarded heart.

HER MOTHERHOOD WISH
by Keli Gwyn

When Callie Hunt and Chip Evans discover two orphans and become their caregivers, neither is ready for a relationship. But can the children draw Callie and Chip together and convince them to put their plans aside and become a family?

FRONTIER AGREEMENT
by Shannon Farrington

When she goes to live with her Native American mother's tribe after her father's death, Claire Manette is told she must find a husband, but she wishes to marry for love. Is there a chance she can find it in the marriage of convenience Lewis and Clark Expedition member Pierre Lafayette offers?

LIHCNM0217

*Needing a home and a husband to help her raise her
orphaned nephews, Bella Wilson heads to Wyoming
in response to a mail-order-bride ad. But when she
discovers that Philip Young, her pony express rider
groom-to-be, didn't place the ad, she must convince
him to marry her for the sake of the children.*

Read on for a sneak preview of
PONY EXPRESS MAIL-ORDER BRIDE,
by **Rhonda Gibson,**
available March 2017 from Love Inspired Historical!

"I'm your mail-order bride."

"What?" Philip wished he could cover the shock in his
voice, but he couldn't.

"I answered your advertisement for a mail-order bride."
Bella's cheeks flushed and her gaze darted to the little boys
on the couch.

Philip didn't know what to think. She didn't appear to
be lying, but he hadn't placed an ad for marriage in any
newspaper. "I have no idea what you are talking about. I
didn't place a mail-order-bride ad in any newspaper."

She frowned and stood. "Hold on a moment." Bella dug
in her bag and handed him a small piece of newspaper.

His gaze fell upon the writing.

November 1860

*Wanted: Wife as soon as possible. Must be willing to live
at a pony express relay station. Must be between the ages
of eighteen to twenty-five. Looks are not important. Write
to: Philip Young, Dove Creek, Wyoming, Pony Express Relay
Station.*

Philip looked up at her. He hadn't placed the ad, but he had a sinking feeling he knew who did. "Did you send a letter to this address?"

Bella shook her head. "No, I didn't have the extra money to spare for postage. I just hoped I'd make it to Dove Creek before another woman. I did, didn't I?"

"Well, since this is the first I've heard of the advertisement—" he shook the paper in his hand "—I'd say your chances of being first are good. But this is dated back in November and it is now January so I'm curious as to what took you so long to get here."

"Well, I didn't actually see the advertisement until a few weeks ago. My sister and her husband had recently passed and I was going through their belongings when I stumbled upon the paper. Your ad leaped out at me as if it was from God." Once more she looked to the two boys playing on the couch.

Philip's gaze moved to the boys, too. "Are they your boys?"

"They are now."

Sadness flooded her eyes. Since she'd just mentioned her sister's death, Philip didn't think it was too much of a stretch to assume that the boys had belonged to Bella's sister. "They are your nephews?"

"Yes. I'm all the family they have left. The oldest boy is Caleb and the younger Mark." Her soulful eyes met his. "And you are our last hope to stay together."

Don't miss
PONY EXPRESS MAIL-ORDER BRIDE
by Rhonda Gibson, available March 2017 wherever
Love Inspired® Historical books
and ebooks are sold.

www.LoveInspired.com